PROHIBITION ORCS

MICHAEL WARREN LUCAS

Tilted
Windmill
Press

ACKNOWLEDGEMENTS

I wrote a silly story about orcs bootlegging bad whiskey into Detroit during Prohibition. I sent it into the world. I forgot about it—after all, I'd had *my* fun, why would I care what happened next?

Readers demanded more. And more. The word "voracious" might even apply.

Here are all the Prohibition Orcs tales so far. If they leave you hungry for more, please dig up the companion novel *Frozen Talons* or seek out further tales. Turns out I have a deep and abiding empathy for huge people in a world too small and fragile for them.

As always, I must thank my Patronizers for their support. They make it possible for this full-time writer to do silly things like "eat" and "bathe" in between book releases. Kate Ebneter, Stefan Johnson, Jeff Marraccini, Eirik Øverby, and Phil Vuchetich throw so much cash at me, I thank them in in the ebook and print versions of everything. If you also desire blame for everything I do, check out https://patronizemwl.com.

This collection, along with the accompanying novel *Frozen Talons*, was the first fiction project I published with Kickstarter support. At the end, you'll find a list of the folks brave enough to admit that they helped drag this collection into the world. I must also thank them for making Robert Jeschonek's lovely introduction possible, and Bob himself for writing it.

This book is for Liz.

CONTENTS

INTRODUCTION TO PROHIBITION ORCS

By Robert Jeschonek

How would an orc write an introduction to a book about orcs?

The easy answer is, he or she just wouldn't *do* it. Orcs, as presented in the *Prohibition Orcs* stories collected in this volume, are no-nonsense beings of few words and little sentimentality, exclusively focused on hard work, practicality, and survival. "Harsh" doesn't begin to do justice to the orcs and the lives they lead.

That doesn't mean there isn't a stark poetry and universality to their existence, though. As written by the unique and insightful Michael Warren Lucas, the orcs of Prohibition-era Detroit, Michigan, circa 1927, personify the American immigrant experience in all its complexity and resonance. Their appearance may be decidedly un-human, with purple-green skin, razor-sharp talons, and two sets of tusks, but they embody human striving, determination, and familial connectedness with great fidelity. Their traditions (like eating the dead) may be unfamiliar and in some cases repulsive to us, but the *importance* of those traditions is very recognizable. The lives they carve out in their new home of Detroit may be strange and brutal, but the faith they show in daring to carve them out at all is stirring.

Nevertheless, if central character Uruk-Tai or one of his fellow orcs were asked to write a book introduction, they might likely do much worse than simply refuse the offer. It's not hard to imagine an orc being insulted by such an invitation and perhaps even mortally wounding the person who made it. They'd have much better things to do with their time, like hauling bales at the docks on Lake Saint Clair, cleaning the vast automotive plants of Detroit, or smuggling bootleg booze (fit for orcs and elves as well as humans) from Canada in defiance of Prohibition-enforcing Feds and rival bootleggers.

The orcs don't have room in their lives for creativity and lack respect for those like the "paper men" who make their living from words. Putting effort into creative work seems like a waste of time, lacking the immediate, tangible results of simple, physical labor. Creative expression of any kind exists on the lowest tier of the orcs' hierarchy of priorities.

Actually, writing *anything* would be impossible for most orcs in America in 1927 because of the simple fact that they are illiterate. That seems likely to change with the next generation, exemplified by Uruk's children, whom he orders to learn to read. "No orc has done this," he tells them. "Maybe it cannot be done. But if orc blood and orc bone can do it, you will do it. You will... *read*."

Literacy may be in the children's future, but the older orcs who moved to the New World from the Old Country have little or no education. Most of the males work as laborers in shipping and manufacturing facilities and have no need for any kind of "book learning." Most of the females fill domestic roles in the home, pouring their energy into cooking, cleaning, and raising children according to orc traditions; learning to read and write would be as far out of reach for them as for their husbands.

Being illiterate, ill-tempered, and uncreative are all part of what makes the orcs so interesting and worth reading about...though you'll find there is much more to them than that range of qualities. In the hands of Lucas, a master craftsman of character development, the title protagonists of *Prohibition Orcs* possess complex inner lives and symbolic resonance far beyond their apparent surface simplicity.

For one thing, the orcs function as stand-ins for put-upon, hard-working immigrants throughout American history. Like so many European, African, Asian, and Latin American immigrants before them, they take jobs that no one in the upper classes would stoop to fill, all in the hope of securing a place in American society and a decent future for their children (though orcs would have you think they don't believe in hope at all). They live in rundown tenements, dress in rough-hewn garments, and eat scraps that the well-to-do consider unfit for consumption. Even their culture has echoes of Eastern European culture, emphasizing a somewhat fatalistic worldview, unswerving devotion to family, and a belief in hard work as the most redeeming pursuit and means of survival (if not success). As explained in "Final Gift," "An orc lived for their clan and their work."

An equally fascinating aspect of Lucas' orcs is their willingness—in the New World, at least—to reach for something better in spite of their tendency toward hopelessness. As Tara-Tai says in "Degreased Hopes," "Proper orcs didn't dream. They didn't expect. They held no hope because orcish gods only demanded, never gave. And they so loved to demand what an orc had the temerity to hope for."

The Detroit of *Prohibition Orcs* is a dark place, and the orcs exist at the bottom of the socio-economic totem pole, expecting only struggle and suffering as their lot in life...but something about the time and place inspires them to aim higher anyway, almost against their will. Sometimes, this comes in the form of lawful ambitions, like pushing for a better job at a factory. Other times, it takes the shape of activities that are unmistakably illegal —the committing of crimes to circumvent the social contract that keeps them down in spite of America's proclaimed status as "the land of opportunity."

All of this harkens back to our own ancestral immigrants, as well as those of today and tomorrow. We see our own origins and striving in those of the orcs, a marginalized people who nevertheless find it in their hearts to reach for something more, to expect better treatment from those around them, and to reach an understanding with those who are different from them.

Perhaps that willingness to change—even masked as it is behind posturing and signaling—is what makes Uruk and the other orcs so sympathetic. It is this optimistic thread that runs through all the stories and links them thematically—that the orcs are changing and being changed by their new home, adapting to the American melting pot that frees them, gradually, from the limitations of the past to which they've been bound.

As methodically, absorbingly constructed by Lucas, each story is a poignant step forward for an individual orc... and, by extension, all orcs inhabiting America. In "Spilled Mirovar," Uruk and members of his family face off against elvish and human bootleggers while crafting a vision of a more positive future for his offspring...a possible greatness he had perhaps not considered before. "His sons, janitors. Or drivers. Or plasterers. Or, one day, one grandchild... a wizard."

In "Final Gift," an elderly female orc faces the tradition of preparing and eating her dead husband, meanwhile coming to terms with her grief and starting a friendship with a human female who has also lost her mate.

In "Drowned Mirovar," a human lawyer seeks Uruk's help to save his wife, in the process becoming a partner in the orc's bootlegging operation.

An aged orc shaman faces off against an aggressive human preacher in "Witness November," ultimately proving the power of orc gods and finding new purpose that will drive him to engage more fully with the world again.

In "Degreased Hopes," Tara-Tai pursues a promotion at work when his supervisor retires, only to face the disappointments of his station in life... and be gifted with compensation that inspires him to consider a different path. Just such a path leads Tara in a new direction in "A Debt of Meat," changing his life through a gesture of kindness from a dwarf.

Finally, "Woolen Torment" presents a new kind of grueling struggle for Uruk—a fitting for a new business suit he can wear to enhance his image in the bootlegging business. His human lawyer partner helps him reinvent himself, even as Uruk resists and finally embraces the new wardrobe as a way to achieve greater success.

Finding success and overcoming obstacles—external and otherwise—is a central theme of this collection, one that dignifies characters we might under other circumstances see as having limited potential. Clearly, Lucas is making a statement with his aspirational orcs, telling us something about America and the dreamers who come from the far corners of the world to build new and better lives there while holding on to the best parts of the ways and places they left behind.

It's because of this that I wonder if, under the right circumstances, an orc might try writing an introduction to a book like this after all. Though most orcs might reject the task out of hand, possibly damaging whoever brought it up in the first place... though they might complain about the unimportance of creative expression... though they might not have the reading and writing skills to compose the text without help... some might also respond by trying as hard as they can within their capabilities to make the most of the opportunity. They might see it as a chance to show what they can do and reach for something better for their family.

In such an introduction, an orc might write about the struggles of life beyond the Old Country. They might share their memories of the dreams that inspire them—as well-hidden as those dreams might be—and also remember the little victories that keep them going along the hard road, the uphill climb. Maybe such a high-minded orc would express gratitude to Lucas the author for getting at the heart of their people, for identifying with them so strongly that his love for them—flaws and all—comes through loud and clear.

Maybe such an orc writer would even point out the ways in which orcs in these stories represent not just immigrants, but all the diverse beings of the world who could demonstrate true courage if they chose to and make a real difference by bridging the gaps between them.

Or, as you will no doubt realize when you read the tales assembled in this book, such an orc might just as likely get fed up with the whole project, tear the pages to shreds, and proceed to inflict extraordinary damage on not just the room in which they were writing, but the whole building and the neighborhood around it.

And if Michael Warren Lucas happened to get in the way, he might get a little more than a black eye for writing the stories and giving the orc such an annoying task in the first place.

 **SPILLED MIROVAR**

1

Uruk knelt on one knee on the verge of the rock-strewn gravel beach, letting his thick wool coat almost brush the ground and give his legs a little more protection from the sleet screaming down from Grosse Pointe's furious night sky. He had yanked his collar up and jammed his corduroy flat cap tightly over his scalp, and crammed his strong hands into the coat's pockets.

One hand bore brutal brass knuckles. He'd chosen the braided knuckles, the ones without the spikes. The other hand cradled the wooden grip of an orc-scale revolver, slightly too large for humans and chambered for .75-caliber bullets. Spare bullets rattled in the bottom of the pocket.

Like any American orc, he kept his talons trimmed so that they wouldn't tear out his pockets. Or the rest of his clothes.

Or other soft things. Like bricks.

If events continued as they had, though, he might have to let them grow.

The modern year of 1927, and orcs *still* had to fight elven asshole bullshit.

Lake Saint Clair wasn't really a Great Lake but tonight it raged like one, thrashing up waves that clawed their way fifteen or twenty feet inland before they collapsed, sometimes even sluicing over the macadam of Lakeshore Drive. Each wave discarded a fresh skein of noxious seaweed, dead from the November cold, and the greatest surges sprayed the stink of dying algae across his face.

Uruk wondered if the lake felt like an orc. Lake Huron, Lake Superior, they all got the glory. They were strong and angry lakes, yes. They demanded sacrifice of blood and bone, on their own calendar. But even little Lake Saint Clair, when roused, devoured those who disrespected it.

An orc with any sense would be at home. Even his family's seething, roach-ruled tenement apartment in Hamtramck would be nicer than this freezing, angry midnight. Grandpa always said *anger keeps you warm enough*, but the icewater punching the gap between cap and collar and shivering down his spine disagreed. Still, his heavy boots with the layered leather soles repulsed rain and cold alike, and beneath the pleated wool coat his thick black sweater and brown canvas pants kept his vitals warm enough.

Fury did not keep you warm.

It just kept you where you needed to be.

Elves could see in the dark—but not on a night like tonight. Even orcs couldn't see in the dark when the screaming wind and sleet stole the heat from the air. The sprawling mansions facing the lake across Lakeshore Drive were merely darker shadows buried in trees.

A wave crashed up towards Uruk. Behind him, Daka cursed in Orcish. His brother had planted himself too close to the water, again. He probably had wet feet. Again. Daka always put himself too close to the edge, any edge. Uruk had tried to ease him back for years, but finally resigned himself to the fact his brother liked wet feet and dented fenders and angry landlords.

But for something like this, Daka was on the side of right. As were Tara and Kaba.

Uruk had tried to fit into America. He'd listened to all his father's stories about the Old Country and what it meant to be a *real* orc. Uruk saw a difference in the United States, though. He'd gone to school for two whole years, and could sign his name and count and knew the sagas of General Presidents Washington and Lincoln. He'd learned English, though he spoke Orc at home. He let the humans and dwarves call him Urka—their feeble misshapen mouths and flimsy voices could never properly pronounce his good, traditional Orcish name.

Uruk might show a fang at a bar, but had never killed anyone. He'd never even broken a jaw, no matter what some ignorant human or dwarf said.

Even Uruk's aging father had learned the comforts of the overstuffed chair. Now that he'd become Grandpa, he spent his days grumping at how things had changed and how much more Orcish the Old Country had been. He watched the children with not-so-secret pride, though.

Detroit was a wonderful place.

But some things went too far. Like the Eighteenth Amendment. Humans could ban their own booze all they wanted. It was feeble, not even fit for washing floors. They'd left exceptions for their church, for the elvish sacraments, even for the dwarven rituals.

But the elves in Congress insisted that orcs had no sacraments. Elves had supported that Prohibition, and immediately started smuggling their mirovar from Canadian distilleries. As the orcs had done with their draught, until last month's disaster.

Without the Orcish draught, without the rites, Uruk's fine strong boys might grow tall. They might earn respect. They might have many fine children of their own and, in time, name Uruk Grandpa.

But they would never be orcs.

There—a sudden flash of light, right on the point!

And again!

Elves.

Guiding their pet bootleggers in.

Uruk raised his left hand in a fist, just like Grandpa talked about, and rose to his feet. "For our children," he snarled in Orcish.

Even with sleet pelting his cap, Uruk heard the gravel behind him shift as his brothers rose with him. "Our children."

An orc who wanted respect had to take it by force.

2

The quick dash down a quarter-mile of grassy, squelchy verge between the broken rocks of the beach and the muddy mess of Jefferson Avenue felt like nothing, even in the cold darkness and the pummeling sleet. Uruk's heart beat steadily and his breath came easily. He worked as a laborer down at the Port of Detroit with Daka and Kaba. Hauling boxes and toting bales that would cripple a human or crush an elf had only strengthened him.

Tara lagged a little behind. The youngest brother had gotten himself apprenticed to a janitor—honorable work, yes, but not labor that would make him strong. Uruk didn't question his brother's heart, though. Tara's weakness might kill him. But if needed, he would fall with elf blood under his trimmed talons and an elven throat in his teeth.

Uruk had passed this place before, driving the clan's rusty decrepit Model T. During the summer, the narrow spit of land stabbing into Lake Saint Clair was a pleasant, grassy picnic spot for elves and humans and even a few dwarves. A dozen families with basket lunches could comfortably sprawl on that peninsula, leaving room for their children to run and play, surrounded on three sides by water and watching the sailboats and freighters and the distant Canada shore. Maybe even flying kites.

There was no law against orcs stopping at that little park.

Laws are written down.

Tonight, though, Lake Saint Clair battered the peninsula, clawing at the tumbled boulders along its edge, spitting and spraying like a rabid wolf. Lightning shattered the sky, and thunder demanded obeisance.

The flash of light exposed a fifteen-foot boat wedged up on the peninsula, through a narrow gap in the rocks. Rowboat? No, in a storm of this madness it had to be a powerboat. Crewed by madmen, or elves. A four-wheeled delivery truck with a giant tomato painted on the side sat facing the road.

The tomato convinced Uruk this was the rendezvous.

Anyone could have a new truck. The lightning had reflected off the great swooping fenders in even curves, unmarred by dents and bumps and all the other damage of Detroit's busy traffic. Maybe they'd just bought the truck today.

But the sole tomato on the side wasn't the work of a sign painter. Nobody had dropped a sawbuck in an artist's hand and said "Gimme a great big tomato." No, even in the quick flash of monochrome lightning, this tomato advertised richness and flavor. The artist had poured the very essence of tomato into the paint, and brought the perfect ripe tomato to life on taut waterproof canvas.

The tomato was elf art. And elves painted only for elves and Presidents.

The informant had been right. The transfer was tonight.

Right now.

Between the truck and the road, two men.

Uruk held his hands out to warn his brothers, and stopped behind an ancient oak tree. His heart suddenly beat more quickly, and a ripple of tension flowed up his spine and tensed his shoulders. Grandpa talked about preparing for battle any time you were willing to listen.

Grandpa hadn't mentioned the sudden spike of fear through the gut, though.

Turning to face his younger brothers, sleet spattered Uruk's face and the sharp wind burned tears from his eyes. Daka, in his fedora and long coat of rough brown leather, looked almost relaxed. As Tara panted for breath and hugged his thinner wool coat his mouth hung open a little, exposing his two Great Tusks but not the Lesser. Surprisingly Kaba, the strongest of them all, looked the most nervous. His leather-gloved hands were clutched into almost human fists.

Uruk had planned to take Tara, the weakest of them. But Kaba's eyes flickered nervously between the lake and the road. *There is more than one kind of weakness*, Grandpa said. While Tara's weakness might kill him, Kaba's might murder them all. "Kaba, with me. We take the one on the left. Tara, Daka, the right." Uruk raised the hand with the brass knuckles. "Do not kill unless we must."

Little Tara nodded and slipped on his own pair of knuckles. These had inch-long steel spikes above each hole.

You'll need every advantage, littlest brother.

Uruk put a heavy hand on Kaba's bicep. "We have not done this before," he hissed in English. "But we are orcs. It's in our blood. We can do this."

A stream of water spilled off of Kaba's flat cap. Then his chest heaved with a deep breath and he gave a quick nod.

"Good orc." Uruk looked at his brothers. "Go!"

They charged.

Uruk could barely see Kaba thundering beside him. Grandpa was right—an orc's matte purple-green skin was made for the night. If he couldn't see his other two brothers from ten feet away, the guards would have no chance.

The guard stood with his back to the thrashing lake, silhouetted against the crazy reflections of the incoherent water. Almost big enough to be an orc, the outline of his fedora showed him swinging his head one way, then the other, looking for lights or motion. Not complacent, but not alert enough. Uruk gave heartfelt thanks to the lake for the spray and the splash and the pounding waves that covered his thudding feet.

The guard had a short-barreled Tommy gun with a big round magazine slung over one shoulder, barrel pointed down to keep the rain out. The weapon could down an orc in two seconds, and the sight sent fear fluttering through the bottom of Uruk's guts, but he used it to charge faster and harder.

They were maybe ten feet away when the guard caught the motion in the darkness. His head snapped towards them, and his hands fumbled at the submachine gun.

A high-pitched human scream pierced the spray and crash.

The guard wrenched at the Tommy gun, spinning towards the darkness that hid his partner. He might have opened his mouth to shout.

Uruk hit him like a freight train striking a dog, sheer momentum throwing the brawny human to the ground. A second later he heard an *oof* of exploding air, and glanced over his shoulder to see Kaba pulling the Tommy gun off the guard's shoulder. The guard lay still on the ground.

Kaba saw Uruk's expression, and pantomimed a punch to the guard's gut.

Shouts rose from behind the truck.

Uruk charged again.

Four humans stood behind the truck, each lugging a wooden milk crate from the boat to the back of the truck. A couple of bigger humans, the sort the elves passed off as muscle, loomed near the boat.

And near the truck, in an immaculate yellow rubberized rain slicker, an elf.

Uruk had hoped he'd finally get to see an elf look surprised. Instead, the elf gracefully pirouetted out of the path of Uruk's charge, raising his hands as if waving a red cape for a bull.

The workmen didn't matter. Not now. The elf was the threat.

Uruk scrabbled to reverse course, but the leather soles of his boots wouldn't grab the slick grass. He barreled into one of the workmen, feet-first, sending the human tumbling aside.

The crate spun through the air.

Glass bottles shone in a barrage of lightning, then the crash of glass breaking against stone introduced the thunder. The smells of honey and roses and tulips and a dozen other flowers pierced the air.

Uruk had never smelled mirovar, the sacramental—no, *sacred*—drink of the elves. It smelled just as stuck-up as he'd thought.

The elf shrieked, "Unspeakable cretin!" He raised a finger at Uruk.

Lightning crackled again, this time from the elf's outstretched finger.

Sudden pain lashed up Uruk's legs, scorching through his chest and out towards the sky. Uruk smelled burning wool and hair and something like scorched bacon.

The blast left him hollow.

The spray and storm flooded in to fill the space with darkness.

3

The darkness slowly filled with Uruk.

The taste of honey and lilies came first, burning into his nose, making him cough. Lungs. He could breathe, cool moist air filling his throat.

Uruk sat up quickly, head twisting one way and another. His head ached, and his mouth felt swollen. But his heart beat steadily and his muscles gave only annoying twinges when he shifted from one side to another. A good hit of draught would take that away.

He sat on the vibrating plank bed of a delivery truck, half-filled with rattling milk crates. His night vision plucked out the canvas awning overhead, the drawn curtain at the back of the truck bed. The truck's engine had a steady thrum. Rain and sleet pelted the canvas overhead.

No rain dripped from the steel arches supporting the canvas. No wind slipped through cracks. The air felt damp with the storm, but no more so than a snug warehouse might. The engine purred without rattle or cough, and the stink of exhaust felt gentle on the nose. An Elvish truck.

Perched on a bench along the front of the bed, Kaba's warmth made his exposed face glow deep red in the darkness. More light oozed from his wrists, where his coat didn't quite touch his gloves. Even among orcs, Kaba was a giant. "Are you all right?" Kaba said in English.

"Yeah." Uruk worked his jaw. "How did we do?"

Kaba held out his hands, grinning widely enough to show Greater and Lesser fangs alike. "We won."

"Our brothers?"

"Well and safe."

Uruk felt his own grin stretch his face. "And the men?"

"We encouraged them to flee."

The men wouldn't recognize Uruk and his brothers. Orcs joked about their terrible vision at night and their weakness in the day. Besides, to a man, all orcs looked alike.

Memory came flooding back. Uruk's grin dissolved. He licked his lips and tasted old blood. "The elf."

Kaba looked at the floor.

Uruk's heart sank. His own brother, looking at the floor in shame? Uruk rolled to his knees. *And the elf?*

Kaba glared into Uruk's eyes. "Dead."

Uruk worked his jaw in surprise. "You killed a wizard? An elf wizard? How?" A wizard who could steer the storm should have killed them all. Elf wizards could turn Orcish bullets. Before Kaba approached closely enough to use his knife, the wizard should have turned him to cinder and salt.

Kaba smiled and hoisted something off the bench beside him. Something that cast long, sharp metallic glints through the darkness.

The guard's Tommy gun.

"Elves protect themselves against all but their own," Kaba said turning the weapon in his hands. One finger caressed the circular magazine. "This gun—the ammunition, maybe the gun itself."

Dread and elation churned in Uruk's bowels. "You have turned every elf against us." Elves lived for centuries—well, no, not *lived*. They existed. They persisted. They did not seize that life by the throat and squeeze it for all the blood it held, yet somehow they treasured their bland centuries.

Kaba nodded. "But they murdered our neighbors, our friends. As they always have. I thought he had struck you dead. The elf would have killed us all."

Uruk's fierce grin returned. "They started it." If the elves wanted blood, they could have it. "How much did we get?"

"Sixty-three cases." Kaba waved his free hand. "Swill."

A fortune in swill. But swill was worth what one would pay for it.

"One case lost?"

Kaba nodded.

So sixty-three, plus one. Sixty-four cases. And the wizard's death might convince the elves they were serious.

Tomorrow, the real work began. The true danger started.

But Kaba still looked away at the floor.

Ч

Uruk awoke the next morning to the sound of his children grunting and chortling at the breakfast table. His wife Vara shushed them in Orcish-accented English. "Your father sleeps! He works hard, you do not wake him!" The heavy smell of porridge with lard tickled his nose.

Uruk dragged a hand across his eyes, sweeping away grains of crust from their corners. Three hours sleep? Grandpa would tell them how he'd marched for days without sleep, but Uruk had grown accustomed to a good eight hours a night, stretched out on the cozy taut canvas mattress and wrapped in a heavy quilt, Vara slumbering as a puddle of comforting warmth by his side. America must make orcs soft.

His breath didn't cloud when he exhaled—the landlord must have finally fired up the boiler.

Uruk yanked the tattered wool comforter aside. The wooden floor sent tiny nails of cold up into his feet. The boiler might have turned over, but the heat hadn't yet sunk into the building's bones. When he stood, he could feel the ache of the wizard's lightning in a jagged line from his ankle, up through his leg, into his hip, and out his chest. The delight of victory had masked the pain, just like Grandpa said.

Uruk pulled on his dungarees, ducked his head to get through the door, and lurched into the family room.

The lathe-and-plaster room was barely large enough to hold Uruk, Vara, the two boys, and Grandpa. Uruk had gotten the couch from one of the humans at the dock. The big monster sagged, and if you sat on the far right side one of the springs would stab you in the hock, but it smelled so much better than the old one had. Next to the couch, Grandpa drowsed in a circle-backed orange horsehair chair so worn with age it had lost any hair. A human had sent it to the trash heap, and Uruk had snatched it before another orc could. Grandpa's immense bulk barely fit into the thing, and his weight squeezed tufts of straw from the rents in its side where Uruk's youngest had slashed it with his new talons when he just started to walk.

Uruk had learned to walk in this room. He'd brought Vara to this room as an eager bride, and they'd savagely, lovingly sanctified and claimed all three rooms as theirs. Uruk's heart flickered with a grin when he recalled the four bare footprints kicked into the wall behind the couch.

He'd brought children home here. And suddenly it looked even older and shabbier than usual. The walls were scuffed and gouged where young orcs had smashed into it, or drawn tusky-faces with their talons. Nobody repaired tenement plaster. The walls had not seen paint since before Uruk was born, since before Grandpa came to the New World. The Hamtramck wind rattling the single window brought a sharp chill and dingy sunlight. The single light bulb in the ceiling cast harsh shadows over everything.

And the smell! Decades of human food, cabbage and leaves and grass and who knew what, boiled on that stove until that sick green steam seeped everywhere. Human shit and piss left in a bowl overnight, to be discarded in the morning, just so the stink would sink into the building's bones.

Even thirty years of orcs couldn't overcome the previous fifty years of humans.

And at the rickety oak table, its surface scuffed by decades of humans and scarred by two generations of orcs, Uruk's honor and pride: his wife Vara in her cotton housecoat, and the nine-year-old boys Oscar and Ivan, both still in canvas pajamas.

"Dad!" the boys shouted, hopping down from their blocky stools and charging to his side.

Uruk accepted their simultaneous hugs. They were growing so quickly! He'd need to get more money somehow. Young orcs could eat their weight in cow each day, let alone bread. His parents had fed him porridge and oatmeal by the vat—they'd done their best, and he'd grown up strong, but he wanted better for Oscar and Ivan. His fine American boys.

Oscar was a fraction taller than Ivan, and Ivan a touch broader and an hour older. But both twins had strong arms and big fine heads, legs that could carry an orc for miles and miles, and appetites—oh, their appetites! Neither could get enough, of anything. And their grip! Both could break a cow's thighbone with a squeeze of a hand. And at only nine years old. Almost ten!

Uruk clapped one arm around each, slapping their backs just enough that they'd think he thought they were strong. A little air huffed out of Ivan—had Uruk struck too hard? The pride that bubbled in his soul made him push too hard sometimes.

Nine years old. They would be ten in a month. On the way to becoming orcs. He had four weeks to gather the draught, or his children would pay.

"That's enough!" Uruk said in English. "Eat! You must grow strong. Next year your school ends, and we must find you work. You must be strong to find good work."

The boys scooted back to their chairs. Vara looked up from the tiny cast-iron coal stove, the giant pot of porridge balanced ridiculously on top of it. "Morning, my warrior."

Warrior. A traditional Orcish greeting—with the *my*, meaning that he belonged to Vara. He was her property, and she would fight to keep him. Uruk let a tiny bit of his smile show—not enough that the boys would notice, but enough that Vara would see. "Morning, my woman."

Uruk took a step towards his spot at the head of the table. He felt soft, worn plaster brush his bare scalp, and ancient white dust powdered down on his shoulders. That hadn't happened for years—he usually remembered to keep his spine lowered that critical half-inch so he cleared the ceiling.

Tired or not, he felt good today.

He had hard work in front of him, but it would succeed.

"Uruk," Vara said as she brought him a decent-sized bucket of porridge with a razor-thin slice of lard melting on the surface, "the boys have a request for their father."

Grandpa suddenly coughed. "Uruk!" He hacked a nugget of phlegm and spit in the cracked earthenware bowl by his feet.

Uruk felt a tingle of excitement. The boys would ask for things of their own accord—a hat for the winter, a penny for the candy store. If Vara brought it up, it meant that she already knew and approved. Yes, they should have presented their wishes to their father first, but he'd been busy yesterday evening, preparing for the hijacking.

"Uruk-Tai!" Grandpa coughed in Orcish. "How did it go? Tell me, were you successful?"

Irritated, Uruk glanced over his shoulder. "Yes," he said in Orcish. "The enemy has fallen." He used the form of *fallen* to indicate that blood had been spilt and enemy corpses left on the field.

"And your brothers?"

Uruk choked his impatience. If his two sons had been the ones to steal a shipment of bootlegged elvish mirovar, he would not rest until he knew that they had returned honorably breathing, or at least honorably. "All are well." He turned back to the boys.

Grandpa coughed, pounding his lungs. "You cannot put me off, son. A battle? A true battle? Tell me the saga, my boy. Every detail!"

My boy. Uruk clenched his teeth. Many of his fellow orcs did not permit such informality from their elders. His father, wheezing and stinking of age and cheap bootleg whiskey, claiming he would fight for his child? Ridiculous.

But striking your elders... that was not American. Forget roasting them on an open fire, as his great-grandmother had done to her elders.

"I will tell you, my father. But the boys leave for—" There was no Orcish word, so he used English—"*school* soon, and then I must join battle again. You shall get the saga, the true saga, when I can tell it correctly."

The old man nodded, wattles flapping under his saggy face. "*School.* Yes, yes."

Uruk turned back to the table, where his sons waited expectantly. Ivan's eyes were raised in hope. Oscar sat ramrod straight, face stilled, like the human soldiers at attention they'd seen when President Commander Coolidge had visited Detroit and they'd gone to see the crowds and the parade. Orcs did not stand at attention, but Uruk had to suppress a smile. A father must be firm. "Yes," he said in English.

"Father," Oscar said.

"Sir," Ivan said.

Tension made Uruk's back quiver. He'd felt a frisson of fear as he charged the bootleggers last night, but if the boys stretched this another heartbeat he thought he might burst.

"They have a program at school," Oscar said.

"What? Like the play last year?" The school had wanted a quarter. A whole quarter, one for *each* boy, for tickets!

"No," Ivan said.

The boys looked at each other. Uruk saw Oscar twitch, like he wanted to glance at Vara but didn't dare.

Uruk's heart beat even more quickly. What could be so terrible as this?

Vara stood still at the porridge pot. Her spoon worked slowly, sending the rich heavy smell into the air. She might have been humming to herself, or counting the number of times she'd stirred the pot. She was a picture of peaceful beauty at work, dark skin glistening in the naked light bulb.

As if she was paying no attention at all, her head slowly rocked, up and down. Her thoughts to Uruk? Encouragement to Oscar, who could see his mother from the corner of his eye? Both?

Encouragement was fine, but enough was enough. "An orc does not cower!" Uruk snapped, letting his own tension lace his tone. "If you would ask, ask. If not, then to school with you. I would have you count to a thousand before the year is out!"

Oscar took a book out of his lap and handed it to Uruk. "We were each given this."

Uruk had seen books before, but this one was weird. Uncanny. Somehow wrong. It was brand new, and had the woody smell of the cardboard boxes he lugged, without the mustiness of age.

The cover was made of stiff cardboard—dangerously flimsy in Orcish hands, but better than most of the impossibly fragile paperwork that men insisted had such importance. It was larger than most human books, too. The cover was mostly the bright red of old blood, but a black stripe the width of a thumb ran down the left and right side. Human letters cluttered the clean black stripes.

Between the stripes stood a black and white horse, reared on its legs as if angry. Its front hooves lashed out, ready to fight.

It faced a tall green creature—a lizard? Its tail had lashed around front, and ridged scales along its back hinted at armor. Great sharp claws stuck out from its front paws, and its long snout hung a little open, lined with white jagged teeth.

They faced each other across a field of stacked symbols. Uruk had seen the symbols before. Some of the human dockworkers had pointed them out while they ate lunch.

A

B

C

Oscar quivered with tension, as if he was about to charge the enemy line.

Ivan swallowed and said "It's for—"

"I know what it is for!" Uruk shouted. He carefully did not crush the fragile thing with his hands. If he broke it, the school would demand he pay for it. Shoulders quivering, he reached and flipped the cover open in a fragrant cloud of fresh ink fumes.

The A symbol. And a round, red apple. An simple apple, drawn by a human, without the life that an elf's hand would have granted it.

At the back of the room, Vara stopped stirring.

The boys sat still.

The pages were thick cardboard as well. Human paper would dissolve into mush if you tried to wipe your ass with it.

But not this book.

Uruk's pulse thudded in his ears. His breath felt short and hot. His heart felt like it might explode in his throat. He carefully put the book down in the middle of the table, where he could see it. Moving with deliberation, so he didn't destroy his chair, he scooted himself away from the table and stood.

"Is that—" Grandpa began.

"Quiet!" Uruk snarled in Orcish, spinning to glare at his father. He turned back to the boys.

Oscar shook with fear, but met his father's eyes.

Ivan sat perfectly still, jaw set. He wanted to run, he ached to run. His body burned to flee. But his mind won, and he met his father's gaze without flinching.

"I am Uruk-Tai. Leader of this clan. And this is my will," Uruk said. He kept his Orcish words slow and clear—the boys spoke English most of the time, but some things, the important things, should be in Orcish.

His bare back suddenly felt cool. Was he sweating?

Vara stopped pretending to pay attention to her pot.

"This—thing." Uruk pointed a blocky finger at the book. "They want you to stay in school. They want you to not *work*."

Both boys stopped breathing.

"No orc has done this thing before. No orc has thought to do such a thing before."

The room was still.

"This is my will." He plucked the book up, dangling it between thumb and forefinger. "You will attack this. You will master this." He looked from one child to the other. "No orc has done this. There is no shame in failure here. There is only shame in not trying as hard as you can, in every way you can. Maybe it cannot be done. But if orc blood and orc bone can do it, you will do it."

"But jobs—" Oscar began.

"This is my will!" Uruk shouted. "My will. My family. Mine!" He did not shake the book. It might have been made for orc hands, but it had been made by humans with no true understanding of orcs. "I shall find the money." *Somehow.* "You—you will do this thing. You will... *read*."

Behind him, Grandpa wheezed.

"Now go," Uruk said. "Dress. School. You do not get the easy life of carrying freight."

The boys glanced at each other.

"*Go!*"

They dashed into their room and slammed the door to get dressed.

Vara stirred the pot, set it to the side of the stove, and came to Uruk. Her arms slipped around him. A jerking squeeze nearly—*nearly*—hard enough to break a rib, then she relaxed into him. "Well done," she murmured in his ear. "So well done."

Uruk thought his heart might burst. The school thought they could teach his boys to read!

And Oscar and Ivan had both faced him. They'd been terrified, and never looked away. Such wonderful boys they were.

Even in the circle of Vara's arms, his elation faded.

Today, Uruk had to prove himself worthy of them.

5

Uruk knew how to find Celebrimble's people. *Everybody* knew how to find Celebrimble's people. The Cadieux Café, down on Cadieux just north of Mack Avenue. The problem was, no orcs ever walked in there.

Oh, orcs sometimes visited, usually by being carried in. And those that got carried in got dragged out. But orcs were never actually *found* there. They were usually found down the river, at the bend near Zug Island where the rest of the garbage washed up.

Uruk shivered. The rain had stopped, but the wind hadn't died down. Expensive new Model As and some fancy Packards trundled down the two-lane asphalt of Cadieux Avenue, splashing icy puddles up onto the grassy easement. Weak November noon sunlight shunted down from just above those huge five-room human houses across the road.

The sooner he got this going, the sooner he could get out of that feral wind.

Uruk tugged delicately at the jacket. He'd found it in a shonky shop—a suit jacket in white linen, with shoulders the size of a barrel. Cut for an orc. It didn't exactly fit, but he'd been shocked to find it at all. Combined with his best dungarees, the ones that didn't need patching yet, and a sharp black cotton button-up shirt with comfortably large glass buttons about the size of hen's eggs, he felt like the best-dressed orc in town. The boots were working-orc's boots, but they were the only ones he had. Orc boots cost a week's wages. Ones that looked good would probably cost two legs and both feet.

With the back of his knuckles, Uruk rapped on the Café's heavy oak door.

A panel slid aside, revealing a gap just large enough for two human eyes to peer out. A burly voice, for a human, said "We're closed."

Uruk bent to put his hands on his knees so he could look at the eyes. "I'm here to talk to Celebrimble. Or his elf boys."

"And I said we're closed." The eyes glanced him up and down, then rolled in contempt. "You should head back to your part of town. Pigs can become bacon around here, even if you do dress 'em up."

Pig. Uruk filed the insult away for future vengeance. He gave a sunny smile showing all four tusks. "Tell him this involves sixty-three crates of Mirovar. It should have been sixty-four, but one got broke. Oh, and a bottle is missing out of the last crate." Uruk gave a mid-sized belch. "I'd hate to see anything happen to the rest of it. It might even go to people who wouldn't—" *belch* "—appreciate it properly."

The eyes narrowed, then peered behind Uruk at the trucks, Model Ts, and Model As puttering down Cadieux Road. A bus trundled past, stuffed to overflowing with humans and dwarves crossing town. "I can't stop you from hanging around," the voice said, "but at least get your ass behind the building."

Uruk nodded. If he accepted the invitation, eventually a door in the back of the building would open. He might get invited inside. Or, a bunch of big humans with guns and cudgels and hammers might come out for their afternoon break.

If he stayed out front, he'd get cold until he decided to give up.

They kept him waiting for an hour before the door opened and the men came out. But at least it was out of the wind.

6

Nine muscular humans, with felt Fedoras perched on their bulging heads and pricey wool suits cut just for them, surrounded Uruk. They left a path clear to the back door. Uruk nodded politely, gave a smile, ducked his head to get through the door, and sauntered in like the owner owed him his kidneys.

The inside of the Cadieux Café was all dark varnished wood. A tiny, shaded electric light above each of the cramped booths gave just enough illumination for the drinkers to see each other. This place didn't exclude orcs just by attitude. The booths were too tight. The tables too tiny, and while the frames were rolled iron the tops were panes of breakable leaded glass. The ladderback chairs were both too small and too flimsy. The plastered ceiling had all kinds of decorations, like an artistic orc had sketched out lots of fiddly bits with an extended talon. The bar along the back was so short that Uruk really *could* act out that old joke—lay his tackle out across the bar and dare someone to punch it.

Walking in here, that was pretty much what he was doing. At least that bar would break before his dick would.

The place stank of that weak ale the humans drank and that fruity elven crap, weirdly plastered over a delicious base note of fried meat.

And everywhere, people dressed in clothes that cost more than Uruk made in a month, drinking from fragile little glasses.

In an Orcish speakeasy, the lookout would give a shout and the drinkers would immediately slam the contents of their glasses, whatever it happened to be. The police would find nothing but fumes, belches, and annoyed orcs.

Uruk suspected that a human speakeasy had a more elegant system.

The humans guided him to a huge round booth near the back, with a stuffed bench seat quilted in rich purple leather and a curved table in expensive mahogany. Two more men sat at each end of the bench, each casually holding a small silver handgun in his lap like it was an inconvenient thing he'd just happened to find, and when the time was right he'd go drop it in the garbage for an orc to take out.

A slender human sat near the middle of the curved booth. Uruk had seen his like before, going in and out of the Port of Detroit shipping office. Prissy mustache. Suit not only cut for him, but made out of some expensive-looking fabric Uruk had never seen before. Narrow face and perpetual frown from staring at too much paperwork. Some reading might be good, but too much of it turned you into... into... *that.*

And next to Mister Prissy, the elf.

Uruk did not know Celebrimble by sight. The elves pretty much all looked the same to him anyway, for as often as he got to see them. This elf looked off into middle space as if he'd bet money on the feather bowling in the next room, looking nowhere near Uruk. His clothes were perfect. His hair was perfect. His nose, his chin, the pursed lips and relaxed pose, perfect. It made Uruk want to reach across the table and squeeze that neck until the elf's eyeballs popped, just to mess up that forsaken perfection.

Elves were everything orcs could never be. And the bastards reminded orcs of that with every breath, just by breathing. No elf would even condescend to speak to an orc, lest he have to chop off his tongue as soiled beyond redemption.

They'd put a splintery wooden packing crate in front of the round table. Uruk couldn't decide if it was a mockery of a chair, or if it was the only thing they had that wouldn't break if he sat on it. Maybe both.

The human thuglets formed a semicircle behind Uruk, just out of clawing range.

Mister Prissy held out a hand. "So kind of you to come visit, sir Orc. Very few of your people choose to grace our establishment. And you dressed up so nice, too."

Uruk glanced at the box, then relaxed his stance but kept standing. If the elf wanted to offer contempt, he would return it. "Humans say you dress like those you want to talk to," said Uruk.

"And you want to talk to us? Charmed, I'm sure."

"Actually," Uruk said, "I wanted to talk to the elf. But I didn't have a two-by-four to jam up my ass, so this is the best I could do." *Contempt returned.*

Mister Prissy flinched. "Indeed. What could we do for you, then?"

"I told your little boy at the door."

One of the humans glared at Uruk. If the human had stretched, he might have been able to head-butt Uruk's nipples. One at a time, at least.

Uruk glared down at him.

The human's eyes stayed on his for half a second, then flickered away.

Pathetic. Uruk's boys had done better when they were four. No, *three*.

"We did not hire him for his messenger-boy abilities," Mister Prissy said. "Would you be so kind as to tell me yourself?"

"I have sixty-three cases of Mirovar. Each has nine two-quart bottles. Minus one bottle because, well, orcs happen. We don't like honey and flowers and crap like that. I will trade them for an equivalent amount of proper Orcish draught."

Mister Prissy smiled. "No code words? No evasions?"

Uruk shrugged. "If you're the Feds, I'm screwed."

Prissy laughed. "Indeed, sir, indeed!" He slapped the table. "My, to have such business partners!" He straightened his black bow tie. "So, if I should learn of someone who would be interested in such an exchange, how could they reach you?"

"Tonight. One AM. State Fairgrounds parking lot. Open space, lots of exits. I'll be there, ready to exchange the goods."

Mister Prissy nodded thoughtfully. "I don't suppose you might have some token of your word?"

Uruk reached for a pocket.

The two men with guns suddenly had them pointed at his face. Behind him, he heard the click of hammers pulling back.

Uruk froze. An orc is tough, but he had nothing worth getting shot for. Yet.

"Slowly," Mister Prissy said. "If you please."

Uruk reached into the pocket with two fingers. He touched the cork with the softness of down, slid his fingers down to the glass lip of the neck, and drew out a lone bottle of Mirovar.

The fluid in the glass bottle looked perfectly transparent, but it seemed to draw in the dim lighting and spit it back out brighter and cleaner. The elegant, perfectly symmetrical bottle bore no label. It didn't seem to need one.

Mirovar. The sacred elf wine.

Mister Prissy's eyebrows rose. "Oh, my."

"If you like, I'll leave this here," Uruk said, holding the bottle aloft. "I think they call it a 'sample.'" He held one hand over the cork. "Or, if you prefer, I can prove it's not poison and chug it right here. I'll even do a handstand after. Bounce up and down a couple times, and I'll be able to fart flowers."

The elf ignored him, still staring through the doorway at the feather bowling.

"I don't think we will require any olfactory demonstrations," Mister Prissy said with a strained smile. "Right on the table will be fine."

Uruk polished the bottle with the jacket sleeve and set it on the table. Despite his efforts, his huge hands left a faint swirl of fingerprints on the bottle. The sight gave him a twinge of satisfaction. "So, any interest?"

"I can talk to some people," Mister Prissy said.

Uruk nodded. "Well, I'd like to know if I have to get it out there tonight. Because if not, I'll start to work on it myself. If I cut that crap with enough horse manure, it's almost drinkable."

This time, the elf shuddered.

Contempt returned, with interest.

"So," Uruk said. "Can someone make the trade?"

"I'll have to ask around!" Mister Prissy said. "These things, they take time."

Uruk stared directly at the elf. "It's a simple question. Yes? Or no. I'm a simple creature, so if there's no answer I'll assume it's a no."

The elf stared into space, not looking at Uruk.

Slowly, reluctantly, his chin dipped once and came back up. Uruk got the impression that the elf would scurry off to bathe his chin in lye the moment Uruk left.

"That's a deal, then. We'll have the goods in a truck—your truck, actually. It's a nice ride, but you'll probably want to get it fumigated or something. Bring ours in another truck. Pull in from Baseline Road. Send a man out front to talk to me. Both trucks pull forward at the signal. We swap trucks. Tell us where you want your truck left when we've unloaded it."

"Very well." Mister Prissy's smile turned predatory. "I must ask, though. Just for my own edification. What made you think we would not have taken you into some quiet place and beaten the mirovar's location out of you?"

Uruk laughed at that. "Have you ever tried beating knowledge out of a brick?"

"Orcs are tough. But we would eventually succeed."

Uruk shook his head. "Orcs are tough. And we're not smart." He scowled, letting a hint of his fury leak out. "But we're not stupid. I have no idea where it is. All I know is, if I don't walk out of here very, very happy, my boys find out just how well that stuff burns."

The elf shuddered again.

Enough interest. "The same thing happens if the deal starts to go sideways. If my boy in the truck gets nervous." Uruk nodded to Mister Prissy. "Pleasure doing business with you—sorry, *your people.* Sir."

As they walked him to the back, Uruk heard a door creak near the elf.

He glanced back to see a shoulder slipping out of a concealed wooden door next to the booth.

Then the men gave him a shove, and he was in the cold again.

But the deal was on.

7

One AM. The vast, empty lot of sticky rutted mud that was the Michigan Fairgrounds parking lot.

The incandescent streetlights of Baseline Road gleamed a block to the north, made hazy by the cold soft mist drifting from the sky. The wind had died. The oak and beech boughs, November bare, cast clawing shadows across the grounds.

Uruk huddled in his coat, flat cap once again pulled low over his ears. The smells of decaying leaves and dying plants filled his nose. Cold ate at his wrists and oozed up under his coat. His clothes hadn't quite dried from the night before, despite Vara's most valiant efforts. No orc could fight the weather. That tiny core of last night's stormy soaking drew tonight's chill even faster. His stomach grumbled with fear, but he didn't let it show in his posture.

Finally, one set of headlights coming down Baseline Road turned into the lot and started bumping across the ruts, weaving back and forth to cast its headlights across the expanse.

Uruk-Tai raised his arms over his head and waved. With each swing of his arms, his coat flapped around him. Fresh cold sloshed down his sleeves and through the neck. Nobody made a good, snug orc coat.

The headlights caught him on a pass, then settled straight toward him.

A hundred feet off, they stopped.

The headlights went off.

Uruk pumped his fist three times in the air.

A couple hundred feet behind Uruk, another truck engine rumbled to light. Headlights came on. Gears ground against each other, then the headlights lurched forward until it was a similar distance away.

Those headlights went out.

Uruk stood in the darkness, watching the distant truck.

Three figures, glowing deep red, climbed out of the new truck and started towards Uruk.

Patience, Uruk told himself. Patience does not come natural to an orc. He relaxed himself by tightening and untightening his hands, his shoulders, his biceps, his jaw. Should the evening demand any rending, he would provide it.

The figures came close enough for Uruk to make them out in more detail. The elf, his aloof face gleaming white even in this dark, draped in some jackass silky drapes that shifted around him with the breeze of his steps. He stared into the mist as if it was fascinating, refusing to let his eyes fall on Uruk. Seeing an orc might give him the personal disease or something.

Mister Prissy, wearing a long black coat and a heavy black muffler. If Uruk was that small, and had so little body heat, he'd want that kind of outfit too.

Forget body size—come February, Uruk might want that big scarf anyway.

Uruk didn't know the third man. Slight, wearing an expensive white wool coat and a black bowler hat. Despite the cold, he somehow had a flower, a red carnation, tucked into his buttonhole. But his face—Uruk had seen that kind of face before, on some humans at the docks.

This was a human orc. What they called a "killing gentleman." The sort who would gut you if he thought it was best.

"Do you have it?" Mister Prissy said.

"I am an orc," Uruk said.

"Doesn't mean you're not too dumb to lie," Mister Prissy said.

"Send your man to my truck," Uruk said. "I'll send my orc forward to check your cargo. Assuming you brought the draught, that is?"

"Proper draught," the Killing Gentleman said. "I checked it myself. Been sealed in those casks for a few weeks now. But do have your man—my apologies, your *orc*—check. "

A few weeks? The last Orcish boatload, Uruk thought. *Where other Tai died.* He waved his right arm.

Kaba trotted out of the darkness.

"How many with your truck?" Uruk said.

"One," said Mister Prissy.

"Two in ours."

Killing Gentleman cocked his head. "You have not done this before, have you? One is traditional. But I commend your honesty. It speaks well for this exchange. Peterson, check the orc's cargo. And count the orcs."

"There's two of them," Mister Prissy—Peterson—said.

"Oh, really?" said the Killing Gentleman. "Two whole orcs? One of them could take your head off with a sneeze. I suppose two could play football with it." He waved his left hand. "You won't be any more dead. Run along, then come back and report."

Peterson cast a tremulous glance at Uruk, then dashed towards the dark shape of the truck.

Uruk waved Kaba forward and said in Orcish "Check their truck. Make sure there's only the driver. Come back."

Kaba thumped his fist to his chest. He cast an angry eye on the elf and the man.

The glare Kaba gave the Killing Gentleman warmed Uruk's heart. Kaba's fire was not the strongest of them, but when it mattered, he was an orc.

Uruk turned to face the elf.

The elf stubbornly looked into the distance, as if counting the motes of fog passing before the streetlights.

"Before they come back," Uruk said, "I have to say to you. The draught is ours. The draught is sacred. Without the draught, my sons cannot become orcs. If this had been the Old Country, this would have meant war. This is America, so we do things the American way."

Uruk shifted his weight and hardened his hands into flat planes. Humans use fists, but orcs use their talons.

An orc's talons can cut bone like butter.

Elves live a long time. They all know this.

Uruk leaned forward. "But break our sacrament again. Interfere with our families again." He took a deep breath. "And it will be war. Many orcs will die. Each dying orc will lose decades. But dying elves will lose centuries."

The elf didn't even veer from the darkness. But words formed distastefully on his lips. "Orcs have no sacraments."

"Our sacraments are as meaningful to us as yours are to you!" Uruk shouted.

"The draught degrades orcs," the elf murmured. "Lowers them even further into the mud."

"Maybe no orc is a wizard," Uruk said. "But now, today—my boys, they learn to read! Maybe one is a driver, or a janitor! Maybe his son a plasterer!"

The elf snorted. "Orcs have nothing." His eyes almost twitched towards Uruk. "They are nothing."

Uruk drew a deep breath. "An orc has everything. An orc lives. We endure. An orc can withstand everything. Why do we need the draught? To teach our children to stand tall, no matter what. No matter how the world attacks them, they stand and face it. No matter what kind of asshole tells them they can't."

The Killing Gentleman gave a small nod to Uruk. "I think I understand what has happened here. This little adventure nearly derailed an important party. For an important customer in Chicago." He turned cold eyes to the elf. "Interfering with one's children is bad business. I don't want to see this again."

Peterson's voice called out of the darkness. "All here!"

The Killing Gentleman showed his teeth, like an orc. "Then we're almost done." He glanced at the two trucks in the dark. "You. Mister Orc. What's your name?"

Uruk glared at the elf. "Won't not say at the moment."

"Understandable. Should you find yourself in need of employment, come to Chicago. Look for people who know the local businessman Al Capone. Describe me. I think you would do quite well with us."

Uruk-Tai nodded. "I just might do that."

At two hand signals, two trucks started. Two sets of headlights started forward.

Uruk-Tai watched the elf the whole time.

His sons, janitors. Or drivers. Or plasterers.

Or, one day, one grandchild... a wizard.

# FINAL GIFT

I

When November's wind clawed at the plank walls of the old wooden barn where Mha lived, when it set the flames in the rusty coal stove of the grooms' quarters to flickering, when the hard-used joints between her ancient orcish bones swelled enough to make every motion torment, when her crumbling guts refused to release the giant turd-brick wedged inside, Mha couldn't help asking in the secret pit of her heart: why hadn't her children eaten her?

She already knew the answer, even on this bitterest of days.

Mha had borne two sons for her Uraz-n'Tass. One son died in the Great War; the other, crushed beneath a falling crane at the Port of Detroit. Other clans had claimed her three daughters.

They had done right by their children.

Even if it left them alone.

Even if a son had survived and kept the clan alive, she would still draw breath. This horrid America of 1927 left the old to rot alive.

And she and Uraz had rotted. Mha couldn't remember ever seeing an orc as old as them. Her beautiful bald purple-green scalp had sprouted long strands of hair, like a human's or a dwarf's but far coarser. Her steel knife couldn't hold enough of an edge to shave away the shameful strands no matter how carefully she worked the whetstone, so she used a piece of old tack she'd found in the barn to tie the strands into a lump in the back of her skull. During the Spanish-American War, her hands had been dexterous enough to work Lord Gatling's famous machine gun, but now her knuckles were the size of walnuts. She'd broken a tusk off short gnawing on a marrow-bone, and the roots of the rest of her teeth felt only tenuous. Her nose had grown weak, but not weak enough she didn't know she stank of something that wasn't quite mildew or decay or foul meat, a stench that could only be called *old orc*.

At least the barn had plenty of space to do the butchering, even with the giant heap of coal and the age-warped timbers wasting away and the open-top carriage that hadn't been used since before Mha's birth. Scattered barrels held scraps of wood and bits of iron and other detritus someone hadn't bothered to properly discard. Dusty shelves offered tools so corroded they imploded at a touch and mysterious half-full bottles. The six stalls hadn't seen beasts for ten years at least, but the stinks of hide and manure and horse-sweat had sunk into the dirt floor like wasted blood. Not that Mha would waste any of Uraz's blood.

The barn was for lost and useless things.

Like an orcess with no clan and no labor.

Like Uraz, Mha was naked. She didn't want to get his blood or grease on her clothes. The grooms' quarters had the tiny stove, but out here in the main barn, November's chill whistled between gaps in the plank walls, turning her breath to white plumes and raising bear pimples on her sagging skin.

Mha knotted the heavy hemp line around Uraz's ankles. She needed two tries to toss the line over the central beam, a mere fifteen feet up. Rusty saw blades in her spine and an even more agonizing brick in her throat, she hauled the line hand-over-hand to hoist her warrior's naked body so that his dangling hands hung inches above the floor. A double loop and quadruple half-hitch around one of the beams supporting the hayloft held him there.

Had the wind picked up? Did November approve of her efforts?

No, she couldn't think that. Orcish gods never gave. They only took. They commanded, never succored. She only thought she'd lost everything. If she dared protest to November or the Sun or Moon or even the sleeping soil, they would find something else to claim.

Watching Uraz's empty shell swing from his ankles, arms dangling almost to the hard-packed wooden floor, Mha fought for her own breath. It wasn't enough that her bent back cramped her lungs and the brick in her throat nearly choked her, the sight threatened to squeeze gasping *tears* from her. She knew every inch of his skin. That long twisted scar on the back of Uraz's ribs, where he'd had taken a sword blade meant for the human Lieutenant Harrison. The thick knot of scar where an overstrained rope had snapped, burning through his skin clear to the muscle. A lump where the first orc to try to claim their daughter Vara had gouged a talon's width of meat away. And so many smaller scars, where she'd marked him each time they joyfully ravished each other. Though those lusts had died twenty years past, her memory held each scar as firmly as his flesh did.

Her warrior's body mapped their lives together.

Uraz had left her this final gift. She had not dishonored him by sobbing when she woke to find him cold. She had not cried when she'd undressed him, gently tracing each of his scars for one last time. She would not soil his memory by even hinting at ingratitude. Even if she was alone for the first time in forty years, even if the rocky lump in her throat swelled enough to wholly choke her, she would not cry.

An orc lived for their clan and their work. She had neither, but Mha would show the gods that taking everything but her breath would not break her. Like the warrior she had been.

When Uraz stopped swinging, she set the broad tin pan beneath him. As she'd hoped, it was exactly wide enough.

Now the worst part.

The first worst part.

Mha didn't dare hesitate. November would think her reluctant. She would not tolerate that.

So many orcs in America, not that she and Uraz had seen any in the last few summers, kept their talons indecently trimmed. How could an orc be an orc without talons? She set her thumb to the side of Uraz's neck. "Thank you for your final gift," she whispered. Not that Uraz would hear, but November would know that she honored her warrior.

She needed to be gentle. She didn't want to set Uraz swinging and disrespect his blood by splashing it across the dirt. She wanted to savor every bite of blood sausage.

Mha flicked her thumb against Uraz's still carotid.

Her talon hit hide—and cracked.

The pain in her thumb was minor, but the shock of breaking a talon on Uraz's hide wholly halted her breath. She stared at the cracked talon, heart thudding in her ears.

She'd cracked talons before, of course.

But age had taken even the power to truly claim her warrior.

Maybe her breath would never start again. Perhaps November would decide she had finally earned death.

But in another heartbeat, her treacherous ruin of a body demanded air.

She had to use the feeble knife to cut Uraz's throat. It wasn't sharp enough to cut him properly, but at least it wouldn't snap. She cradled the back of his head with one hand as she sawed, trying to keep the swaying to a minimum.

An awful minute later, thick red blood pinged into the tin pan.

Mha's vision blurred. How *dare* she? The barn seemed even colder than before—had November witnessed her shameful tear? She refused to raise a hand to wipe her eyes. If the tear had been seen, she had condemned herself. If it had not, she would not draw November's eye.

The barn's chill would slow his blood. He would be there for hours.

She couldn't put it off any longer.

If she could preserve Uraz's meat and tan his hide properly, so that his remains could succor her for as long as she lived, she could choose a proper final sacrifice for him. If she couldn't, if his whole body had to be consumed in a single feast or be wasted, she would have to sacrifice it all.

You couldn't smoke meat over a coal fire, so she'd have to salt-cure him. A lot of salt. The little box in the groom's quarters didn't come close.

If she found salt, she would tan Uraz's hide with his brains. If she couldn't make the necessary sacrifice, she'd surrender his hide with the rest of him.

If she found salt before she needed to eat or drink, her warrior could still shelter her against the world.

And in the pit of her heart, Mha so desperately wanted something of Uraz to stay.

That meant calling upon that most un-orcish of human customs.

A *favor*.

2

Stepping out of the dim barn into the clear morning, Mha blinked and raised an arm against the painful light. The winter-weakened Sun had dragged itself a quarter of the way across the sky, but November stole so much of its warmth the frost still gleamed across the vast grassy lawn. Drifts of dead leaves from the surrounding forest raised a stink of decay from their sheltered steaming innards, almost smearing the crisp cold air. November's wind slipped through gaps in the old horse blanket she'd stitched into the coat and cut straight through her canvas dress. She'd debated over the skulls of her three failed suitors, but decided to leave them on their shelf. Humans wouldn't understand the significance.

Her warrior hung in the barn behind her, his turgid blood draining into a bucket before he froze, and the Sun shone as though the world hadn't ended. Maybe this year would be different. Maybe December Sun-Eater would fully devour the Sun. Plunge the world into a darkness as complete as that inside her.

December would not grant that fiercely held hope.

If she was to have anything at all, she must find salt.

Her only hope was the big white farmhouse at the far side of the meadow.

Frozen dirt crunched beneath her boots. The Army had issued her these misshapen boots when they'd claimed her labor for the Spanish-American War. Thirty years on, she'd worn the third set of soles so thin that only the cardboard liners kept the dirt out. If she could keep some of Uraz, she could make new boots. Truly orcish boots.

Every other step sparked a flare of pain in her left hip. Each month, each week, that hip ached more. A slow-growing pain, demanding a hair's thickness more from her every day. Perhaps she needed to finally surrender to the humiliation of a staff? Using a staff while Uraz lived would have been an admission that she was too feeble to be worthy of him, but now...

She brushed the thought away. She would deal with Uraz's gift honorably. Making that last sacrifice, she would stand on her own feet. She could bear the pain one more day.

Nothing compared to the pain of relying on a *favor*.

Uraz and Mha had saved Lieutenant Harrison's life in the war. They had only done their duty as soldiers of the US Orc Army, but Harrison claimed a human sort of blood debt. Not a proper blood debt, where Harrison would serve the n'Tass clan all his days, but a human *favor* as feeble as a man's thighbone. The young human had fumbled trying to explain *favors* to a young Mha and Uraz, finally settling on *When you can't take, I will give.*

Senseless, senseless words behind a senseless human idea.

But *favor* had sheltered Mha and Uraz in Lieutenant Harrison's barn for these last three summers, even after the Lieutenant's death. It had granted them the freedom of the woods, a heap of coal every month, oats and beans and bacon and a handful of salt or sugar or lard left at their door every week.

A feast of humiliation every day, for orcs who did nothing to earn it.

And now, Mha needed to invoke *favor* again.

A ten-pound bag of salt was nothing to a man. Perhaps Mha could do some service to earn it without the demeaning *favor*. The humans here didn't work the soil, or care for cows or horses, but surely they had some labor that would merit a bag of salt? Even age-twisted, she could carry a load that would cripple all but the biggest men.

Her finger caressed the knife-trimmed edge of the talon she'd broken against her warrior's neck, and wondered if that was still true.

A horseless carriage growled down the road beyond the line of trees at the front of the property. One of the new Model Ts, or Model As, or Model Another Stupid Meaningless Human Word. What was a T? Or an A? You couldn't point at a tree or a human or dirt or the Sun or even a despicable elf and say *This is a T.* More than one human had told her they were marks on paper, but that had to be a human prank. Why would you give marks on paper a name? You could make countless marks, of any sort you wanted, before using the paper to scrape your ass clean.

Perhaps the walk would shift the brick blocking Mha's guts.

It wasn't as painful as the brick in her throat, though.

Mha trudged past the human outhouse to the farmhouse's back door. The farmhouse was built so sturdily that it might have been intended for short orcs. The doorframe was timber, painted a shining white, and the door was solid planks of oak fit tightly together, sanded to be inseparable to human eyes, and stained a dark brown.

Mha had grown accustomed to the barn. The ceiling of the groom's quarters was so low, her awful *hair* brushed the plaster. The barn doors were comfortably tall. In the time since Uraz had brought them here, Mha had not once approached a building truly meant for humans.

The sight of this door added another layer of self-revulsion to her heart.

She had been strong. She had been tall. Her heart remembered being the sort of orcess that picked up a young recalcitrant cow under each arm before tossing them up onto the scale.

A normal human door should come up to her chin.

Her head could clear the farmhouse door without so much as a nod.

Heart shuddering anew, Mha's breath trembled. Had age stolen so much from her? Was she so stooped? Her traitorous eyes threatened to erupt with tears again, so she squeezed them shut until they obeyed her.

If she'd worn her skulls, any orc that saw her would challenge her boast.

Humans wanted you to knock on their doors to request admission, then built doors that would fall off the hinges at the lightest touch. She rapped the back of her knuckles against the door, light as she could. The dim thud, inaudible even ten feet away, sent another shudder through her.

She was weak. Old and weak and useless.

Maybe once she'd cared for Uraz's gifts, the gods would let her die.

She knocked again, a little harder.

A muffled cry beyond the door answered. The humans knew she was present.

Mha made herself relax. She needed to be calm. Humans worried when an orc showed so much as a tusk, or breathed too deeply, or farted. Her sharp ears picked up the sound of slippered feet crossing a wooden floor, along with a peculiar double thump. Moments later, the door rattled and swung open.

The gaunt human wore a faded white house dress—*she*, the human had to be a she, only women wore dresses, even though her skin hung so loose she might be sexless. She was even more bent than Mha, relying on a cane in each hand to keep her upright, head twisted almost cruelly forward so that she could see ahead. Wire-framed glasses with heavy lenses loomed on her beaklike nose, transforming her rheumy eyes into giant bloodshot orbs. She stank of grease and spearmint.

"Yes?" The woman started. "Oh, it's you!" She leaned on one cane to peer around Mha's flank. "It's usually your husband."

"Woman," Mha said formally. "I must invoke *favor*."

Before Mha could explain the woman said, "But of course!" She retreated a step, working her canes and legs in combination like a nightmare spider-horse. "Come in, come in! Wipe your feet, come in!"

What sort of human invited an orc into their home? Even in Mha's decrepitude, too bent to breathe well, one sneeze would shatter the old woman's spine. Human homes were full of breakable things spaced too closely together.

But Mha was completely, un-orcishly dependent upon Lieutenant Harrison's *favor*.

Mha stepped inside and meticulously wiped the soles of her boots against the boar-bristle mat.

"Shut the door, shut the door," the woman said. "These old bones freeze too easy."

This had to be a kitchen. It had a coal stove, and a counter, and even one of the fancy iceboxes just like an Army mess hall. It didn't look anything like a mess hall, with smooth-plastered walls painted a pale blue and a pristine white ceiling. The smells of a dozen different dried spices and baking bread filled Mha's sinuses. A china cabinet displayed delicate white porcelain plates and tiny cups, all bearing identical intricate blue sketches that Mha's old eyes couldn't quite make out. An antique wooden claw-foot table dominated the room, surrounded by masterfully carved ladderback chairs that any of Mha's children would have broken with a hard look. The floor was so brightly polished that Mha could see the shape of her reflection, if not her features.

Mha had never smelled any place so weirdly clean.

The woman waved to a sturdy-looking bench. "Sit, sit. At our age, our bones need all the rest they can get. I was just putting water on for tea, it's no problem to add a little more."

Did *favor* require tea? Uraz drank tea each time he begged for food? What were *favor*'s rules?

"Could you grab one of those big brown mugs off the top of the china cabinet before you sit?" the woman said, pouring water into a kettle. "I'm afraid it's a mite too heavy for these old bones."

The woman wanted her to go near the most breakable items in the kitchen? Was this a test? Did aged humans test orcs the way the Army had? And why would she keep a mug she couldn't reach and couldn't use? Keeping her steps as light as her treacherous hip permitted, Mha held her breath and plucked a mug down. It would hold perhaps a quart, and had a nearly orcish heft.

The woman set the kettle on the stove and tottered towards the table. "Sit, sit, my dear."

Mha sat. The bench was almost high enough to be comfortable.

"While that heats—oh, dear." The woman blinked. "I fear we've never been introduced, have we? And you, of course, are Mantis."

Humans! They couldn't speak an Orcish name properly if you stuffed them with apples and fennel and slow-roasted them over a hickory fire. "Mha-n'Tass." Maybe a little garlic. Garlic went well with man.

Ignoring her correction, the way humans always did, the woman turned a chair to face Mha and settled down. "My name is Rose, but everyone calls me Thorn. You must do so as well."

She had a name, but others refused to use it? Perhaps "Mantis" was as close a feeble human throat could get to her name, but "Thorn" sounded nothing like "Rose." How did humans stomach such disrespect?

Still, the woman had demanded a labor of using a wrong name. Mha would swallow the insult, so long as she didn't have the gall to ruin Uraz's name. Mha sucked her cold-chapped lips to moisten them. "Thorn."

"Just so!" the woman said. "What brings you out here, and not your fine orc husband?"

The knot in Mha's throat swelled until it threatened to burst. She didn't dare shout past it. Such words demanded to be shouted, but shouting would scare Thorn and might make her summon the police. "My warrior is dead."

The woman leaned back. "Oh, you poor thing! I am so sorry. How can I help you? Do you need help with arrangements? Should I send word to someone?"

Mha's heart pounded. This tiny sparrowlike woman, intruding on Uraz's final gift? Her hands twitched with the instinct to leap across the room and swipe her talons across the old lady's throat. The urge lacked heat, though. Mha's old blood didn't boil the way it once had. And could her talons pierce even human hide any longer?

"No," Mha said. "I need salt."

Thorn raised a hand to her mouth. "Orcs bury their dead with salt? I had no idea! Bristol would never talk of his time serving with orcs, you know.

Except for the part where you and your husband saved his life." She leaned closer and reached out a hand, almost as if she wanted to touch Mha. Which was silly. Humans didn't touch orcs if they could avoid it. "You gave me another twenty-nine years with the man I love. You don't have to worry. The barn is yours as long as you live. It's in my will."

What did Thorn's willpower have to do with the barn? Mha was sixty years old, and still understood nothing of humans. "It was duty."

"Now don't discount yourself!" Thorn lightly slapped both her knees. "Your man shoved Bristol out of the way and took a bayonet meant for him. The fall popped his knee, so you carried him away to safety before he got trampled. I know the whole story, see?" One side of her mouth cricked upwards. "By the time he healed up, the war was over. You were sent by God to keep my man safe, and I won't forget it. Whatever you need that I can give you, is yours."

Mha needed worthwhile labor. She needed a hip that didn't pain and hands without giant swollen knuckles and a back so bent that she could walk through a human door. She needed the hair to fall away, restoring her beautiful green-purple scalp.

Thorn's offer meant nothing.

And sent by God? Human gods did not even notice orcs.

On the coal stove, the warming kettle hissed and spat.

"I can work," Mha said. "For salt."

"Oh don't be silly!" Thorn said. "How much do you want?"

Silly? Mha's pulse throbbed in her vision. How was offering labor for salt silly? No, she couldn't let human strangeness distract her. The best way to deal with humans was to ignore the senseless things, swallow the insults, and say what you needed. "Ten pounds. I can move firewood. Or rocks."

"Nonsense." Thorn waved her hand. "In the pantry. Let's take a look."

Would she refuse labor? Did humans count *favor* so strongly?

Mha set the mug on the bench and followed.

In the Army, a pantry was a food warehouse. Thorn's pantry was the same, on a smaller scale. Big enough for Mha and Thorn to stand side by side, with wooden shelves lining the walls and tiny cans and boxes and jars lining the shelves. Sacks of flour and sugar and rice filled the floor space beneath the shelves. Mha had never imagined one person having so much food, so many different kinds of food. She recognized the beans and the red goop of tomatoes. But what were the jars of yellow orbs suspended in dark liquid standing in precise rows, ready for inspection whenever the Lieutenant returned? Were those peaches? Humans could have peaches all year long? Mha's mouth watered at the thought.

"My nephew, the ungrateful wretch, comes by every weekend to make sure I have everything I need and to do a few chores," Thorn said. "He brings me more than I can possibly eat. He *says* it's because he's afraid I'll get snowed in, but I'm sure it's just because he doesn't want to drive all the way out to Clinton Township when the weather's bad." Her head turned as she studied the bags and boxes. "He thinks I should move down to Detroit near him, like I would ever leave the home Bristol made for us. My son thinks I should move out to New York City with him, where he's got his fancy bank job. He's a vice-president, you know. He had the phone put in and everything." Her cane thrust out. "There. That little cask. That's the salt, left over from last year's canning. Here, let me out and you can pick it up."

The cask was big enough for twenty pounds of salt. How full was it? Mha's hope thrummed. She tried to dampen it before November noticed and was compelled to thwart it. She made herself watch Thorn's two-cane shamble back to her seat, refusing to surrender to dangerous hope.

"Go on, then," Thorn said. "Pick it up. I'll make the tea."

Mha lifted the keg's loose lid.

It was nearly full.

If Thorn permitted her the whole cask, Mha could accept every scrap of Uraz's final gift. Not just the meat, but the organs and bowels as well.

Mha commanded her heart to slow. "I could move coal for this,"

"Oh, you go on," Thorn said. "Take it, take it. You more than earned a few pounds of salt."

Earned? How had Mha *earned* this?

No, she couldn't get angry. She'd already lost her pride by living too long.

The cask felt far heavier than twenty pounds.

Thorn said, "I have a jar in the cupboard I use for cooking. When Pete shows up this weekend, I'll send him tooty-sweetie for another box."

Escaping the pantry had its own challenge. If Mha turned around, her back side would probably bump the canned peaches, or maybe the bag of flour. Or the sugar—how did humans stomach that awful stuff? Mha backed up, each unnatural step triggering an unfamiliar ache in her rotting hip, glancing left and right before each motion to be sure she wouldn't accidentally knock down a wall.

Not that she could wreck a human's house. Not anymore. Not like when she was young and worthwhile.

She emerged to find Thorn had set a china cup and the mug on the table, and was pouring hot water into a teapot barely bigger than the mug. "Set that by the door and have a sit. I still have some cookies left from yesterday's baking. And prunes, but you don't want them. Nobody wants them, but I get stopped up something fierce and nothing clears you like a prune. It happens to old ladies like us."

Thorn thought she was like Mha? An orc was nothing like a human!

But...

They were both old.

Both lived alone.

They'd borne their children. Those children had gone away.

Like Mha, nobody remained to eat Thorn.

"Sit a spell," Thorn said.

Mha shoved her disquieting thoughts away. Even if she wanted to eat with a human, she could neither eat nor drink until she made Uraz's final sacrifice. "Uraz-n'Tass needs me."

Thorn's entire face drooped. Was she disappointed? "Of course, of course. It's selfish of me." She set the kettle back on the stove. "Listen. It's just us ladies now. We can't be all formal. If you get lonesome, you just come up and knock on that door. We'll have tea and chat, and you can tell me what you need my nephew to bring for you. I'm sure you get tired of oats and lard, don't you?"

Get lonesome? Mha's entire life would be lonesome. Uraz had nuzzled her neck before sleeping last night. That would be the last true contact she would have in all her days, and she would treasure that memory in the pit of her heart as long as she lived.

And when she died, she'd rot until she was found.

Chatting with a human would shorten her days when her heart burst from frustration.

And what sort of human would welcome Mha to her fragile dainty kitchen?

3

November had stripped away the forest's greenery, leaving an impassable tangle of vines and low-hanging branches on all sides. Every time the breeze surged, it carried scents of burning leaves and distant coal and November's constant decay. Leaves crunched beneath her bare feet as she trudged down the path, a knot of bloody gristle in each hand. The knot in her throat had not eased, but thirst had added its burn.

Make sacrifice, then she could drink. Eat a scoop of leftover porridge. Spend half an hour in the outshed Uraz had built behind the barn, heaving at the brick in her guts. Begin cutting and salting and tanning.

And dress.

An orc's final sacrifice must be made naked. Anything she wore, anything she carried, the gods would strip from her like the scudding clouds stripped the Sun's warmth from her skin. Mha kept her thoughts as empty as she could. Her greatest treasure were memories of Uraz. She would not offer any more of those than she must.

A few minutes hobbling through the woods brought her to the clearing she and Uraz had chosen. Wide enough for a dozen orcs to brawl, with long brown grass that cracked and crackled at each step, just like her bones. The ankle-deep stream still flowed freely, but its mocking laughter sounded cold.

The Sun was almost at its highest point when she reached the rock. She and Uraz had sat on it yesterday on their daily walk through the woods. They had stopped here more and more often, Uraz saying he would share the Sun's gift of light with his woman. She had thanked him, refusing to shame him by noticing his shallow breath.

Even when Uraz could no longer claim her body, he claimed her heart every day.

Her warrior had fought for her until the end.

She knelt before the rock.

Sobs threatened to come ripping straight up from her and out her face, spilling scornful tears and broken breath. Swallowing them was even harder than cutting Uraz's throat, harder still than choosing what to sacrifice.

Mha opened her hands.

In the left, Uraz's heart.

In the right, his privates.

The blood hadn't finished draining, but they were still pale and shrunken.

The cuts should be smooth, like orcish talons. Not brutally hacked from his flesh by a knife more saw than blade.

Mha took a deep breath. She must say this clearly. She must not be misunderstood.

When she thought she could speak, she raised her face and stared at the Sun. "Sun! Light of day. I thank you for Uraz's life. He fought for me all his days."

Her throat tightened again, her guts clenching around the brick of turd.

The Moon was not visible, but it would hear. The Moon knew everything.

"Moon! Keeper of secrets! I thank you for Uraz's nights. He brought me pleasure in every one!" The pleasure had faded, but as she aged she'd found warmth alone a milder pleasure.

Her next breath was brazenly ragged, a disgrace. Her chest refused her commands, so she pushed her air out as hard as she could, hoping that volume could make up for shakiness. "November! My Uraz sought death all his days. I thank you for granting it to him."

She should be surrounded by the clan. Even if orcs born in America would not end their elders, would not take those final gifts, she should at least be surrounded by sons and their wives and their babes. She should be living with her own blood, not left alone in a barn in the wilderness with a strange human woman who would offer her *tea*.

No. No distractions. Complete the sacrifice.

Mha bowed her head to stare at the rock. The heart that had driven the passion of his spirit, the privates that had driven the passion of his flesh. Two pathetic shriveled offerings, left on cold stone.

More of an offering than she would leave of herself.

She could barely force the words out. "I thank you for my love. My warrior. My Uraz."

There. She'd left his name for the gods. She would never speak it again.

Bitterness overwhelmed her. She had lived her whole life as an orc ought. And she would end her days here, without a warrior? Without useful labor? With no reason, no purpose? The gods took everything from an orc, but couldn't they at least grant her death in return? Why couldn't someone, anyone, just eat her?

The Sun peered around a cloud.

Mha's breath caught.

She'd knelt at her warrior's last sacrifice, and dared to demand?

November had certainly witnessed her. Had the Sun seen as well?

It didn't matter. There was nothing November or the Sun could take from her. If either claimed the barn she called home, December the Sun-Eater would freeze her blood to her bone.

And she would welcome it.

Swallowing a groan, she heaved to her feet and walked from the clearing without looking back, leaving her warrior's shriveled heart and orchod and name behind. When she returned, if she ever returned, they would all be gone.

The wind gnawed at her bare skin, sucking away what little warmth she still held. She refused to let it speed her step. An orc endured, even when the wind tried to make her skin as cold as her heart.

She'd left her coat and dress by the outshed her warrior had built. Before pulling them on, she dipped water from the ice-crusted rain barrel and washed the heart's blood from her hands and empty breasts. Five orcs had suckled at them. Another had once admired them. Now, as useless as the rest of her and even more annoying, the way they flopped around.

It was done.

And he would still nurture her. A bite of meat, every day. New boots. A leather dress. Bits and drabs of her warrior, to shelter her and warm her and protect her.

Mha was reaching for the barn door when she heard the soft cry.

Between the human outhouse and the farmhouse, a figure in white flailed at the ground.

Grateful for any distraction, Mha stomped towards the farmhouse.

Thorn had fallen, arms and legs and canes flying every which way. The woman sucked in breaths bigger than a tiny human should be able to hold. One hand still held a cane. The other cane lay well out of her reach. Eyes watering and blinking, she stared up at Mha. "I seem to have fallen."

Humans, explaining the obvious, would never stop annoying Mha. But she needed to think of something else, anything else, other than her warrior and the gut-wrenching task that would fill the next few days. "Are you hurt?"

Thorn raised her hands and flexed her legs. "I don't think so. My other cane is missing, though. Can you see it?"

Mha knelt to pick it up.

"It's my own fault," Thorn babbled. "It's the prunes, you see. They help when things stop, but when they start again I get in such a rush and the grass was still icy underneath. I can't abide the old chamber pots."

Mha offered her the cane.

Thorn said, "Could you offer a hand?"

Mha had helped wounded human soldiers to their feet before, helping them get upright so they could keep a little self-respect by hobbling off the battlefield. Thorn's tiny hand felt like helping a butterfly aloft.

"Thank you, my dear," Thorn said.

Did the woman think Mha roamed the woods eating grasses?

Getting her canes braced beneath her, Thorn said, "If you'd care to come back in half an hour or so, or any time, we could have that tea. Just knock on the door."

Why did she persist in that offer? Was Thorn so lonesome she would take an orc as company? The only thing Mha could think to do was offer the human parting respect chant and walk away. "Thank you, human."

"Do call me Thorn, I said."

Mha nodded. "Thorn. Thank you, Thorn."

Halfway back to the barn, Mha stopped.

She had knelt at Ur—at her warrior's final sacrifice, heart overflowing with bitterness at not having her clan or labor or her warrior.

November and the Sun *had* heard her.

And answered.

An old, decaying, worthless orcess wanted labor? Then let her help an equally rotting humaness. She'd thought the gods could take nothing more. They had taken the dare, and followed it by claiming her dignity, her patience, her peace of mind.

Mha ached to bellow reproach at the Sun itself.

But if she did, the gods would find something else to take. She couldn't imagine what remained, but they would find it.

Instead, she trudged back to the barn, fragrant with long-dead horses and the coppery stench of her warrior's still-draining blood. November's chill would help preserve his blood and meat.

She found her boots. Sat on the chunk of tree stump she used as a stool. Tried to ignore the aches in her heart and her throat, and the more concrete pain in her gut. And thought.

She must have a reason. An orc could not pound on a human's door without a reason.

Some time later, the outhouse door slammed on its spring. In another dozen breaths, the farmhouse door shut. Thorn was back in her home.

Mha steadied her breath. Hoisted herself to her feet. Perhaps she should carve a cane from her warrior's thigh bones? That would allow him to support her even more. No, that was for later. For now, she would obey the commands of season and Sun.

Heart pounding and November wind at her back, she trudged across the yard and knocked on the door, as instructed.

When Thorn's delighted face appeared Mha said, "Tell me of these *prunes*."

DROWNED MIROVAR

1

Orcs had built the Baksh-Ka speakeasy to keep humans out.

It started with the biggest, heaviest human door they could find, salvaged from a burned-out slaughterhouse near Detroit's Eastern Market, where it had withstood frightened bulls. An added inch of lead on the inside made it so heavy that even an orc needed a shoulder and a shove to force it open.

Not that a proper orc would complain of such an effort.

The door was mounted on a tiny angle, so that the moment it was released its own weight slammed it shut. Anyone who tried trailing an orc in would get crushed between the door and the steel frame. A dwarven family would get back a corpse with a big head-to-gut crease down the middle. A human? His children would find a bucket of gore wearing their father's shoes on their doorstep.

Uruk-Tai idly wondered how this human had gotten in.

And how long the tidbit would last, standing there at the top of the half-flight of stairs that led into the speakeasy.

He was skinny, even for a human. His "business suit" was ready for the shonky shop—worn elbows, threadbare knees, the tweed so battered that its previous owner might have been chained behind a Model A and dragged to death. The human's wide eyes circled the bowing hard brick walls of the converted basement, taking in the battered Old Country axes and clubs on the walls. Sweat shone on his forehead, and not only from the red-hot coal stove in the back of the speakeasy. There at the top of the cement stairs, pulling in his shoulders to make himself smaller, he somehow looked even more fragile than humans usually did.

Uruk pivoted on his stool to wrap one heavy hand around his clay mug, resting his elbow on the dented oak bar but keeping one eye on the intruder.

The orc outside the door had seemed sturdy and attentive. How had he let this feeble thing slip past him?

It wasn't that Uruk hated humans. But an orc needed a place to be an orc. Even in America, an orc wouldn't feel at ease unless surrounded by purple-green skin, bare scalps, and strong shoulders.

That morsel would break his neck trying to climb down the stairs.

Uruk sipped his whiskey, rolling the pale flavor around his mouth. He should be drinking proper draught, but the foolishness of Prohibition meant he had to make do with this weak whiskey. Taba-Kahk kept a bottle of draught in the back for Uruk. Uruk hadn't even broken the seal on it yet.

Once he had a taste of draught, he wouldn't be able to drag any pleasure from the shallow Canadian Club for weeks. Months, maybe.

Now the human was breathing through his mouth. Panic, maybe? No, probably the thick air. The speakeasy had no windows and almost no ventilation beyond the stovepipe. Tonight's horde was small, a dozen or so orcs in canvas dockworker dungarees. The aged shaman Azok-Snaka sat at a small table near the fire, his heavy sheepskin cloak thrown back to expose the twisted ropes of muscle in his chest, tough purple-gray hide covered with the honors of slash-like tattoos and the ragged scars of ceremonial bloodletting, snarling as he advised a young orc in a janitor's uniform. An orc with more dick than brains had accepted Dona-Feg's standing offer to wrestle for drinks, and their struggles in the shallow challenge pit raised concrete dust stinking of decades of such struggles.

With air this thick, Uruk felt somewhat surprised that a human could breathe at all.

At least the man promised Uruk a distraction from his problems. Raising twin orc boys ate money like porridge. They had the chance to stay in school, to even learn to *read*, but that meant they wouldn't get jobs, wouldn't contribute to the clan for years more. Rent—the landlord raised his rent every year. Everything got more expensive every year. And his woman, Vara, deserved better than a Port of Detroit dockworker could give her.

Uruk's brother Kaba, perched on the upended shipping crate that served him as a stool, drained his mug in a single swallow. He opened his mouth to speak, but something in Uruk's face made him close it almost immediately. Casually, he turned his head a little more towards Uruk, turning his eyes still further.

Seeing the human, Kaba's lip curled a little more, exposing the tips of his Greater Tusks behind his heavy purple lips.

Kaba wasn't Uruk's bravest brother, but a human who dared come in here didn't deserve the bravest orc.

Still... a dead human meant trouble.

"Hold," Uruk growled in Orcish.

Kaba relaxed his stiff fingers. Where a human would use his fists, an orc used his talons. Even close-cropped claws could gouge human flesh like warm lard.

The human's gaze flitted around the room, from the ancestral weapons to the massive boiler than had once warmed the warehouse overhead. In the years since Michigan had banned alcohol, orcs had used the rusty rupture in the boiler's flank to settle bets and test their strength. A proper orc could grab the sharp steel edge and bend the metal. Yes, he would cut his hand—but so what? Today, the contorted edges of the rupture twisted in every direction.

Uruk drew a heavy breath. The speakeasy's comfortable warmth filled his lungs. After working all day loading and unloading at the Port of Detroit in the chilling November sleet, broken only by a few minutes in the orc lunchroom, a few moments of proper heat was a deserved reward.

But a human would find the heat oppressive.

And the dust. And the smell.

Most humans called it a "stench." Never mind that they had their own stench. Perfume could conceal the reeks of garlic and boiled cabbage and old sweat from human noses, but not orc.

Behind the bar, Taba-Kahk stopped wiping the wood. His three-fingered hand still held the rag, but the other slipped beneath the bar. Only then did he focus his remaining eye at the door.

One of the orcs gathered around the big steel-topped gaming table stared flatly up at the human. In seconds, the others fell silent to glare up.

The bar's conversation drained away.

In the corner furthest from the fire, aged Koba-Tran turned his white-blind eyes towards his son and quietly asked in Orcish, "What is it?"

His son answered in a whisper that carried through the room, in the first English spoken in the Baksh-Ka in years. "A Pale Meat."

The human flinched. One hand reached up and snatched the flat cap from his head, exposing black hair cut short enough to show his scalp. His legs trembled, his hands shook. Thick fear-sweat oozed down his face.

But faced with a room full of orcs, he stood his ground.

Brave human.

Stupid. But brave.

The cast-iron stove ponged in the silence.

The human pulled his shaking shoulders back. Even his breath shivered. "Excuse me."

If he was any more scared, Uruk thought, he'd soil himself.

Good.

The man licked his lips. "I'm looking for an orc called..." He cleared his throat, preparing to twist his tongue around syllables humans found unspeakable. "Urka-Tai."

Uruk didn't let his thoughts show.

What could a manling like that want with me?

How could he even know my name?

The man looked like an, an accountant. Maybe an inspector. Or a doctor. Some kind of ink-weakened paper man. What could make a human like that come to an orc speakeasy? A place where orcs came to drink and boast and brawl?

Kaba pulled his lips back, exposing both his Greater and Lesser Tusks. Another orc would recognize it as a challenge. He pushed his heavy clay cup further back on the bar and heaved himself to his feet.

Even among orcs, Uruk's brother was a giant. The ceiling was high enough for most orcs to comfortably swing an axe, but if Kaba raised a hand he could seize one of the heavy wood rafters. His shoulders strained the canvas dungarees. His hands were large enough to fold over the human's scalp, wrap beneath the jaw, and lift the little thing.

The man quailed in his battered shoes, but didn't shift his feet back.

He must be drunk. Or perhaps those jazz cigarettes some humans broiled their brains with.

At the top of the stairs, though, with that massive door at his back, he had no space to retreat.

Kaba let extra Orcish color his English. "Who are you, that you think you can walk in here to seek Uruk-Tai?"

"I'm—I'm..." The man swallowed. "My name is Peter Sanford."

"Zhan-Fhort," Kaba said. "So. Who are you, that you can walk back out of here?"

Sanford licked sweat from his upper lip. "Nobody. If you decide to, to do away with me—there's nothing I can do." He gathered a shred of nerve from somewhere to hold his hands open at his sides. "I was told that if I wanted to find him, to come here and ask."

"Decide to *do away with* you?" Kaba gave a quick, guttural laugh. "That's not a problem. Now, you want to change our minds."

Angry Orcish laughter from two dozen throats echoed off the cracked brick walls.

Sanford grew even whiter.

So he's not completely stupid, Uruk thought. But he hasn't broken and run.

"Koba-Tran!" Kaba shouted. "Old one! You remember how to roast a man?"

The ancient orc raised his chin. "In the Boer War," he said, his accent making his English almost indecipherable. "Slowly, over low flame. They're best smoked over apple-wood. Stuff with garlic. Or fennel."

Sanford's hand flew up.

Uruk tensed. Surely now the human would pull out his weapon. A gun? Or something more decent, like a knife? Maybe even brass knuckles?

Maybe his weak body would betray him, make him fall unconscious without a touch. The orcs could put him outside the speakeasy, someplace a little sheltered from the November cold. Maybe he'd survive. Maybe he'd freeze, or succumb to pneumonia or chicken pox or one of those other human diseases. If he lived, he'd tell other humans to never disturb orcs at play.

But the human only put his hand on the brick. The ratcheting shake in his legs grew worse, and it seemed that only the wall held him up.

A dark patch appeared at Sanford's groin, spreading down one pant leg.

Orcish laughter erupted.

This little man had courage.

Men did not belong here. Bigger, stronger men than Sanford sometimes forced their way in and demanded respect. They left in tears and blood and bone.

This tiny man, though, somehow stood above the stairs and refused to even try to flee, even when his body betrayed him.

"Enough!" Uruk shouted.

The laughter choked off.

"I am Uruk-Tai," Uruk said, deliberately keeping his English clear.

Sanford's eyes swiveled in their sockets to focus on Uruk. The man's fear narrowed, as if Uruk alone could dictate his fate.

Which was true. It wasn't that Uruk ruled anything beyond the Tai brothers and their families, but if a man wanted to see Uruk, the disposition of that man belonged to Uruk.

"You buy me a drink," Uruk said. "I drink. You speak. When the drink ends, you go."

The man's courage outweighed his flesh. Uruk could drink to that bravery.

3

With Uruk's declaration, the orcs turned back to their drinks in a rumble of Orcish. Some dismissed Sanford's bravery in coming to the speakeasy, while others were curious what could drive such a feeble man here.

Uruk waited impatiently as Sanford half-crawled down the orc-sized stairs, each twice the height and width of a human stair. Orcs weren't nearly twice as big as men, but adding a shell over the pathetic human stairs was much simpler than tearing them out and building risers meant for orcs.

The tiny man crossed the room without taking his gaze from Uruk, even when he stumbled on the broken bricks of the floor. He kept his shoulders pulled in, trying to make himself too small to even accidentally bump one of the orcs sitting at a table. About two yards from Uruk-Tai, he stopped. The quiver in his shoulders had tightened—not gone away, but somehow focused. The man's jaw was set firm, though. He stood with the defiance of a man who hadn't pissed his pants in fear.

Without taking his eyes from the human, Uruk raised his mug. "Whiskey." He felt Taba-Kahk lift the mug from his grip. "And you, man?"

Sanford drew a breath. "Beer."

Taba-Kahk laughed. "Your beer is what *we* piss. Whiskey? Or are you foolish enough to try the draught?"

"Whiskey, then. But a smaller glass." Sanford tried to make his voice firmer. "I never drink anything bigger than my head."

The stab at bravado must have been what softened Taba-Kahk's next laugh. "A thimble for you." The bartender produced a glass cup no bigger than Uruk's two thumbs from beneath the bar, placed it next to Uruk's mug, and filled it with exaggerated delicacy. Uruk's mug was filled until the Canadian whiskey slopped over the brim. "Five dollars, man."

An outrageous sum, but Sanford only let out his breath and gave a single nod. With a trembling hand he extracted a money clip from one pocket and extracted five silver notes. The clip looked considerably less full when he returned it to his pocket.

Taba-Kahk held out a hand. He could have reached further, but kept his palm over the bar.

Sanford looked at the narrow space between Uruk and Kaba, took another breath, and darted forward. The bills fluttered to the abused wood even as Sanford snatched the cup and slipped back.

The little man was fast as well as brave, Uruk had to admit. He raised his own mug. "No man chair here."

Kaba crossed his arms and glared down at Sanford, exposing his Greater Tusks in gentle menace.

Sanford raised his cup to the height of his head. The tiny cup looked as large as a mug in that puny grip. "To your health, Mister Urka-Tai."

A toast? This human dared offer Uruk a toast? They didn't know each other, let alone struggled together—but the human had to be ignorant of orcish ways to even show up here.

And the toast had been to him.

Uruk grunted and raised his own mug. The gentle whiskey soothed his throat.

Sanford broke out in a barrage of coughing.

Kaba laughed again, this time from his belly, with more honest humor.

"The rules," Uruk said.

Sanford looked up through streaming eyes.

"You talk while I have drink," Uruk said. "The more interesting you are, the slower I drink. When I'm done, you go. Understand?"

Sanford drew himself up straight. Even that pallid Canadian whiskey seemed to have kicked him in the heart. Draught would have burned a hole straight through him. Fresh sweat had broken out on the thin hair of his scalp. "I understand."

"Boring," Uruk said, sucking in a mouthful. He'd offered Sanford the respect of a chance—but he was still a human, in an orc speakeasy. Any victory this human wanted, he would have to earn.

"Wait!" Sanford coughed. "I—you're the only one who can help me! In Detroit!"

"Boring," Uruk said. He rolled the next swallow around his mouth as Sanford's mouth worked.

The brave little human was going to lose his chance in another gulp.

"Celebrimble!" Sanford said. "Celebrimble the elf!"

Uruk paused, the mug inches from his lips. Celebrimble ruled the elves of Detroit—not that elves had rulers, of course. The elves merely did what Celebrimble said, because they always thought he was correct.

More importantly, the Tai clan's greatest secret? They'd killed a wizard of Celebrimble's.

Sanford's gaze flickered to Uruk's stationary mug, and the little man gasped for air. "You're the only one who's ever stood up to him, you and yours. The only one brave enough, tough enough, to get away with it."

How did the man know? Sanford had Uruk's interest now, but an earned compliment like that—even from a human—demanded a deep drink.

Regretfully, Uruk touched the mug to his lips.

Kaba grunted loudly and hoisted his mug. "Tai!" A single mouthful drained the mug.

Honor satisfied, Uruk contented himself with a sip. "Even the Lord of the Elves risks his life, threatening us."

"I don't want to, I *can't* threaten you," Sanford said, his words tumbling out like a ruptured bale of raw cotton spilling on the dock. "I want to hire you. I have a boat, I have cargo, but Celebrimble's put the word out on me. Nobody will crew for me, they're all afraid. Just one night, tomorrow night, to Windsor and back. You and a couple of other orcs, a hundred dollars."

Uruk made his face stay still. The four dollars a day he brought home barely held his home together. He took a single sip, rolling the soothing fire around his teeth before swallowing. "You are no bootlegger."

Sanford stood straight, but the whiskey cup trembling in his hand betrayed his terror. "I am now."

"You are brave, to walk in here," Uruk said. "You are smart enough to offer an honorable amount." Uruk shook his head. "But your stupidity is greater than either. Paper men are not bootleggers. Courage is not success. Your flesh is weak. Your plan, it will fail. You will die."

Uruk drained the mug, tipping his head back to dump every last drop straight down his gullet. Whiskey fumes burned his sinuses. "I will not die with you. Take your courage and go. Do not return."

Sanford opened his mouth, as if he thought he could argue.

Or maybe he'd ruin everything, by begging.

Sanford wasn't one of those men who thought he could out-punch an orc. Breaking him would feel like kicking an infant.

But if Sanford begged, Uruk wouldn't have a choice.

Uruk showed an inch of fang, scowl on his face and hope in his heart.

Something broke inside Sanford. All that courage shriveled, leaving him somehow even smaller. His chin trembled, and—was that a tear in the man's eye?

Before Uruk could get a good look, though, Sanford turned back towards the stairs.

"One last thing," Uruk said.

Sanford stopped, looking over his shoulder. Fevered hope burned in his eyes.

"Tell me who gave you my name," Uruk said, "and I'll have my brother open the door so you *can* leave."

4

November's night wind howled down Grand River Avenue, seeking its due sacrifice of warmth from blood and marrow. Uruk-Tai had the heavy collar of his wool coat turned up and his head pulled down almost between his shoulders, but the wind still burned in the gap between the collar and flat cap, stabbing up the sleeves.

Fortunately, the fire in his belly would warm him.

The clan's battered, rusty Model T offered no shelter, but at least the lap rug kept his legs from freezing solid. Heavy, stiff gloves protected his fingers enough to grab the bone knob of the gearshift and the hide-wrapped wheel. Crisp dead leaves whirled around the ridiculous little windshield, and the line of cars ahead of him made every breath stink of exhaust.

If Uruk stopped on Grand River, between the mansions of Detroit's newly rich, the police would appear in minutes. Men put great faith in the importance of their written laws, and proclaimed that there were no laws against orcs in a prosperous neighborhood after dark.

Orcs knew that the most important laws were not written.

Best he didn't stop.

A left onto the two-lane Mack Avenue. Past the human's massive Roman Church, the electric lights behind its stained-glass windows staining the night with a rainbow shout of wealth. Orc gods demanded proper bone and flesh. Human gods demanded wealth, only to clad their churches and priests in gold and glitter. Even an orc could see through that scam.

Uruk didn't have time for this. He needed to be home asleep, preparing for work tomorrow. The rent was due at the end of the week.

Another left, at a smaller street, between tight-packed two-story homes, and a right into the factories.

Lord Chrysler's factory distorted the land as much as any emperor's castle. Iron railways crossed the macadam road, allowing locomotives the size of homes to haul machines from one plant to its twin across the road. Coal smoke blacked out the sky, replacing the scudding clouds with embers spiraling up to eternity. The land felt like Grandpa's tales from the Old Country, when a Lord demanded service.

America was better. But it still had its lords and emperors.

A stark, windowless brick building, maybe four stories tall, had two dwarves in medieval armor guarding the lone knee-high door; an apartment building for the dwarven craftsmen that dominated "skilled trades" in the surrounding plants.

Uruk-Tai kept the Model T's speed comfortably below the limit, deferring to other drivers. The police always blamed orcs for accidents.

One little side street hadn't surrendered to the factory. Massive but dilapidated two story brick homes stood here, looming close enough together that an orc couldn't hope to squeeze between them, all facing the back end of a decrepit warehouse that loomed high enough to block out the sky. Lights flickered between heavy drapes. The few cars on the street were Model Ts as old as the one Uruk drove, many with their flimsy cloth roofs gone but carefully blanketed in canvas tarps by protective owners.

Most orcs lived in Hamtramck, with their ancient tenements and speakeasies and repurposed temples. Some had found places elsewhere.

Like here.

Uruk found the boarding house he sought. He ignored the open space by the side of the road right in front of the stoop, instead squeezing into a tiny gap across the street, facing the warehouse. If he'd been home he would have covered the clan's Model T with its own tarp, but he didn't expect to be here long.

With exaggerated, practiced delicacy he tugged the key from the dashboard and trudged up the muddy verge to a door in a house much like all the others.

Unlike the speakeasy, the door on this exposed cement stoop was only a suggestion. A human would call it sturdy, yes, but Uruk could bash it to kindling with a shoulder. The hard part of passing through it would be crouching so he didn't rap his skull on the wooden wall above it. Instead, he used one finger to lift the heavy cast-iron knocker and let it fall.

The rippled glass in the door's twin curtained windows rattled with the thud.

Three knocks was customary, but the door rattled after the second. "Hold!" someone shouted in Orcish, the words muffled by the wall. "Weakling human thing!" Wood groaned against wood as the door swung in.

The orc behind the door wore a flannel house dress and a heavy burlap apron. While she had a black kerchief demurely over her scalp, she had her mouth open barely enough to expose her gleaming Greater Tusks and one hand raised to show the trimmed talons.

Uruk-Tai lifted his cap with one hand, letting the cold wind abrade his scalp. "Pardon, home-keeper. I hunt my brother, Tara-Tai." He pulled the cap back down, trapping the fresh cold against his head. "Uruk, leader of Tai."

Her tusks remained visible for another moment—*my home, I will defend it*—then her scowl swallowed them. "Tara-Tai!" she shouted. "Door!"

"Worthy home-keeper," Uruk said to the closing door. Etiquette said she should have allowed him to offer his respect before departing, but he couldn't blame anyone for barricading their home against this cold.

Seconds later, Tara-Tai swung the door open. "Brother?"

The heat burning in Uruk's belly burst into incendiary flame. He grabbed his smallest brother by the front of his dungarees, let out a wordless roar, and flung Tara out of the house and through the air.

5

His brother crashed on his back with a satisfying *oof*, right in the freezing mud at the edge of the dirt road. Tara's head hit so hard that Uruk heard teeth clang together—better still.

Uruk mustn't break his brother. Not yet.

No matter how hot his blood burned.

Uruk heard the boarding house door slam. The home-keeper had closed them out—a brotherly dispute wasn't a spectacle for a woman. The night engulfed Uruk, leaving only the coal-dark sky and stabbing wind as witnesses. The only light came from Tara's face gleaming in night-sight, as cloying mud sapped the warmth from the rest of him.

Uruk took two steps to stand over Tara. Tara's hands thrust against the cold mud, scrabbling for traction, one knee rising, the foot slipping through the tire-pounded wet sludge.

"You betrayed us," Uruk said. Lightning-quick, he knelt and straddled his brother, digging in until the edge of Tara's ribcage gouged his knees. The warmth of his brother's gut rose into Uruk's seat.

Tara's feeble breath rushed out.

"A paper man comes to me today," Uruk said conversationally, ignoring the cold mud seeping through his dungarees and into his shins. "He walks into the Baksh-Ka like a landlord. He asks for me."

Tara started to get more air, the beginning of a proper breath.

Uruk gave a little bounce over his brother's gut to crush that air back out. In the dim light reflected off the clouds, the purple-green of Tara's face faded to a pleasing pale red.

Right now, his brother didn't deserve air.

"He tells me," Uruk said. His voice dropped to a low hiss. "He tells me that me and mine stood up to Celebrimble. He wants to pay us to do it again. He tells me that an orc gave him my name. An orc they call," and Uruk bent forward to hiss into Tara's face the unfamiliar English word: "Terror."

Tara's hips wrenched up from the road, launching Uruk forward off Tara's belly. Tara kicked and whirled, and suddenly Uruk was rolling to the side, Tara on top but trapped within Uruk's interlocked heels.

Uruk kept his elbows at his sides, but raised his hands talon-first towards his brother's face. "Did you forget that *we* killed Celebrimble's wizard?" he hissed as the mud's chill seeped through his coat and into his back. "No orc has stood against the elves but us. Why did you not simply tell the human police everything?"

Tara wheezed out, "He knew."

Uruk leaned his head back in surprise, then jerked up at the freezing touch of chilled mud. "He knew? How?"

Tara shook his head, heaving in more air as he shifted his weight back onto his knees, out of reach of Uruk's talons. "He knew. I said only, if he wanted to," another deep breath, "do business with our clan, he must speak to Uruk-Tai." Proper color had begun seeping back into Tara's cheeks, but the skin around his mouth and eyes were still pale and sweat steamed on his bare head.

Uruk's clench had loosened with his surprise. He squeezed his legs together again, squeezing a whooshing exhalation from Tara. "What did he know?"

"He said I had been with some orcs that had killed an elf," Tara wheezed. "He wanted to know," gasp, "if he could hire them."

"And you sent him right to me?" Uruk snarled.

Tara shook his head. He braced his hands on Uruk's thighs, pushing them apart for a little more breathing space. "I asked him why he thought that. He said, everybody knew."

Uruk raised his head, staring into Tara's face. "Everybody knew? Who is this *everybody*?"

"Everybody at the factory," Tara said. "All the men. Even the dwarves."

Shock flooded Uruk. He'd sworn his brothers to silence. The few humans who had been there had fled, seeing only tall shadows in the dark. Humans thought all orcs looked alike anyway. How could men know which orc had been there? His ankles slipped apart, releasing Tara.

Tara's chest heaved. He glanced up and down the street, back at the boarding house.

Quick as an enraged lightning bolt, Tara slammed the edge of his hand down on Uruk's chest, right below Uruk's ribs.

The impact crashed through Uruk like a falling ore crate. He felt his liver crash against his spine, and the air rushed from his own lungs.

Tara leaned forward, trading his voice for his own angry hiss. "You doubt my loyalty? *My* loyalty? I do not meet women you would not approve of. I do not make myself out to be more than you even though I'm apprenticed to a janitor. I could have my own apartment, my own woman, but no—I send you every dollar I earn, I live *only* on what you return." Tara bared his Greater Tusks, adding the Lesser to them a blink later. "I give the clan *everything*, and you reward me with distrust."

Uruk's tusks ached, but he kept his teeth clamped tight shut and his lips together.

Tara spat into the mud. "If you were not my brother, I would scar your face. Let others know. But that. Would hurt. The clan." Tara threw himself to his feet and stomped away.

Uruk's lungs felt unsteady and his liver begged for respite, but he couldn't lie in the mud while his younger brother stood. The wind stabbed into his wet clothes, sucking heat from his back and legs, but Tara's unmoving back seemed more implacable than the night.

6

The last leaves of fall whirled down the frozen dirt road, trapped between old homes on one side and the looming warehouse's back end. The frozen street was empty—Tara had looked for observers before landing that strike and snarling his rebuke. From the way Uruk's liver burned, Tara wasn't merely angry. To pound Uruk that hard, Tara had to be *furious*.

Embarrassment shivered in Uruk's spine. Tara had always been a proper orc. Uruk had let a human's words drive him to anger against his own brother.

Uruk stilled his face. "There is a woman?"

Tara didn't look back. "The apprentice sweeper. He has a sister."

Uruk firmed his voice. "Why have you not brought her name to me?"

Tara glanced over his shoulder to spit, "He is of the Morannod clan."

Uruk's coughed in surprise. He'd absorbed the Morannod marrow feud in Grandpa's lap, from his father, his mother. He'd chanted the oaths of retribution before every sleep, as every orc did. The feud had immigrated from the Old Country, and while it lay dormant in America he felt sure the Morannod chanted it to their children. Marrow feuds were part of being an orc.

"And I have obeyed our laws," Tara said.

"How long?"

Tara spun. "How long have I been an apprentice?"

"Two years."

"Two years. I work with her brother every day. I clean toilets and windows and machines. He sweeps the floors. She brings his lunch—and mine. I pay her to bring mine." His voice dropped. "I pay her for lunch so I can see her. Hear her voice." He shook his head, face bowed.

Uruk said nothing. Tara's shame at paying for a woman's attentions came through as clearly as if he'd shouted it.

"Last week," Tara said, "she brings pasties. His, turnip. Mine, not just meat. Cow. Not organ, not gristle—sweet cow muscle."

Uruk grimaced. "Forward."

"You say this is America," Tara said. "That things are different here. I told Gashmor-Morannod that his sister had mixed up our lunches. He said only, 'no.'"

"Does he ignore marrow feud?" Uruk said.

"I knew you would say that!" Tara raised a fist to the blind sky. "Work is more important than whose grandmother ate whose grandfather! We make ourselves better every day." He took a step towards Uruk, keeping a finger's length out of reach. "One day, one day soon, the janitor stops work. He—" Tara struggled with the English word. "He *re-tires*. Do they hire another? Or does one of *us* get his work?"

Uruk shook his head. "You dream, brother."

"Yes," Tara said. "I dream. But I hold the clan first. So I do not gather allies and storm her home. I do not claim Kiva as my marrow shrieks I should."

Uruk held silent a moment. A windblown leaf brushed against his wool coat and stuck to the mud. What would he have done, if his own woman had been a Morannod? "We *will* discuss this later." Wool held heat even when wet, but after rolling in the mud the November chill had stabbed its talons through the coat into his skin. No matter what an orc did, the wind always claimed its sacrifices. "But tonight—they know. We must protect the clan. Tell me what you know of this Sanford."

Tara spoke.

Uruk listened.

They'd hardly begun when the boarding house door swung open, casting light onto the churned-up road and both muddy orcs. The home-keeper stood with her arms crossed, glaring into the night. Her Greater Tusks stood out against the warm glow of her face. "If you two are done," she barked, "get out of the road. Morda and Bakh-Hai have to settle something."

7

Tara had followed Sanford home one evening, to a little cluster of human homes south of Cadieux Avenue, near Vernor. A suitable place for low-level paper men. Go east, you'd hit the wealth and elves of Grosse Pointe. West would bring you to immigrant Hamtramck, where orcs and the poorest men lived in buildings discarded by the wealthy decades ago. A few miles south, the glorious glittering heart of Detroit. Close enough to Chrysler's factory for laborers, but upwind enough for the paper men to not smell the coal or the chemicals. Rich enough for tidy, well-patched macadam streets, but not wealthy enough to light those streets.

Here, squares of straw-covered dirt showed where men grew vegetables for fun, although they could afford to stuff their puny bellies until they ruptured. The homes glowed in the dark where heat seeped through the brick, revealing tight brickwork and snug mortar beneath well-build shingled roofs. This late, only one house had a lit window, and that at the far end of the block. Other windows shone only with the heat seeping through heavy winter drapery. A man would think this street impassibly dark, lit only by the Cadieux streetlights two and a half blocks away.

Uruk thought it looked almost perfect.

Without streetlights, nobody would notice how decrepit their Model T looked parked on the side of the road. Nobody would see the two bedraggled, muddy orcs walking up to a home. Elves could pick out their body heat against the night, but an elf would find these even these luxurious four-room bungalows unspeakably drab. And an elf wouldn't condescend to go near air that smelled of coal. Not even pricey, clean-burning anthracite.

Even the hungry wind seemed gentler here.

Or maybe Uruk's hide had gone numb under his wet wool coat and mud-drenched dungarees.

Sanford's bungalow looked exactly like the others around it, as if Lord Chrysler had built another plant that spat out identical shallow-roofed brick rectangles. Maybe he'd colored it differently, but such trivialities were invisible in orcish night-sight. The stoop wasn't big enough for both Tara and Uruk, so Tara waited behind Uruk, on the path leading to the street.

Uruk rapped the door lightly, using the back of his hand.

The flimsy pine door shuddered in its frame.

Uruk imagined the human newspaper vendors, waving their unreadable broadsheets and declaiming: *Orcs Break Into East Detroit Home! Are You Safe? Read All About It!* He tried to make the second knock even lighter, but the feeble wood quavered at his lightest touch. Annoyed, he tapped the wooden doorframe with the tip of a finger.

"Just a damn minute!" a muffled voice shouted.

Footsteps approached. The door rattled and swung open.

Sanford had exchanged his formal suit for a relaxed pair of cotton pants and a thin cotton shirt. He clutched a heavy wool robe around him. The man blinked as he realized he was looking at an orc chest, then his eyes grew round and he hugged his robe more tightly as his gaze traveled up to Uruk's face. His jaw hung open beneath red-rimmed bloodshot eyes.

Uruk ached to push Sanford back into the house. Follow him in. Learn what he needed directly. But an orc who attacked a human went to jail, no matter the provocation. Human courts, human laws, ruled America. And a human jury always declared an orc guilty.

Instead, Uruk tipped his head. "Man Sanford."

"You're..." Sanford said. "You're Urka-Tai."

Uruk swallowed his frustration. That butchering of his name was as close as humans could get without vomiting up their voicebox. "Most men can't tell us apart."

"Wh-what are you doing here?"

"You answered my question." You're in human-town. Speak quietly. Respectfully. "You did not tell me what I needed to know."

Sanford gave a little shudder. "What do you need?"

"Who told you this tale that Tara had fought the elves?"

"Everyone knows it," Sanford said.

Uruk's feet tried to drag themselves forward. He needed a moment to restrain them. "Who? Who is this everybody?"

"I..." Sanford tried to speak, but he'd run out of air. Even Uruk's gentle questions and polite manner had driven him to paralytic terror.

Uruk stilled his hands. "I am not here for your blood, man." No, humans liked names. "Sanford. Someone spreads tales about my family. I must find out who and stop them. You understand?"

The words seemed enough for Sanford to breathe again. "Okay. Yes. I'll tell you, all right?"

Was it all right? How had Uruk not been clear? "Yes. All right."

Warmth spilled out through the open door, richly layered with human food—cabbage, potatoes, a trace of corned beef. A trickle of chemical taint turned Uruk's stomach far more than its feeble strength should have allowed.

And beneath it all... was that blood?

"I heard..." Sanford sucked on his lips. "I heard it first at the coffee shop. One of the old guys there told me about it."

"What 'old guy?'" And how far back would this chain go?

"He'd read it in the paper."

The frustrated anger in Uruk's belly flared high, rushing out his nose in a huff.

Sanford lurched back a step, raising his hands protectively. "Paper. You know?" He spread his hands in a pantomime. "Broadsheets?"

"I know of newspapers, man." Don't claw the human. Don't claw the human.

"It was one of the back pages," Sanford said. "Someone saw a bunch of orcs attack an elvish rumrunner."

"Why—" No, quieter. Don't scare the human any more.

Scare him less, if you can. "What made you think Tara was among those orcs?"

"I heard..." Sanford drew a shuddering breath. "It's all over the factory. The coffee shop girl told me, too. She asked me over breakfast a few weeks ago, if it was true that the Orcish janitor at our place had gone up against Celebrimble."

"Rising above our place?" The words growled out of Uruk's heart before he could tame them.

Sanford raised his hands back before his face. "No, no! She said it was great, that the elves needed reminding that they're flesh and blood like the rest of us."

Uruk trembled with frustration. "So, this coffee shop girl?"

"No, that's just where I heard it first. Sal—uh, she hears all the gossip first. But we had reporters coming around the plant and everything."

Uruk glanced over his shoulder. Tara stood a few steps behind, exactly out of reach. "You did not tell me of reporters," he snarled in Orcish.

"I saw no reporters," Tara said.

Uruk turned back to Sanford. The human had retreated another step. In that brief interruption, he'd snatched a wrought iron poker from beside a cold fireplace and raised it like a sword.

Humans! All the memory of a babe. "I am not here for your blood, man."

Sanford didn't lower the feeble poker. The pointed metal tip shook so badly that the paper man might put a hole in the wall or himself.

It's his home. His flesh. If he wants to put a hole in either, that is his business. "What did the reporters do?"

"They talked to the first orc they saw, Gash-mur, the sweeper."

Gashmor Morannod! Even speaking of the Tai-Morannod marrow feud to a babble-mouthed human reporter would cover the Tai clan with suspicion. Uruk stilled his voice and commanded his blood to ease its roar, before the human's own fear killed him. "What did the sweeper say?"

"He pretended to not speak English."

Uruk sucked in a surprised breath, accidentally dragging the house's thick potato-scent deep into his lungs. He coughed in revulsion. "Good." Worry seeped into his gut, stirring the storm of anger.

Tara had spoken truly. Everyone knew... meaning *everyone*.

"So, when I needed help," Sanford said, "I asked Terror. He sent me to you."

"His name is Tara," Uruk said.

"Tarr... Tero..." Sanford coughed. "Te—"

Feeble human mouths! "Never mind." No, *quieter*. And polite. "Man. I thank you for sharing your knowledge." Uruk nodded formally. "No blood tonight."

He had to get home. Figure out how to protect the clan.

Prepare to fight.

Uruk had both feet on the frozen lawn when Sanford called, "Wait!"

Uruk stopped, looking over his shoulder.

Sanford stood in the doorway, silhouetted in the glaring light and heat bleeding from his home. He'd lowered the poker, almost as if he'd forgotten it was there.

"What?" Uruk said.

Sanford licked his lips. "Now that you know how I knew... might you reconsider the job?"

Uruk's worry and anger burst into laughter. "Work for you? Going against an elf?"

"Keep your voice down!" Sanford hissed, glancing at the dark houses around them.

Uruk turned to face Sanford. Sometimes you had to tell humans the simplest things more than once. They had a terrible time accepting truths they disliked. "I told you. Any errand you might have will end with the earth claiming your broken body. We have work. We will not serve you." Uruk shook his head. "You are a paper man. Paper men surrender. They give up."

To Uruk's astonishment, Sanford inflated.

His chest swelled as his face grew bright with heat. His spine straightened, and his breath turned hard and hot in the night. The poker dangling from his hand came up, as if the man might use it as a weapon.

"I will not give up," Sanford hissed.

Was he actually... angry? Not the pallid thing humans called anger when they wanted to brawl, but true passion?

The thought shocked Uruk out of his worry.

"I will never give up," the little paper man snarled. "And I'll prove it to you."

8

Uruk's night-sight showed steam from Sanford's soft pink feet as they touched the frozen concrete stoop, but his face didn't even twitch with discomfort. The wind ripped Sanford's wool robe open, sacrificing hoarded heat to the icy November night. Uruk didn't deal with humans other than the dockyard's boss, but his every instinct screamed that proper passion burned in the little man's every motion, his every word.

"This is my home," Sanford hissed, "so these are my rules. You are silent inside. You touch nothing. You see what I have to show you. And you walk out in silence. You disturb *nobody*. Am I clear?"

The challenge shocked Uruk. Was this paper man really—

Yes. He was. He was demanding Uruk's labor.

His obedience.

Uruk stilled himself. "This is America." He trembled with the urge to fling himself at Sanford, restraining himself only with the thought of police. "You are not in the Old World. You are not a lord building troops for battle."

"I am no lord," Sanford said. "But you think—you doubt my—my *will* to see this through. Walking into an orc bar wasn't enough?" His eyebrows bent into his nose as he snarled, "Then *follow me*."

Uruk instinctively straightened his hands, raising his talons to slash.

No, no—nothing had changed. If Uruk treated Sanford properly, Uruk would go to jail. Tara, too. Maybe the whole clan. Human police weren't too selective when it came to "crimes" against humans, no matter than the humans only got what they requested.

That only left one option. "Stay," he growled to Tara.

"But—" Tara began.

"Stay!"

"Yes, brother," Tara said through clenched tusks.

Uruk glared at Sanford. "You would find holding me difficult."

Sanford didn't even flinch as he spat "What was it you said? No blood tonight? Well, there's blood here—but do what I said and none of it will be yours."

"Let me pass through in peace," Uruk said, "and none of it will be yours."

Sanford nodded and stepped back. One hand still held an upraised poker, but the other waved Uruk in.

Uruk had never been inside a human home before. He'd been born in a tenement built for humans, but orcs had lived there for decades before his birth. Sanford's home was impossibly small and ridiculously clean. Yes, a home should be clean—but it should also be lived in. The walls should have patched holes where children ran headlong into them. These walls weren't even scuffed. A carpet was fine, but it shouldn't be *white*. How could anyone keep a carpet white? And the tiny furniture! Humans didn't need a couch that could hold an orc, that stood to reason, but even a human child could break that ruffled blue thing with a good bounce or two! And on the wall—a telephone. A telephone for this tiny house?

At least the ceiling was high enough.

Sanford closed the door after Uruk, blocking out the wind, the night, and Tara. Not that it mattered. If Uruk needed out, that door would shatter with a half-hearted charge.

Sanford's anger still held him upright. "I'm told you can see in the dark." He reached onto the mantle to snuff out an old-fashioned lamp burning cinnamon-scented oil. The flimsy electric table lamp beside the couch still cast its pool of illumination across the floor.

Uruk couldn't explain night-sight in silence. Chafing at the man's ignorant claim to knowledge, he forced himself to give a single stiff nod.

Sanford raised a finger across his lips. "This way." He turned his back on Uruk and stalked into the hall.

Uruk had to duck beneath a curved archway to follow. Why deliberately divide these high ceilings?

The halls beyond had walls almost too narrow for Uruk's shoulders. He tried to pull himself in tighter, but still felt his coat brush the pale green walls.

Sanford stopped before the door at the end. "Stay here," he whispered as he reached for the knob.

The door had barely cracked open when the smell hit Uruk.

Blood.

No, not only blood. Woman's blood.

Too much woman's blood, as well as heart's blood.

Seasoned with a thin aroma of forget-me-not flowers, as if someone had tried to cover the stench and failed.

Uruk put his hands on his knees to peer through the short door.

A human lay in a narrow bed, a thick quilt drawn up to her neck. Her face shone bright with fever. A long, low table was covered in salves and unguents and medicines, tucked between folded towels that looked too soft and fluffy to be real. A plain wooden cross from the human church hung on the wall above her head.

Sanford faced the woman long enough to take a deep, soft breath of the fetid air, then glared at Uruk.

Uruk nodded. His blood still burned with frustration and fear for the clan. The tight space made him feel ridiculous. But somehow, this intimate, vulnerable glance into the human's life laced all of that with embarrassment.

Sanford closed the door and pointed back to the front room.

Uruk followed his own muddy footprints and the dirt his coat had left on the walls back to the front door. Sanford marched him out, heedless of the wind.

"My wife is ill," Sanford snarled, bare feet again steaming on the stoop. "There's a surgeon downtown that can help her, but he wants paying. In advance. Two hundred and fifty dollars."

An unimaginable sum for an orc making four dollars a day and struggling to feed his family.

"I've sold about everything anyone will take," Sanford said. "My good clothes. My new car, traded for cash and that junker outside. I'd sell the house if I wouldn't lose money. Everything I have? Ninety-two dollars."

Uruk could almost imagine that much money. Almost.

And if his Vara fell ill, but money could cure her? Orcs had no doctors— but if such a thing existed?

"Tomorrow night, I make the money that saves her." Sanford's mouth tightened under distant eyes. "Or I die trying." His vision suddenly tightened on Uruk. "Is that enough *will* for you, orc?"

The tangled feelings burning inside him demanded he strike, or run, or scream defiance at the sky. Uruk's fingers were straight again, the carefully trimmed talons ready to rip flesh. Instead, he deliberately relaxed his fingers and lowered his hands.

"Maybe you won't surrender," Uruk said. "So talk to me of the work, man. Is your plan as strong as your passion?"

Sanford looked puzzled for a second.

Uruk made himself wait. Humans were not very quick.

The anger bled out of Sanford's stance. A smile crept across his face. "Yes," he said. "Let's talk."

The wind gusted, sending Sanford's robe lashing around him. The man glanced at the sky. "Damnation, it's cold out here. Let me get some clothes."

9

Sanford sent them around to the carriage house to wait while he dressed. The carriage house's twin wooden doors, sturdy enough to discourage a horse, swung aside to expose a single Model T, not much newer than the Tai clan's but not nearly as rusty and with all its fenders. The other side, roomy enough for a second automobile, had been a victim of the most un-orcish transformation Uruk had ever seen.

Orcs knew carriage houses and barns. Generations of orcs had worked shoveling manure and loading wagons. With the automobile, innumerable carriage houses had become home garages.

Sanford's garage, though—someone had dug out the dirt floor and poured concrete. Rather than bare two-by-four studs, second-hand pine panels stained dark covered the walls.

The side window opposite the Model T had a ruffled curtain.

And beneath that window, a paper man's lair.

The desk of pale wood featured innumerable tiny drawers. Cabinets beside it had larger drawers, the kind humans used for their precious paper records. A silly padded human chair—on *wheels!*—sat beside them.

A carriage house should smell of old horses and gasoline, but this place stank of motor oil and inked paper.

Uruk stopped in astonishment. Did all paper men use their carriage houses to store yet more paper? Were they never satisfied? Or did their wives banish their shame to the garage?

Tara knelt by the potbellied stove in the corner and sniffed. "The ashes. Three days old at most."

"Light it, brother." Even if Sanford eavesdropped, Uruk felt confident the man didn't understand Orcish. "He's offered a hundred dollars for one night's work."

"Generous," Tara said, using two fingers to delicately swing the iron stove's fragile door open. "The work must be substantial."

Uruk pulled the first broad door closed, but left the second open a couple of feet so Sanford could enter. "Only dangerous work could make a man offer such to an orc."

"Sanford..." Tara squeezed a handful of coal into the stove's minuscule opening. "Sanford is a strange human."

Uruk stopped. "Oh?"

"He knows my name," Tara said. "He says *hello* as he passes. When I'm burdened, he steps aside to let me pass."

"An apprentice janitor gets burdened?" Uruk snorted in disdain.

"*He* thinks it's a burden."

"He has no understanding."

"Still." Tara blew into the stove, encouraging the early flickers. "I do not believe he would thrust us into the dragon's maw. He has no marrow for that."

Uruk saw a second chair, but it was too small for one of his sons, let alone Uruk. "The only way to earn that kind of money is bootlegging."

A burst of flame lit Tara's face. "A hundred for us. One-sixty for himself—more, if he's smart." He closed the stove door and stood. "That much profit means a large boat. He needs stevedores. Engine crew."

"He wants me, and a few more orcs." Uruk took two paces, all the tiny carriage house permitted, and spun about. "This does not make sense."

"Maybe it's not bootlegging."

"What other work pays that much?" Uruk said.

Outside, a door shut in the night.

"Let's ask him," Tara said.

A breath later, Sanford staggered in through the gap in the door, waddling beneath a paltry two-gallon cooking pot. "You got the fire," he gasped. "Good."

Uruk smelled fresh water. Why did Sanford need such a thing? Was he trying to prove his strength, by carrying a load Uruk's sons could have borne more smoothly as soon as they learned to walk?

"Excuse me," Sanford said, staggering towards the stove.

Tara stepped aside, allowing Sanford to place the pot atop the black metal.

Sanford wore ridiculously snug pants of dark wool and a sweater. His shoes had once been that weird shiny leather humans liked, but the shine had worn off with use. "Close the door, would you? Nobody needs to hear this, and the place will heat more quickly."

Not an order. A request? A command given after a display of weakness? If his father had said such a thing, Uruk would have snarled him down.

Sanford clearly knew nothing of proper behavior.

And yet the man was willing to be closed into his carriage house, with two orcs.

Uruk tugged the door shut.

The latch clicked into place.

Sanford said, "Take a—" He stopped and glanced around. "I'm sorry, I don't have any orc chairs." His face grew pale. "I, I wasn't expecting you."

"We stand," Uruk said.

"As you wish." Sanford pushed his absurd rolling chair beneath the desk. "It'll take time for the water to heat—Mister Burr tells me that you take your tea black, Terror?"

"Tea?" Uruk turned to his brother, tongue stretched by the improbable word. He reverted to Orcish. "You drink tea?"

Tara answered in the same language. "Master Janitor Burr drinks tea. So I drink tea. Humans offer tea or coffee before fighting their money-wars. It's part of their respect chant. They call it, *ne-go-ti-ation*."

"Negotiation, yes," Sanford said. His face lost that fake human chumminess. "You know my concern. It's late. I don't want to rush things, but shall we talk while it heats?"

Finally! "This work. What is it?"

"Bootlegging. What else?"

Uruk nodded. The human Prohibition had made Detroit America's biggest border crossing. Distilleries in Canada provided beer, whiskey, Orcish draught, even the elves' precious sacred mirovar. "I do not believe you're a bootlegger."

"Never done it before," Sanford said cheerily.

In the corner of Uruk's gaze, he saw Tara's jaw tighten as he restrained himself from speaking. Uruk needed to strengthen Tara's bond to the clan— but for tonight, it would hold. "How do you think you can do this, man? Paper men do not bootleg."

"Paper man." Sanford chuckled—he actually chuckled at the insult! "That's fair. I'm a lawyer, and 'paper man' sounds better than 'hot air man.'" He lost his smile and crossed his arms. "I've found ways to make it work. I've borrowed a boat from my brother, and I'm getting a truck from the plant. The buy is complete on the Canadian side. I show up, pick it up, we load it, we go. I have a buyer and everything."

"Boat? To make two hundred fifty dollars on one run, you need a full ship."

Sanford leaned his rear against his desk and grinned. Had lugging that little pan of water exhausted him? "That's where I've changed everything. That kind of money, you need a freighter of beer. A barge of whiskey." His smile turned predatory. "Or, you can take a twenty-footer and fill it with Elvish holy wine."

10

The carriage house was heating quickly. Uruk-Tai wasn't sure if his sweat was from the coal blazing in the pinging potbelly stove, the body heat of two orcs, or the sheer foolish audacity of the tiny little man insolently slouching on his desk.

"The elves control mirovar," Uruk said. We're still in human land. Speak quietly. "Nobody but elves may touch it, may use it." And be polite, or he'll call the police. "You are a gullible fool."

Sanford laughed. Standing before two orcs who had challenged him, he dared laugh. "Here, Mister Urka-Tai, is where us paper men get ahead." His face became serious. "Booze is illegal in Canada, too. You can make it for export, but you can't sell it within the country. There are all kinds of laws on how you can use it, how you can buy it... and who can buy it. There is no law in Canada against humans buying mirovar for export."

"Surely the elves will not sell to a human."

"There aren't enough elves to control the distribution chain," Sanford said. "The warehouse is owned by humans. I showed up there three days ago to make my purchase and transport it to a shipping warehouse."

"The elves would not permit that!" Uruk said, his voice rising.

Sanford's smile returned. "The law said that they must. And I, Mister Orc, am a lawyer. I'm sure that the law has changed since, or will be changed soon—but tonight, I have the only supply of mirovar in human hands, secured in a bonded warehouse. I have an export permit, to the Caribbean, but we'll bring it back here instead. And humans will pay *dearly* for mirovar. Especially humans that have tasted it once."

"Elves cannot be that foolish," Uruk said.

Near the stove, Tara stood straighter. Supporting the clan leader, as he should.

"Elves did not think that humans would be so bold," Sanford said.

"You would make enemies of the elves?"

"To save Beverly?" The heat of his voice burned away his smile. "Mister Urka. I would burn down Heaven itself to heal her. And the elves?" His voice shook. "A year ago, Beverly and I, we were expecting our first child. Then Celebrimble's men started trying to take over the Dodge plant—where Terror and I work. It's all through front men, but once you dig through the paperwork, it's Celebrimble's cronies. He's not buying the plant honestly—he's using legalities, little tidbits in different contracts, trying to box us in. Mister Dodge, he's a good man. He pays us well, he takes care of us. I started working more, finding ways to use those same contracts to stave him off. And while I did that... Beverly lost our baby."

Humans. How could they bear to speak of such private sorrow to strangers?

But Uruk couldn't deny the man's nearly orcish passion.

"She lost the baby, and I was not there. I was at work, trying to help my boss, my friend. She never got better." Sanford closed his eyes. "I will lose her in weeks, unless I can pay for this operation. Mister Dodge, he's at his limit—he'd loan it to me, but he doesn't have it. He's put everything into fighting off this God-forsaken elf. We will never have the children we want, but at least we'll have each other. And Celebrimble, he's destroying a good man. If saving my Beverly hurts him, that's a gift from the Almighty."

Uruk began pacing. The garage was frustratingly short, unable to accommodate more than three or four comfortable Orcish strides. "You have the fire to carry you," Uruk said. "You have the shape of a plan."

"There's more to the plan," Sanford said quickly.

"I have listened to your oath," Uruk snarled.

"Quieter!" Sanford snapped. "Don't wake Beverly!"

Uruk trembled with the effort of restraining his answering roar. Even a mild rebuke would alarm every human on the block and summon at least one policeman. Quiet. "I have listened to your oath," he whispered. "Now listen to me."

Sanford drew a breath and nodded.

"You have an opportunity. You have a buyer. But you lack the experience. Your word-fights, they are all with paper. Bootleg buyers do not fight with words. They care not for your 'legalities.' I will not let you lead us to our deaths."

Sanford's face grew tight. "I will see this through, or die trying."

Uruk nodded. "You have the fire. You say you would burn down your after-world for your woman. Would you listen to an orc?"

"Speak, then," Sanford snarled. "What would you say?"

Humans. "That *is* what I say." Uruk tried to put patience in his voice. "Would you listen to an orc? I know more about bootlegging than you. I know how to work a boat. My brothers and I, we know how to fight."

Sanford shouted, "That's why I—" He caught himself, and finished by hissing, "That's why I want to hire you."

"Brother," Tara said in Orcish. "May I explain to him?"

Uruk gave a single tight nod, not trusting himself to speak without exploding.

Tara deliberately lowered his hands. "Uruk-Tai says, if you want this to succeed, he must command."

11

Sanford came up from his slouch against his desk to stand up straight, as if the chill wind seeping beneath the carriage house doors had puffed him up like a laundered shirt on the line. What did the eyebrows drawing together mean?

"Orcs aren't leaders," he said.

Ah, Uruk thought. That's what the eyebrows meant.

More ignorance.

"Orcs have always lead," Uruk said.

"Squads of orcs, in war, sure," Sanford said.

"And what is this, if not war?" Uruk raised his hands. "We sneak into an enemy country. We capture the prize. We bring it back into our land, evading enemy patrols."

"It's not the same," Sanford said.

"If it is not the same," Uruk said, "how is money-war the same? You file papers and call them law!"

Sanford's mouth worked silently, lips closed. Was he chewing his tongue?

Uruk said, "My clan, we are dockworkers. We haul cargo. We move boats. We are stronger. We see at night, when you are blind and helpless." Uruk lowered his arms, but straightened his hand to ready his talons. No—humans didn't have talons, and he needed to make this human understand. He rolled his fingers into a clumsy but huge fist.

"You need us," Uruk said. "And we know how to do the work."

"My people," Sanford said. "They won't give you the mirovar. And the buyer, he's expecting me."

"Then you come," Uruk said. "You are needed. You speak to the humans. But I know how this is done. *I* speak. You listen. I..." What was the word Tara had used? "I *command*."

Sanford shook his head. "I must be mad."

Tara cocked his head at Uruk.

He knows humans better than I do. Uruk gave a nod of permission.

Tara spoke more quietly than Uruk had ever heard an orc speak, but the whisper had proper deep passion behind it. "You would burn down your after-world to save your woman. That is a great madness. That madness might save your heart. But half-mad, it is not enough. If you would use madness, only complete surrender to it can save her."

Humans. So many words, for such a simple orc idea!

Sanford's chest expanded with a deep breath. "I've seen orcs settle arguments. One slap would kill me."

"I will not beat you," Uruk said. "But when I order, you obey."

"I know how this works," Sanford said. "I've set up all the deals."

"You will tell me everything," Uruk said. "You will speak to humans, you will be our messenger. But as we travel, as we fight—you obey."

Sanford rubbed his face with one soft hand. "Very well. I'm crazy. You command."

Uruk turned to his brother. "Tara," he said in Orcish. "When the humans need an orc shaman, we shall send you."

"I still don't know Orcish," Sanford said.

"If I wanted you to understand," Uruk said, "then I would have spoken your language."

Sanford blanched.

The man might have walked into an orc bar, but in some ways he was very human: soft, unable to accept the mildest correction. Commanding him would be like pushing a rope.

"You are not hiring muscle," Uruk said. "You hire skills."

The human gave a small nod.

"Skill is more expensive than muscle."

One side of Sanford's mouth quirked upward. "How does one-fifty sound?"

"Half," Uruk said.

Sanford firmed. "No."

Uruk bristled. "No? You need us, and would withhold fair wealth?"

Sanford took a step forward, arms fisted at his sides. "Listen, *orc*. All that matters is Beverly. I've put every penny I have into this. Yes, I should bring in about eight hundred dollars—but what if Celebrimble reaches the surgeon? What if he doubles the price to hold me off ? If I'm successful—

we're successful—but I cannot get the operation, then you can burn with Heaven for all I care!"

Uruk studied the little man. Eight hundred dollars from this one night? And half that? Uruk painfully worked the math. Four hundred dollars—three months' hard-earned wages! The boys could stay in school until they not merely defeated *reading*, but until they crushed it.

But without Sanford—nothing.

"Your woman," Uruk said. "She gets her healer. If it costs more than half, you owe us. You pay us a few dollars a week. You, though. You listen to me, until the end of the war."

Sanford drew a shaky breath. "Agreed."

Uruk squatted comfortably on his heels. "Tara! Make this—this tea. Man, use your chair. Do not waste what strength you have. And tell me... *everything*."

12

The next evening burned cold. Somehow, the back of this delivery truck seemed even colder despite the five orcs filling it. The wooden slats of the floor fit poorly, and the stretched canvas had been so long-used it no longer fit snugly. Traffic wind poured in from every gap and seam. Uruk's every breath turned to steam and was sucked away.

At least he'd dressed for it. Vara had brushed his coat free of mud and hung it in the warmth near the kitchen, but not so close to the stove that it shrank. Uruk wore a ragged wool liner beneath his heaviest dungarees, and heavy leather gloves to repulse the damp. His corduroy flat cap was pulled as far down over his head as he could wedge it.

If this was successful, if they really got four hundred dollars, maybe he could spend a couple on a warmer hat. No, he was the clan leader—he had to set an example.

Four brothers in the clan. Two sons. Tonight, brother Daka guarded their home, leaving five for the work.

Six hats? As a reward?

Stop dreaming, Uruk told himself.

Dreams are for the dead.

The truck bounced on some rut, and Uruk heard the transmission grind again. He winced. Sanford had borrowed this truck from the Dodge plant, with his employer's blessing, but that employer had demanded Sanford be the only one to drive it. Sanford drove like a dwarf ran—slowly, with stumbles and stops and lots and lots of complaints from down below.

They'd been in the back of this thing for almost an hour, rattling up Lakeshore Drive until it turned back into Jefferson. He'd peeked through the canvas back flap to see the macadam turn to mud and the fancy houses grow smaller and further apart. Uruk had never been this far north, all the way past Saint Clair Shores, where the rich humans had their weekend cottages.

Cottages.

Two-story cottages, with lawns the size of Uruk's whole tenement.

Cottages with leaded glass windows and concrete sidewalks and extra little pavilions in front of them, in case the owners wanted to... be outside without being outside?

The sight set fresh frustration burning in Uruk's gullet. He did his best to lead the clan. His brothers labored every day, just as he did. They pooled every dollar they made. They spent only what they had to.

But somehow, it was never enough.

And no matter how hard they worked, they would never spend a day in such a glorious place as any one of these weekend cottages.

A spare house? For weekends?

The only thing special about the weekend was that the human church required the orcs get an extra quarter for working Sunday. Uruk worked every Sunday he could.

It didn't feel fair.

Not that he wanted a cottage. These places were built for humans, like Sanford. The furniture was feeble, the walls fragile. The fireplace probably wasn't even big enough to roast cattle. Not that the clan could afford a cow—but if they could afford a cottage, they could afford a cattle roast to go with it.

Forget fair. Orcs didn't get fair. They endured.

But for some to have so much while Uruk struggled so hard felt... cruel.

An orc would have no use for a weekend, he reminded himself. An orc must work. Work is what made an orc. America had work for every hand. Sometimes you carried freight, sometimes you cleaned factories, and sometimes you hauled rum.

The transmission ground again, and Uruk felt the truck's turn urge him towards the far side of the truck bed. Another complaint from the transmission, and the truck jounced furiously up and down.

"Soon," he growled.

Around him, orcs grunted assent.

Impatient moments later, the truck lunched to a haphazard halt.

The abused motor cut off.

The door slammed. "Everybody out," Sanford called.

The truck sat in a small clearing, surrounded by thick trees. The cloudless sky still gleamed with the banded colors of the sun's surrender, but the brightest stars had already made their marks in that banner. The November wind had claimed its sacrifices and moved on. Uruk-Tai wondered how an evening without wind, without the frozen clouds, could be even chillier than one with those cold omens.

The air smelled strange, laced with unfamiliar scents. It's not what's there, Uruk realized—it's what was missing. There was only a trace of coal smoke. There was no manure, no sewage, no exhaust but the narrow stream fading from the truck. He could smell the water, but it lacked the tangs of rot and metal and coal that marked the Detroit waterfront. The smells of trees and plants and decaying leaves dominated.

The loamy air satisfied Uruk's lungs in a way he'd never expected.

"Gentlemen," Sanford said. "Welcome to our first port of call."

Uruk straightened. Calling them gentle? Was Sanford already trying to start a fight? Leading a mad orc would cause problems. Was leading a mad *human* even possible?

"It is a human greeting," Tara said in Orcish. "He offers respect."

He truly knows nothing, Uruk thought. It is best that I lead. "Sanford. You are ours tonight."

Sanford leaned back in surprise.

Good. He must remember we are orcs. "You know Kaba."

Sanford looked up. Kaba, tall even for an orc, looked down.

"I know you," Sanford said. "You threatened to cook me."

Kaba grinned, showing all four tusks. "I would not cook you, man. Too thin. No marbling, no flavor."

Uruk joined in the laughter. Sanford looked pained for a moment, then gave his own weak chuckle.

Uruk couldn't help smiling a little as he said, "Oscar. Ivan."

"Unusual names for orcs," Sanford said.

"They are American," Uruk said. "My boys, they have American names."

"Your sons?" Sanford studied them both. "Fine boys."

Human praise should mean nothing to Uruk, but Sanford's words fanned the burning pride in his heart. "Their first battle is tonight," Uruk growled. "They speak when spoken to. They obey me. They obey the clan." He glared down into Oscar's eyes. The boy stood straighter, and did not flinch.

Uruk's pride grew brighter still.

When he turned to Ivan, the boy could not stand any straighter than he already was.

Well done.

Uruk kept his face still and turned to Sanford.

The man stared back—but flinched.

Pathetic.

Uruk breathed, "You would do well to emulate my boys."

Sanford took a shuddering breath. "Tonight… you are in charge."

"Then we go."

13

Uruk had seen many boats on his days at the docks. He'd seen boats like that of Sanford's brother, tied up at the marina. But the sky's dimming light made it clear that he'd never seen a boat like this before.

This was not a boat for working. This was a cottage boat, tied to a human dock so flimsy that Uruk sent his clan across it one at a time. The boat had no real cargo space, merely an open space in the middle where boxes could be lowered to rest on the hull. Bench seats surrounded the gunwales, where humans could sit. It had four tiny oars, inadequate for any distance.

Uruk shook his head. Were those fishing poles? Humans fished with nets. He'd seen them. One man, alone, might use a pole because he had no-one to help him with the net. Why would anyone feed their family one fish at a time? But the smell alone told him that the boat had been used for such.

The captain's chair was padded. What sort of commander sat in luxury?

Fortunately, Kaba's arms were long enough to reach over the ridiculous seat and work the wheel and throttle.

Oscar and Ivan climbed in last, each heaving a bulging canvas-wrapped bundle almost as large as they were into the belly of the boat.

Uruk and Tara settled in the rear, between the flimsy human seats. Uruk tucked the long sack containing their best weapon beneath his feet and leaned back.

Sanford struggled with strapping a bulky yellow contrivance around his neck and torso before perching on one of the seats along the side. "Do you need help with the motor?"

Fortunately, Kaba did not demean himself with a response. Instead, he took the tiny key between two fingers and gave it a delicate turn.

Beneath Uruk's feet, the motor coughed and stuttered, then roared to life.

This whole boat was absurd. It could mock fishing. It wasn't built for proper cargo, and it offered no hiding places for secret cargo. The motor gave it neither speed nor stealth—it was like a weak mule.

The boat was exactly like Sanford.

Who was at that very moment, when battle was about to begin, tying himself to his chair. All of the chairs had thin flat cloth ropes around them, with buckles like tiny versions of cargo straps. What was he thinking? Did he wish to drown with the boat?

"Sanford," Uruk said.

The human looked up.

"Come here."

Sanford fumbled with the rope, cast it away, and stumbled across the narrow deck. "Yes, Captain?"

"Sit with me." Otherwise, you might sink the boat. "What is this boat's name?"

"Uh," Sanford said. "I don't know."

"Kaba!" Uruk cried. "Stop the motor!"

Kaba instantly turned the key.

The motor's growl died, replaced with the splash of waves hitting the sandy shore and the dock's pilings.

"You would have us sail in a boat without a name?" Uruk said.

Sanford's hands jerked up, and the blood left his face. "David—my brother, he has something painted on the prow."

"We should bring him instead of you," Uruk said. "You can read, paper man?"

A spark of indignation flashed in Sanford's eyes. "Of course!"

"Then go read it!"

The boat hardly wobbled as Sanford clambered back onto the dock. He only needed a moment to peer at the prow. "It's called... *Endless Sky*."

Uruk grunted. If an orc owned a boat he might choose such a name, hoping that the sky would act kindly towards it. "Get back in. Cast us off, and come back here."

Sanford hesitated a beat.

Humans! Even when they promised to listen, they didn't know *how*. "Quickly, man!"

Sanford leapt towards the tie-downs.

If only Sanford was not needed. If only no human was needed. He would take a smaller cut for working without that burden.

The name might be almost Orcish, but it was in English. "Endless Sky," Uruk said, before switching to his native language. "Bear us well, and we will protect and care for you as one of our own. Kaba, the motor!"

The motor started with a lion's purr, Sanford flung the last of the tie-down lines into the boat, and they were under way to break written and unwritten laws.

14

Lake Saint Clair felt at peace tonight. Uruk could see the Michigan shore only as a rumpled line of shadow against the last remnants of the day.

Kaba coaxed the *Endless Sky* smoothly through the water, but the prow still rose and dropped with the waves, raising a fine mist that constantly brushed Uruk's face with dampness. The cold had killed the lake greens a month ago, and each surge raised their fetid rotting stink. Traveling at an innocent-looking low speed, the wind barely ruffled Uruk's collar and the lacquered wood beneath him barely moved. The motor's disciplined grumble drowned the sound of the water.

From their seats in the boat's belly, Oscar and Ivan watched the night swallow the sky. Uruk looked at them no more than he did any other orc—but he found himself compelled to spend more time watching Kaba and Tara than he had in years, a transparent excuse to study his boys.

Oscar waited well. Ivan was patient enough, but less so than his brother.

They would give him pride.

Sanford settled in the seat next to Uruk, in the back corner of the boat. Uruk had begun to hope that the human understood him when the man ruined it by speaking. "Is this your whole clan?"

"You should have asked that last night."

Sanford looked puzzled. "Why?"

"It is too late for you to worry about the strength of my clan."

"That's not it at all!" Sanford shook his head. "I was just... making small talk."

Small talk? Tiny words?

Tara said in Orcish, "Humans say 'small talk' when they wish to avoid fighting."

If Sanford didn't want to fight, why had he started this? "We have enough strength here. Brother Daka remains at home, on guard."

"Guarding? From what?"

Uruk didn't even understand the question. Was his English wrong? Had he

82

spoken badly? Or was Sanford truly that ignorant? "They guard the family. If Celebrimble sends his men to attack our clan, he will lose blood."

"He wouldn't do any such thing," Sanford said.

"You *are* a fool," Uruk said.

"Excuse me?"

"I will not pardon you." Out here in the open water, Uruk did not need to soften his voice. No human neighbors would call the police. "Your plan angers the elves. They will fight to keep mirovar from human gullets."

Sanford shook his head. "But they're civilized."

"If you spoke for us," Uruk said, "we would be dead already. You know nothing of how these things are done, do you?"

"It's a business deal," Sanford said. "There'll be a hundred boats out here tonight doing the same thing."

Uruk said, "You haven't even done the first step for a war." He'd known humans lacked wisdom, but he shouldn't have to explain *everything*.

"I've arranged all this!" Sanford said. "I agreed to follow you, but that doesn't mean—"

"You ride to war!" Uruk snarled.

Sanford leaned back, eyes wide.

"You leave your woman behind," Uruk thundered. "Sick. You go to war for her—but what happens if you do not come back?"

Sanford turned even more pale. "We've got a boat full of orcs. Nobody will dare bother us."

"Orcs? Men with mirovar?" Uruk laughed with bitter humor. "Elves will sink every boat on this lake if it means keeping their sacred wine from us."

Sanford clutched the bulky yellow thing he wore around his chest and neck. "That's insane."

"You know less of elves than you do of orcs." Uruk couldn't bear to look at Sanford any more. He turned his sight towards the east and the invisible Canadian shore. "Tonight, we declare marrow-feud with the elves."

"Why are you here then?" Sanford said.

"Because they already hate us," Uruk said. "They know who we are. They intend the clan should pay for the death of an elf. That is why everybody knew Tara was involved. The elves wanted us to know."

"That's really a stretch. Why not just tell you? Threaten you?"

Maybe he could send the man down with Ivan and Oscar.

No, they had never been to war before. In their excitement, they might slap Sanford's back and shatter his spine.

Instead, Uruk contented himself with saying, "An elf would never speak to an orc. And they are patient. They think we fear them."

"But—" Sanford started.

"Enough!" Uruk said. "Silence. Until we arrive at the blue-green-blue dock, I will have silence!"

Sanford held peace for a breath. "Yes, Ca—"

"I said *silence!*"

The bellow echoed off the distant shore.

Sanford shrunk into himself.

Uruk studied the man for breath, then turned to study the shore. It looked peaceful from here, but he'd seen how it was smothered in noisy, foolish men.

Who had enough money for extra homes, for "weekends."

Once the lights of Windsor came into view without Sanford speaking, Uruk turned back to him. "Man," he said. "You did not know enough to ask before agreeing, so I must tell you. If you die obeying me, we will see your woman to the healer. She will survive you."

Sanford took a shaky breath. "Th—"

"If!" Uruk hissed. "If you die disobedient... she dies alone."

Sanford's shoulders quivered.

Then he nodded. His jaw twitched, but his lips never parted.

Satisfied, Uruk leaned back against the gunwale.

If he spoke simply enough, even humans could understand.

15

Brightly illuminated docks and warehouses lined the Windsor shore, snuggled together like herd animals seeking warmth. With the sun gone, the night's chill had deepened with the sky's darkness. Every breath filled the lungs with ice and the nose with the stink of a dozen distilleries and breweries.

Uruk couldn't count how many boats churned the water. Small wooden rowboats with one man in them tossed in the wake of motor vessels the size of the *Endless Sky*. Floating buoys with green and red lamps marked directions of travel, just as on the Detroit side, but with so many craft of different speeds and sizes bickering for dock space the bootleggers crossed each other's path far more often than they should. Shouts of outrage and frustration rose above the countless motors, occasionally trampled by the blare of a horn.

Uruk marveled at the chaos, even as he wondered why he thought bootleggers would concern themselves at all with sea traffic rules.

As Sanford had said, the dock with the blue, green, and blue lanterns at its end was far to the north. Annoyingly bright electric lamps illuminated the dozen yards of dock between those marker lamps and the warehouse's huge sliding doors.

The traffic had dropped to almost nothing, and a few hundred yards further along the well-lit docks surrendered to the night.

Uruk didn't need night-sight to make out the short, heavy figure lurking beneath the lights.

Uruk reached into his pocket to brush against his .75 revolver. His own foolishness—he'd checked before getting in the truck, of course, and if he'd found it missing now he could do nothing.

Still, the grip carved to fit an orcish hand comforted him.

Kaba dropped the motor to a grumble barely above an idle.

"Oscar," Uruk said. "Ivan. The lines."

The boys leapt to the gunwales, taking the tiny human ropes into their hands.

Unfortunately, Sanford had his gaze fixed on the broad expanse of the waterfront warehouse. His lips moved as he studied the unintelligible human runes painted near the roof.

Uruk swallowed his annoyance. "Sanford. It is your time. Speak no more than you must."

The man swallowed and nodded.

As Kaba brought the *Endless Sky* up to the dock, the figure standing on the dock walked to meet them. Oscar and Ivan looped lines around the cleats, but the man made no move to help. Not a dockworker, then.

Kaba cut the engine.

Sanford grabbed the gunwale and stood, wobbling with the boat's lingering motion. "Hello."

"Good evening." The figure spoke with a human's voice.

"I'm here for a pickup," Sanford said.

The man said nothing. Like Uruk, he probably thought Sanford's words didn't deserve a response.

Sanford put his hands on the dock and crawled up, heaving himself to his feet with an assortment of mewling grunts. "Inside, I take it."

The man stood half a foot taller than Sanford, and looked twice as thick through the chest. He turned to study Uruk with the closest thing to an intimidating stare a human could manage, exposing the black and silver gleam of a Thompson rifle over his far shoulder, and drawled his first word.

"Orcs."

"My crew," Sanford said.

The man's eyes flickered from orc to orc. "Take two. No more."

Sanford turned and gave Uruk a presumptuous nod, as if he actually spoke for the clan.

Right now, Uruk reminded himself, Sanford did speak. The man, the warehouse-keepers, wouldn't speak to Uruk with Sanford right there. And they wouldn't give Sanford's mirovar to an orc. Or to a human that listened to an orc. "Tara."

Tara stood.

"Let's go," Sanford said.

Uruk climbed up to the dock far more gracefully than Sanford had managed, instantly standing straight. This dock didn't even wobble with his weight, nor when Tara bounced up a heartbeat later. Good, solid craftsmanship.

Sanford led them not to the loading doors, but to a scrawny human-sized door to their left. His knock sounded feeble even for a man. "Hello?"

Uruk fought the urge to cover his eyes in embarrassment.

The door opened anyway, exposing a human with more bacon in his paunch that Uruk had in his whole body. "Yeah?"

"Pickup. Name of Peter Sanford. For a Caribbean freighter waiting in Lake Saint Clair."

This man scowled up at Uruk and Tara. "Let me get the door."

The loading doors slid silently open, and they were in.

The warehouse stank of whiskey and beer and raw alcohol. Crates and barrels of booze stood everywhere, stacked neatly, all bearing the proud seal of the Canadian government as if that strip of paper stamped with English runes would secure them from tampering. More brilliant lights shone down from the rafters, so widely spaced that they created pools of grating illumination in a sea of darkness.

The human thug that opened the door stepped back into the edge of the light beside a low human desk. The man sitting behind it said "Mister Sanford," like he was holding a festival instead of a committing a crime. And what sort of human wore a striped suit this late at night, for this kind of business?

"Mister Tackaway," Sanford shouted, as if the man was a long-lost brother. "I did not expect to see you this late."

"You're a new customer," Tackaway said. "I'm only staying to make certain you're absolutely happy, then it's home to my children." His gaze flicked to Uruk, then Tara, but he said nothing to either orc.

Uruk preferred it that way. The only proper response to that much bogus cheeriness was a slap across the face.

"Most kind of you," Sanford said.

"I've had your shipment moved over here," Tackaway said, starting up an aisle.

"Excellent."

"And here it is!" Tackaway stood with an arm outstretched, as if revealing a grand surprise.

Six simple wooden crates sat on top of a mostly empty pallet. They looked even more tiny next to the surrounding towers of Canadian Club.

Uruk tromped forward and knelt at the nearest box.

"You'll need to sign before you load, of course," Tackaway said quickly, as if Uruk would stop at the words.

Uruk took one of the slats on the top of the closest crate between thumb and forefinger. It came up with an irritating screech of nail against wood.

"Stop, you!" Tackaway said. "Sanford, stop your orc!"

"Urka," Sanford said uneasily.

"You're responsible for this," Tackaway shouted.

Uruk reached into the open space and pulled out a tall, curved mirovar bottle. Everyone knew the shape of mirovar bottles. You saw them in pawnshop windows sometimes. The Lord of the Docks had one in his office, like it could grant his flab propriety and class.

He'd heard that elves and humans need a special tool to get the cork out of a bottle. Uruk never understood why. You only needed a little gentle pressure and twisting.

A sharp alcohol tang filled the air.

"The law will hear of this!" Tackaway shouted. "You'll never export booze—"

Uruk spoke loudly enough to drown the human's voice, loud enough to be heard out on the dock. "This is not mirovar."

16

The overhead light spotlighted Sanford and Tackaway, frozen in place on the warehouse's concrete floor, mouths hanging open from their useless, amputated argument. Nearby, Tara kept his arms limp at his sides but his hands straight and ready to slice. Uruk's night vision exposed the human thug who had opened the warehouse door standing in the shadows, rolling his hands into fists.

Uruk raised the open bottle towards them. "Mirovar is soft. It hits the throat like water. This—" With a quick twist of his wrist, clear fluid splashed to the floor, raising an alcohol stink that stabbed Uruk's sinuses. "This? Raw moonshine, with *flowers*." He stuffed the cork back into the empty bottle and set it on the offending crate.

"Ridiculous!" Tackaway shouted.

Sanford studied Uruk through narrowed eyes. "Mister Tackaway." His gaze fixed on Uruk's face. "I went to the distillery myself. I purchased the mirovar, with an Ontario customs officer as an escort." He whirled on Tackaway. "I assure you, sir—this smells nothing like mirovar."

"We are a bonded—" Tackaway began.

"Yes!" Sanford shouted. "Bonded and insured. Which means that you're liable for any losses or damages of materials awaiting export. Shall we take these crates to the magistrate? I feel certain *they* can call upon an elf to validate their quality."

In the darkness, Tackaway's thug took a step towards them.

Tara stared straight at the thug. His lips parted to expose his Greater Tusks, then the Lesser.

The thug stopped, uncertain.

Tara held his glare.

The thug stepped to the side.

Tara turned his head to follow.

A man might ambush an orc. But he would never attack one head-on. Even a small one like Uruk's youngest brother.

Oblivious of the battle his man had just lost, Tackaway said "I assure you that the magistrate will support us!"

Uruk eased his stance, loosening his knees and shoulders so he could move more quickly. When the fight began, he'd need to strike quickly. Sanford would stand there like a stunned cow ready for slaughter. Uruk would have to fling the human to the rear and drag him out.

Once Tackaway's reinforcements arrived, this would be bloody.

Sanford's voice lost its edge. "I can see that this is a large warehouse." He might as well be talking about the weather. "The logistics must be overwhelming. I don't think there's any malice here, Mister Tackaway."

Uruk couldn't help a growl. What was Sanford saying? Tackaway had tried to rob them!

Sanford continued, "And there's certainly no need for any trouble. Why don't you double-check your lading? I'm certain that my mirovar is somewhere in the building. There's no need for the law to know about this."

Tackaway glared at Sanford. His lips twitched.

Uruk readied himself to leap.

"Very well," Tackaway said.

What?

Uruk barely smothered his attack down to a shuffle of feet.

Tara shifted his stance uneasily.

"It's possible that my men mixed up two loads," Tackaway said. "Let's check."

"Please," Sanford said politely.

Tara glanced at Uruk, confused, then focused back on the thug.

After an annoying babble of paperwork, Tackaway found the mirovar in the next aisle, behind stacked barrels of rum. Sanford had Uruk check the contents, and the warm spring scent of mirovar silenced even Tackaway. The aroma lingered even after Uruk squeezed the cork halfway back into the bottle.

"Good," Sanford said. He tapped the bottom case on the stack. "And the front right bottle in this case, please. Check it."

Maybe Sanford would have been taken in on his own, Uruk thought as he moved crates aside. But once he'd understood the battle, he'd joined adequately.

The bottle from the bottom proved true as well. Sanford even accepted the man's ridiculous "apologies" for the "confusion," then stood with Tackaway and made more tiny talk as Uruk and Tara hauled six crates out to the boat.

Uruk did not like leaving Sanford alone, but a human in charge of such a business wouldn't keep an orc standing by him. He did return after ferrying the last crate to the boat, though. "Loaded," he grunted.

Sanford smiled. "Excellent." He turned to Tackaway. "That should conclude our business."

Tackaway's smile seemed to pain him. "Happy to help. We look forward to serving you again."

"Oh," Sanford said breezily, "I don't think that will be happening."

Tackaway leaned back like Sanford had slapped him.

"You confused where you stored the most valuable drink in this building," Sanford said. "It's going to be quite the story when I get home."

"You said nobody needed to know that!" Tackaway said.

Sanford grinned. Somehow, the smile showed no anger or malice, merely good cheer. "I said that the *law* didn't need know. Which they don't. But it'll be quite a tale, once I've loaded this on the Caribbean freighter and returned home. I'll dine on it for weeks. Months, probably. And besides, you've upset my orcs."

Tackaway couldn't quite hide his sneer.

"I ask you, sir." Sanford raised a hand towards Uruk. "Does this look like a happy orc to you?"

What madness was Sanford doing now? A truly unhappy orc would destroy this whole warehouse. Is that what the man wanted?

No—what would anger look like to a human?

Uruk bared his tusks.

Tackaway's sneer dissolved, leaving his jaw loose and his eyes wide.

"And now, I have to somehow soothe them," Sanford said. "Do you know how hard it is to soothe an unhappy orc?"

"Maybe..." Tackaway said. "Maybe the case your orc broke into would help matters?"

"A grand idea," Sanford said. His smile now grew predatory. "Only, I'm afraid they're a little more upset than one case of moonshine can handle..."

17

The six crates of mirovar filled the belly of the *Endless Sky*. Uruk approved of how Kaba, Oscar, and Ivan had successfully jammed their unexpected ten cases of Canadian Club between the seats, even though they made the little boat ride low. The weight added tension to the lines, making them difficult to unlash, but soon enough Oscar and Ivan had them free and the boat was off.

With the crescent moon low in the western sky and the sun half through its sleep, boat traffic had thinned. Most of the larger motor craft had departed, leaving the smaller rowboats to squabble over leavings. Kaba held their boat to the shadows furthest from shore, both giving the smaller boats space to maneuver and taking away any excuse they might have to approach before the *Endless Sky* could slip out into the dark water.

The laden boat wallowed more than it had on the trip to Canada, surging and struggling against each wave. Each frosty breath tasted of icy motor oil and smoky coal ash. Even the wooden bench beneath Uruk chilled his bones.

Uruk watched the colored lamps at the end of the warehouse dock shrink and mingle with other lights. Once those lights merged into a distant blur and Kaba had turned back towards Michigan, Uruk said "Oscar. Ivan. Begin."

The two boys squeezed themselves down beside the mirovar crates.

The sound of wood creaking on nails roused Sanford from his empty stare across the lake. "What are they doing?" he said.

"Securing our cargo," Uruk said.

Sanford licked his lips nervously.

If he mewls again, I'm going punch him. To divert the human, Uruk said, "You did well."

Sanford breathed deeply. "Uh, thank you." His gaze went back to the shrinking lights of Windsor. "I hadn't planned on the whiskey, but I couldn't let Tackaway get away with his little scam." His lips tightened. "I'm glad you know what mirovar smells like. I wouldn't expect that from an orc."

"You hired skill," Uruk said.

Sanford nodded and wrapped his arms around his chest. Was he chilled? That coat looked thicker than Uruk's, but maybe his scrawny body didn't generate enough heat to fill it. "I have to say—you were right."

What was the man babbling about now?

"I—Those were mirovar cases," Sanford said. "Mirovar bottles. I would have taken them, the government seals, at face value."

"You will not be fooled again," Uruk said, wondering if the man would even notice the compliment.

Sanford shook his head. "This is my last time playing bootlegger. I'll be happiest if I never see those warehouses again."

Every time Uruk thought he'd reached the bottom of Sanford's ignorance, the man exposed another sub-basement. "You think the elves will forget this night's work? How will you defend you and yours without money?"

Sanford's face grew hotter, shining brighter in night-sight. "Oh, God."

At least the man understood that much.

Wood snapped. Oscar growled in frustration.

"The crate tops are not important," Uruk said in Orcish. "Only speed and correctness."

"Sir," the boys said.

The sounds of breaking wood grew louder.

The noise had alerted Sanford. He peered into the *Endless Sky*'s belly as if his feeble vision could punch through the darkness.

"When the fight begins," Uruk said, "you will lie down. You will hide."

That distracted the man. "What fight?"

"When the elves try again," Uruk said.

"Again?" Sanford shook his head. "Wait—slow down. They haven't..." His voice trailed off. "You think the thing at the warehouse was because of the elves."

Uruk throttled the urge to push Sanford overboard. "What else?"

"I figured Tackaway was trying to get the mirovar for himself," Sanford said.

"Maybe he did," Uruk said. "But the elves, they would bribe him to do the same. Would Tackaway declare feud with the elves? Or would he lap from their hand?"

Sanford made a pained noise, like a stretched-out growl. "You're probably right."

"So. The elves will try again."

Sanford's face grew even brighter in Uruk's night-sight. "You think they'll attack?"

Uruk studied the water around them, so cold that even his night-sight showed only a blackness as deep as a grave. "We've taken their most precious possession."

"Mirovar isn't *that* valuable," Sanford said.

"Pride, you stupid man!" Uruk snarled. "Elves live for centuries, but the slights they suffer, they carry forever. They will send men to fight for them. Maybe dwarves."

At least Sanford didn't cringe this time.

"Silence now, man," Uruk said. "Watch. Wait."

Thankfully, the man obeyed.

With the lights of Windsor and Detroit receding and the dark Michigan coast ahead, Uruk had to rely on night-sight. Exposed skin shone. Clothed skin had a dull sheen. The lake itself looked as black as the inside of the grave, and the countless unnamed stars only witnessed.

Uruk held himself alert, studying the ever-changing water to port. Tara kept his gaze to starboard. When Oscar and Ivan finally finished their delicate work, they joined the watch.

Sanford huddled in his chair. His eyes were closed, but Uruk got the sense that the man had shut off all his senses to curl around himself. Only his breath, too shallow for sleep, betrayed him.

How could this man possibly have ferried even false mirovar back to America on his own?

Uruk should have negotiated a larger cut. Nothing for that now, though.

He settled himself into that orcish patience Grandpa had spoken of so many times. Relaxed muscles, to save energy. Fingers rolled into fists and the meager flat cap tugged over his ears, to hold heat. Breathing deep and easy through his nose, so he didn't pull the night's chill straight into his center.

Grandpa had said that orcs found waiting and watching as much a part of them as the need to take a mate and the need to work.

Once again, the old man had been proven right. Uruk found keeping his mind on the black water easy.

He noticed the tiny, flickering spot of heat as soon as it appeared.

That spot alone wouldn't alarm him—but seconds after, Uruk caught a whiff of something flowery. The November lake had many rich, organic smells.

Flowers didn't belong out here.

In Grandpa's stories, the smells of spring meant elvish magic.

The distant flicker of heat near the horizon grew a little brighter.

Another joined it.

The heat of upraised faces, stalking their prey of orcs.

18

"They're coming," Uruk said in Orcish.

The words sent a sudden thrum of energy through his veins and made the night less dark. The all-engulfing waters of Lake Saint Clair felt no more threatening than a stretch of bare dirt where young orcs played. The low grumble of the *Endless Sky*'s motor suddenly felt like the purr of a sleeping bear. Even the noxious aroma of decaying lake weeds seemed right.

Uruk felt the boat shift as Tara and Kaba straightened, but the motor's growl remained steady.

"What is it?" Sanford said.

"Get in the bottom," Uruk said.

"What's going on?" Sanford said.

The man couldn't even obey the simplest instruction! "If you want to fight, then stand. If not, *get down*." Uruk turned to his sons. "Oscar. Ivan. Up."

The two young orcs bounced to the gunwale.

The human squeezed himself flat into the space they vacated, as if trying to stuff his scrawny body beneath the waterline. Good.

Tara said "My side is dark."

"No light ahead," Kaba said.

One boat? That wasn't like elves. Uruk had expected at least two, pinching them in. Maybe this was another gang of bootleggers, looking to get rid of their competition?

But the thin aroma of flowers—something like tulips—out here, that meant elf magic.

Uruk slipped the spiked brass knuckles out of his pocket and onto his left hand. The cold metal chilled his fingers and cast a line of ice across his palm when he tightened his hand. His talons would slice an elf or a man to the bone, but an orc needed options.

Punching four two-inch spikes through an elf's skull was a very good option.

The .75 revolver's carved grip soothed the heel of his right hand.

Across the water, the flickers of light grew brighter. The other boat wasn't rushing, instead keeping a steady speed as they veered towards a collision.

Were they hoping to take the clan by surprise?

If they wanted surprise, one could be arranged.

"Tara!" Uruk said. "Take the wheel. Kaba, with me."

Without a word, his smallest brother replaced the largest. Kaba clambered back to join Uruk in the rear of the boat.

"Tara," Uruk said. "You see them?"

Settling at the wheel, Tara said, "Yes."

"Turn to them." Uruk tightened his jaw. "Full speed."

The motor's purr awakened to an angry roar. Tara spun the wheel, and the *Endless Sky* sluiced to the side in a spray of fetid water.

The wind of their passage chilled Uruk's face as he joyfully bared his tusks. Work supported the clan and filled the heart with pride. A fight made the soul shine.

But a fight for the clan?

The greatest work of all.

The spots of light grew and separated. In a moment Uruk could make out separate faces. The attackers, they held their route.

"Tara!" Uruk kept his voice just loud enough to penetrate the motor's roar. The boat's harsh bounce across the waves made speaking difficult. "If they do not turn, straight through. Cut them in half."

Would the *Endless Sky* survive such an impact? Perhaps not—but despite its misbegotten, nearly purposeless human construction, it was sturdy.

"Kaba!" Uruk said. "Oscar! Ivan! Prepare to fight."

Ivan hissed with anticipation.

Uruk glanced back at his son. "Quiet! No sound until we begin."

Ivan clamped his lips shut.

Good boys.

Uruk had to lean to the side to peer around the boat's speed-raised prow, letting cold dank water spray across his cheek.

Ahead, the attacker's boat skewed to face them, close enough that Uruk's night-sight could make out the dim shadow rather than only warm faces. It wasn't much larger than the *Endless Sky*. "Tara! Pass beside them. Oscar, Ivan, you defend." Uruk raised his chin. "Kaba. With me."

A gunshot echoed across the water.

Uruk felt his mouth twist in surprise. Almost a flinch? So you've never been shot at before? You knew this would happen—not might, *would*. Quit acting like Sanford.

He tightened his gut.

Wait—that sound. Was Sanford crying?

No. Only the quick breaths of panic.

Kaba's weight beside Uruk made the *Endless Sky* list to port. Tara's back and shoulders showed his struggle to hold the burdened boat to a straight course. "Oscar. Ivan. To starboard. Balance our weight." The change smoothed the boat's rocking, but each violated wave still sent the prow skyward.

Uruk's blood sang.

More gunshots punched through the motor's roar. They might be close enough to hit with a rifle, but the motion of the two boats made actually hitting anything at this distance nearly impossible.

Besides, elves wouldn't handle a firearm. Dwarves wouldn't willingly go on a small boat. That mean night-blind humans were shooting.

Really, Uruk couldn't be safer.

Uruk crouched on the gunwale.

Seconds to go.

Kaba knelt beside him.

Ahead, the attackers' boat slowed.

Uruk couldn't imagine why—but it only made his work easier.

Tara held the *Endless Sky* straight across the endless water.

Uruk tensed his legs.

Through the roar of spray, he heard the abrupt loud growl of the attacking boat. Only yards away, its nose started to turn away.

The *Endless Sky* skipped across another wave.

And rose with the next.

Now.

Uruk leaped off the *Endless Sky*.

19

Five feet of black water flashed by beneath Uruk, then his midriff crashed into a cold metal gunwale. Air exploded from him as he jackknifed, his legs plunging into the freezing waters of Lake Saint Clair as his arms swung into the boat.

Hungry water dragged at Uruk, pulling him back, yanking his body down. Uruk's hands caught for traction as his heart forge-hammered his ribs from within. Eager for its sacrifice, the lake hauled at his legs, his groin, up his belly—

Uruk's armpits caught on the edge of the gunwale. The whole boat rocked at the impact—but the water stopped rising up his body. Uruk clenched his arms, gripping the boat with all his strength.

A mass of heat loomed in front of him—a human, face bright in night-sight. The revolver barrel gleamed brighter still, hot from fresh use. The boat's motor drowned the man's screamed words, but the rising gun spoke for him.

Uruk squeezed his left arm even tighter, desperately thrashing out with his right.

Sensing Uruk's weak grip, the water yanked harder.

Uruk's right hand caught cloth.

He twisted his hand, trimmed talons slashing.

The man's gun jerked down, his scream punching through the motor. Fresh hot blood brightened his leg.

More shouts.

The boat rocked harder.

No time! Uruk grabbed the gunwale and heaved himself up, robbing Saint Clair of her sacrifice. The lake was ice-cold, but somehow the air nailed ice through his hide as he hoisted himself over the edge and into the boat, rolling onto his knees, bringing his talons up—

Bright shadows of men, everywhere.

Another barking gunshot.

A razor line of unexpected pain punched through Uruk's left shoulder, striking hard enough to knock his shoulder back and rock his head on his neck.

He'd been shot.

Uruk screamed wordlessly in rage.

The impact rippled to his feet. Up his head. Cold heat. Ice inside, burning. The water soaking his clothes, weighing him down.

Another human, clutching the gunwale, raised a Thompson machine gun brilliant with heat.

Uruk leaped forward. His left arm didn't want to work so he shouldered the Thompson aside and slashed with his right, bringing claws across the man's face, the torrent of blood and screams splashing across the night before Uruk could spin himself to face the other man trying to bring a rifle into play so close, the barrel wobbling past Uruk where he could knock it aside and throw himself headfirst into the man's gut, knocking him off into the water—*sacrifice repaid, Saint Clair!*—and fling his arm aside to smash through the pilot's flimsy wooden stand, bashing the wheel into kindling, the shards driving into the human at the post, releasing the man's agonized shriek to the sky.

Gunfire ripped through the night.

The boat lurched.

Kaba roared defiance to the night.

Uruk used his working arm to shove the throttle lever all the way back. The boat rocked with the sudden loss of drive. A man screamed.

Uruk whirled.

The human coming up behind Uruk dropped to his knees. "I surrender!"

Behind the man, Kaba let out a victory shriek.

Uruk's chest heaved with exertion. His wounded arm burned.

Bodies littered the deck of the little craft. The wind brushed away tatters of gunsmoke, but spilled blood thickened its stink every moment. Uruk's chest heaved in and out, his pulse drumming fiercely in his temples, his neck.

One miserable man remained—but on his knees, arms upraised, hands open and fingers spread.

Near the front of the boat, Kaba dropped the last broken man to the deck. They'd won.

20

Uruk felt dizzy with victory. The boat's back-and-forth rocking didn't help. His stomach suddenly felt loose, wobbling with the throbbing hot-cold burn of the gunshot wound in his arm. The very air tasted of spilled blood and gunpowder and death, witnessed only by lake and sky.

And the human had to spoil *everything* by bawling "I surrender! I surrender!"

Uruk steadied his breath. "Do you think we take prisoners?"

The man shrieked "You won't ever see me again! I surrender, whatever you say!"

The sight sickened Uruk more than the heavy pulse of pain in his arm. Was it swelling up to his shoulder now? No, no time for that. A leader didn't show weakness. He could feel his hand, even if it had no strength. He would heal.

"Quiet!" Uruk bellowed.

The man cowered—but he stopped begging.

At least this one obeyed better than Sanford.

"Man," Uruk said. "Did you speak for these? Did you *command*?"

The man shook his head. "Karlo did."

The man begged for the right to bargain for his life—but offered his goods freely. How did men rule the world? "His commands?"

The man licked his lips and started to lower his hands.

"Up!" Kaba shouted from behind the man. "Back up!"

The man's hands jerked up.

"You move when I command," Uruk said. A human needed politeness—Uruk didn't want even this wretch to die of fear. "You breathe only by my word."

The man nodded.

Uruk showed more tusk. "I did not command movement!"

"Sir!" the man cried. "Yes, mister orc!"

The sniveling made the nausea in Uruk's gut grow worse. "Your leader. Your commander. What did he command?"

"We—we followed the compass." The man licked his lips. "It led us to the orc boat."

"And when you found the orc boat?" Uruk growled.

The man's face grew dim as blood left his face.

How could you interrogate a weakling? Uruk wanted to scream his frustration. How did men turn feebleness to strength?

If Uruk questioned the man properly, his heart would rupture from terror.

Nothing for it. He had to calm the man. "Speak true, and we will not take your blood tonight."

The man shook like a frightened bear.

What more could the man hope for? "Kaba. You and I, we robbed Saint Clair of her sacrifice tonight."

Kaba bent to seize the broken man at his feet. "For Saint Clair!" The body hit the water with a strangely quiet splash.

A boat motor grew closer. Uruk recognized the putter of the *Endless Sky* at a trawl.

Uruk tried to soften his voice, as if soothing a newborn. "What were your orders?"

"Shoot," the man whispered. "Tommy guns. Fill the boat with bullets. Move up, throw a grenade. Sink it, and everyone on it."

Kaba said, "For Saint Clair!" *Splash*.

Uruk nodded. "How did you find us?"

"Compass," the man said. "A—a special compass."

"For Saint Clair!" *Splash*.

The man shuddered inexplicably.

"Where?"

The man twitched as if to point, stopping himself. "There. By the wheel."

Uruk grunted. He'd smashed the wheel getting to the man behind it. "Kaba."

"For Saint Clair!" The fourth man had barely hit the water when Kaba turned. He trudged carefully past the wretch, trying not to make the boat rock further. Night-sight exposed fresh blood around Kaba's ankle, a line of brightness shining down the shin where fresh blood replenished the warmth.

"Who hired you?" Uruk said.

"Karlo," the man said.

"Who hired him?"

The man shook his head. "I don't know."

"You want me to think you would work for a man you don't know?" Uruk said.

The man cringed. "I don't know, I really don't!"

The sudden stink of flowers came in a wave, smothering the reek of blood. "Found it!" Kaba said in Orcish.

"Bring it," Uruk said.

The man somehow cringed even more without moving. He panted, without his body working hard. Streaks down his face grew colder in the wind.

Wait—was he crying?

Uruk felt even more sick. The boat seemed to be listing with his revulsion. Or was the boat truly listing?

Kaba handed Uruk something flat and small, tiny enough to sit in the palm of Uruk's hand and still leave skin all around. He couldn't study it without light, but the stink of flowers came off it.

The prize boat rocked anew as the *Endless Sky* idled up alongside. Oscar leaned across to seize the gunwale, bringing the two together with a clatter. Uruk grunted in satisfaction.

At the stern, Kaba said "For Saint Clair." That splash seemed louder than the others. Maybe the pilot had been fat?

Splitting the cargo would make each boat faster. "Kaba. This boat."

"Sinking," Kaba said.

Maybe not this boat, then. "Tara! The *Endless Sky*?"

"Sinking."

"How bad?" Uruk said.

Tara said, "A couple bullet holes. Slow leak."

Kaba said, "Many bullet holes. Machine gun to the deck."

"Return to the *Sky*," Uruk said.

As Kaba climbed past, Uruk said to the surrendered man, "I leave you with your blood."

The man's mouth worked.

Uruk reached over to grab the *Endless Sky*'s gunwale.

The man started to drop his hands.

"Do not move!" Uruk shouted. "Move, and you die."

The man's gaze flickered in the night. "This—I'm going down." His voice climbed. "You can't leave me here, I'm sinking!"

Uruk shoved the dying boat. Even his strength could only give the craft a tiny drift away from the *Endless Sky*. "You understand, man. Tara. Full speed to shore."

21

The *Endless Sky* didn't skip across the water as much as wallow. Each surge sent shocking fresh ice over Uruk's boots and down into his socks. The chill had vanished from the gunshot wound in his shoulder, replaced with the heat of a red hot iron rod jammed through the muscle. Uruk kept the other hand clenched to the boat's stern.

Kaba had removed his massive boots, using one to bail water. Oscar worked the other.

But for every bootful of water flung over the side, a bootful and a little more shot through the punctures in the bow.

Sanford huddled on the seat next to Uruk, hugging the ridiculous puffy yellow thing he'd strapped around his neck. His face was pale, even in night-sight, and Uruk heard his quick breath. He'd learned silence.

Ahead, the shadow of the Michigan shore grew brighter. The blocky shapes of houses were close enough to glow as a line of seeping heat, shifting against each other as Tara guided the *Endless Sky* straight at the shore.

Even if they beached the craft behind a stranger's house, Uruk felt confident that Sanford could trade a crate of Canadian Club for a man's silence. Men found that pale whiskey valuable.

Ivan leaned over Oscar, raising his voice just enough to penetrate the growl of the motor underfoot. "Two cases of the whiskey were shot. We lost seven bottles. The mirovar survived—I think the water protected it."

"I did not ask your thoughts," Uruk said, but with only a mild snarl.

Ivan straightened, accepting the rebuke.

Uruk forced himself to hide his smile. Ivan and Oscar both had every reason for excitement. Bullets? In their first war? Uruk's first war had been defending the tenement's sixth floor against the insults of the fifth. He would have given a *tusk* to have gunfire that night.

His boys would remember this night forever. And him.

If they made it to shore.

"We aren't going to make it," Sanford whispered through clenched teeth.

"We offered Saint Clair sacrifice," Uruk snapped. "Do not stoke her greed."

"Sacrifice?" Sanford said, a little louder.

Uruk glared at the man. "Blood, man. Would you suggest she take more?"

"No," Sanford whispered. "No, there's been enough blood."

Weak human. Reassure him. "The man who surrendered." Uruk tightened his mouth. "I heard him cry."

Sanford looked away, into the night.

"When we joined battle, you did not cry." A weak compliment, for a weak race—but an earned one.

Sanford shuddered. "Are you trying to make me feel better? We killed—how many?"

"Kaba?" Uruk said.

Kaba dumped a bootful of water over the side. "Six."

"Six people!" Sanford said. "How am I supposed to feel okay with that?"

One good slap would knock reason into the man, even as it smacked the insolence out. No—he'd promised. And humans understood nothing. "They stood between you and your woman's life."

Sanford stared into the water. After a shaky breath he said, "You're right. They wouldn't have been there unless some elf sent them. Unless—were they really after us? Or did they just shoot because we were coming at them?"

"They had elf magic. A compass." Uruk felt for the round shape in his pocket. "They were sent for us. To let your woman die."

Sanford's next breath shook even more, but somehow seemed stronger. "Then things are... as I wanted them."

One problem dealt with.

Until the man broke again.

Besides Uruk's feet, Kaba and Oscar bailed as quickly as the boots filled.

But the water no longer sloshed over Uruk's boots. The irregular splash had become a surging stream.

Uruk could make out gaps between the buildings on the lakeshore.

Close. So close.

His boots filled. The bones of his feet burned with cold.

And still, the water rose.

"Ivan," Uruk said in Orcish. "We are too heavy. Those broken Canadian Club crates. Overboard."

Ivan nodded and climbed forward. Moments later, the call "For Saint Clair" came, followed by a splash.

Sanford's rabbity eyes peered ahead. "What is he doing?"

"We are too heavy," Uruk said.

Sanford grimaced. "The whiskey?"

"For Saint Clair!"

"The whiskey," Uruk said.

"Overboard," Ivan called.

The *Endless Sky* still wallowed.

"The rest of the whiskey," Uruk called.

"What does he shout?" Sanford said.

"He offers our whiskey to Lake Saint Clair," Uruk said. "A sacrifice, that we may reach the shore."

Sanford gave a little snort. Was it a laugh? "That... makes sense. In more ways than one."

Sanford had acknowledged orcish wisdom. That snort must not have been a laugh.

After four more splashes and four more shouts from Ivan, the boat's prow seemed a little higher.

But chill water, stinking of winter death, still crept up Uruk's ankles.

It spread enough that Ivan could take his boot off and help bail.

Uruk kept his gaze on the shore.

If they made it to land, wealth was theirs. Yes, they'd have to walk a few miles up the road to fetch the truck—so what? The boys could stay in school. They could learn to *read*. His grandchildren would rule a stronger clan, a clan that Uruk-Tai could only dream of. They would name him Grandpa. Give him and his Vara the old chairs near the fire.

The brilliant burst of steady light from behind took Uruk completely by surprise.

Uruk whirled in shock to see a boat behind them—no, not a boat.

A ship.

A ship three times their length, with actual deck and rails and a looming pilot house, fixing a spotlight on the *Endless Sky*.

A titanic voice boomed "UNITED STATES DEPARTMENT OF TREASURY. THROTTLE DOWN AND PREPARE TO BE BOARDED."

22

"Tara!" Uruk said. "Evade the light!"

The *Endless Sky* slewed with a roar, throwing Uruk against the side and spraying water in the air—but a second later, comforting darkness swallowed them again.

A Treasury boat? Uruk cursed himself. He'd expected trouble at the warehouse. He'd expected a fight.

But the elves, of course they would alert the Treasury. They knew the police, the Commander Governor. The elves would offer bribes for intercepting a specific boat.

And the elves would have people on the shore.

Uruk had expected a pincher attack. He'd been right.

But he hadn't expected the law.

A third full of water and inhaling more each minute, the *Endless Sky* moved like a drunken cow. The prow still bravely rose, but the water in the boat's belly dragged it down. They couldn't outrun the Treasury.

Even reaching the shore wouldn't save the clan.

And worse, he'd allowed his mind to drift! The sacrifices of blood and whiskey had only whetted Saint Clair's appetite, and Uruk's hopeful dreams had drawn this fate in.

If the boat didn't sink, but the Treasury caught them with a boatload of mirovar? Maybe the clan wouldn't end—but with the five of them in prison, the remnants would not prosper. Without his sons, the clan had no future.

The Treasury ship was large enough to have dwarves.

The *Endless Sky* would stand out in their night-sight.

Uruk's chest tightened. So close to success! "Tara! Straight in to shore again!"

Behind them, the great Treasury vessel began its slow turn to follow.

Two smaller speedboats swept out from behind it, their motors roaring.

Trapped.

"Ivan!" Uruk shouted. "Oscar."

Both boys raised their faces to look at him, water pooling around them.

Uruk grimaced. "Save the clan."

Both boys leaped to obey.

Sanford glanced back towards the Treasury ship, then to Uruk. "What are they doing?"

"We're trapped," Uruk said. "They're throwing the mirovar overboard."

Sanford's face came to life. He plunged his feet into the flooded stern as if to march forward. "We're so close! We can make it!"

"They surround us," Uruk said. Keep it simple for the human madman. "The elves, they have bribed the Treasury boat. They will have bribed people on shore." The words tasted bitter. "They will have a second elvish compass."

Oscar hoisted the first mirovar crate to the low bench against the gunwale.

"No!" Sanford threw himself forward, arms flailing as he propelled himself a step up the deck's slope. Water sloshed around the man's knees.

Uruk flung his good arm across Sanford's chest, knocking him back onto the bench. The man somehow bounced off the rear and hurtled himself back into Uruk's arm, those tiny fingers snatching at Uruk's coat. Did Sanford think he could toss Uruk aside?

No—Sanford had surrendered to his madness. He would drown himself to save the mirovar, to save his woman.

Uruk felt a moment of helplessness. An orc caught by such a frenzy needed a solid blow to the head, enough to shake the mind free—but if he even tapped Sanford, that fragile skull would splinter.

Sanford wrenched himself under Uruk's arm with a proper, incoherent scream, crashing right into Kaba.

Kaba's face broadcast his surprise.

Sanford squirmed to slither around Kaba.

Uruk snatched the neck of Sanford's coat. Careful! Sanford thrashed, his feet slipping against the submerged deck, his hands scrabbling rat-like at the starboard bench, not even reacting to Uruk's grip.

Uruk yanked.

Sanford's feet slipped free. His hands whirled desperately for half a second before Uruk could swing his arm around—

—and plunge the man into the murky, fetid water filling the stern.

Sanford convulsed, jackknifing. His feet feebly kicked at Uruk's shins.

Kaba shifted back to avoid Sanford's feeble blows. Good. Sanford might break his soft bones against Kaba's hard hide.

How long? An orc would need a good two minutes to start to calm—

but Sanford's struggles had already changed, from pathetically clawing for freedom to animal struggles for air.

Uruk hoisted Sanford up by the neck of his coat.

Sanford whooped, mindlessly coughing dead green water into Uruk's face.

Amazing. How did humans rule America?

"Your woman is yours." Uruk concentrated on making his words soft. "If they take us with the mirovar, she dies alone."

Sanford blinked and coughed.

Uruk studied the man's face. Had he drowned Sanford's madness? Or did the man need more time in the water?

Sanford sneezed.

More fetid water, made even worse with the scent of human, hit Uruk's eyes.

Maybe Sanford's ears hadn't worked yet. "Would you give her a chance, any chance? Or would you have your woman die alone?"

Sanford glared at Uruk. For one moment, pure orcish hatred burned from the man's white eyes.

Then the passion drained away into the hungry water. "No." Uruk barely heard the whisper through the *Endless Sky*'s struggling motor.

Uruk gave a nod, holding his tongue.

Seconds later, Ivan heaved the last crate of mirovar on the gunwale bench, beside the first five.

"Go," Uruk said.

Silently, Oscar and Ivan dropped one valuable crate after another into the hungry lake.

23

Brief minutes later, the bravely wallowing *Endless Sky* hit beach and stopped, nailed there by the brilliant spotlight of the Treasury boat.

Uruk squeezed the gunwale. "Thank you. You will sail again."

The boat wobbled uneasily, then tipped to starboard and stayed there. Water sloshed out, drenching the rock-strewn sand with the stink of dead seaweed.

Icy water drenched Uruk's pants and filled his boots. He couldn't feel his feet. The gunshot wound in his shoulder still burned like a brand, further draining his strength. Tonight made two nights without sleep, and while the sky still loomed in rich black he felt sure dawn approached. Exhaustion or no, the clan had to return to Detroit and prepare for the day. If they did not show up for work, the dock boss would replace them. And Tara, he had to get to the factory—the clan could not lose his apprenticeship. At least the boys had no school today.

If the clan had won the war, the energy of victory would have carried them through.

They hadn't lost. Not yet. But pulling victory from this would take everything he had.

Sanford flung one leg over the edge of the boat, then sat on the edge and inched his way down.

The spotlight illuminated one of those absurd human cottages a dozen yards further inland. A square of light appeared in the cottage—a window? The Treasury boat's spotlight had attracted locals. Beyond that, the headlights of a car traveling down Jefferson came into view.

The car didn't roll past, though.

It turned towards the shore, exposing two pale spots of light.

The lights went out.

The Treasury. Here.

They had seconds.

"Sanford," Uruk said.

The man stood like a sack of broken bones. He didn't flinch at Uruk's voice, but he didn't raise his gaze either. The flat, wet stones at his feet seemed to consume his attention.

He'd shaken the man out of his madness. What was he supposed to do now? "Sanford!"

The man's head jerked up. But his eyes saw... nothing.

"They come," Uruk said. "You must speak. We have no liquor. Tell them. Show them."

Sanford's face didn't twitch.

Did he need drowning again? "Man! Speak for us, or you do not see her again!"

The words shattered something in Sanford. He shook his head as if throwing off ropes. "Yes... yes... Beverly..." He looked up into the endless sky. "Kaba. It's Kaba, right?"

Uruk glanced to the road.

Night-sight showed three figures trundling towards closer.

Kaba sat near the prow, hopelessly shaking and squeezing his waterlogged boots. "Yes."

Uruk couldn't help tensing at Sanford ordering his brother, and his brother's obedience.

The human had to speak now, though.

"Fishing poles," Sanford said. "You see them?"

Kaba bent, raising a spindly twig about as long as Uruk was tall. Metal shone from one end.

"Yes," Sanford said. "Get them all."

What was he going to do? Take the Treasury fishing?

"Urka," Sanford said. "The elf-compass—do you still have it?"

Uruk felt through his coat for the round container. Sanford's command galled him, but the Treasury men were seconds away. "Yes."

"It's evidence," Sanford said. "Break it."

Uruk pulled the compass out. Like any compass, it was a flat glass disk filled with liquid.

But inside floated an orc fingerbone, wrapped in orc-hide leather.

Revulsion curdled in Uruk's gut. He dropped the compass to the rock and brought his bootheel down atop it—not as hard as he could, but hard enough.

Glass shattered.

A wave of flowery stink erupted as the Elvish magic broke with the glass.

Uruk gagged. Nearby, Oscar bent almost double, clutching his face like he could filter the appalling musk with his fingers. Ivan was a little further back, and even he staggered. Uruk heard Tara retch and spit.

Somehow, Sanford only looked on. How did he ignore that reek?

Maybe humans had their own strengths.

Uruk knelt, trying to breathe through his mouth to keep the horrible smell away. From among the shards of glass, he plucked the finger bone and slipped it back into his pocket.

"What is that?" Sanford demanded. "I said break it!"

Uruk's teeth ground at the man's impudence. "What I took—it is orc. The elves desecrated an orc's bones for their magic. I take the bone to the shaman. He will burn the curse from it."

"A bone?" Sanford grimaced. "Fine. Put it in your pocket, they won't ask."

The lake wind was already carrying the flower stink away, beginning to cleanse the lost orc's remains. Uruk tucked the bone into one of the tiny pockets in the coat's chest.

The Treasury men were almost there.

"Remember," Sanford said. "We were fishing. Bootleggers fought nearby. Stray bullets hit the boat." His shoulders slumped. When he spoke again, a shard of his earlier passion broke his voice. "Only... fishing."

24

It wasn't three Treasury men, but three men and a dwarf, all in those dark suit-uniforms the senior policemen favored. Minutes later, a second carload pulled off of Jefferson. Then a third, until a ring of men surrounded them and more climbed through the boat.

Uruk felt feeble, standing on the shore in the lee of the beached boat as Sanford fought his war of words. Not normal words, either, but strange paper-men words.

He stood silent for an hour as the men babbled.

Maybe two hours.

But as the eastern stars surrendered to the approaching sun, Sanford's words sent the Treasury men angrily stomping back to their cars.

Trying to understand their word-war had made Uruk even more tired. Orcs called smuggling liquor bootlegging, or maybe rumrunning. Human words, pillaged into Orcish. Somehow, though, Sanford's repeated insistence that the Treasury agents would never have a corpse finally repelled them.

Uruk would never understand humans.

The moment the Treasury cars turned onto Jefferson and started back towards Detroit, Sanford sagged back. "That's it, then." His voice had no fire.

"The war is not over," Uruk said.

"No," Sanford said. "We still have to go back home."

"Let's go," Uruk said.

In the light leaking over the horizon, Uruk recognized the two lanes of Jefferson Avenue's macadam. They were only a mile, perhaps two, south of the truck and the *Endless Sky*'s dock. A couple hundred feet from the shore wasn't enough to take the edge off the lake breeze. Uruk thought his legs might freeze solid before they reached the truck.

Not that frozen legs would deter an orc. Nor the bullet wound burning in his shoulder.

Thankfully, Sanford held his silence for perhaps half a mile along Jefferson's pebbled verge. He walked slowly, defeat in every step. Uruk didn't hurry the man. Kaba's leg had stopped bleeding, but the massive orc still limped with each step.

"So close," Sanford finally said.

"The war is not over," Uruk said again. "If all else fails, your woman will not die alone."

"I don't want her to die at all!" Sanford shouted, fire burning in his face. Uruk would have rebuked him, but the fire vanished as suddenly as it appeared.

Still—no more. Uruk had been patient beyond the bounds of reason. He'd listened to Sanford's lunacy. He'd watched a senseless word-fight. After a second night without sleep, his very bones ached with exhaustion. He wasn't going to spend any more energy tonight explaining anything to a human.

"You go home," Uruk said. "Get her something nice. Whiskey. Cow. Flowers."

Sanford laughed bitterly. "Beverly can't stand flowers, perfume, any of that. They all make her sneeze something fierce."

Uruk stopped.

Sanford's voice got even weaker. "Besides, I'm broke now. I'm just hoping the bank doesn't repossess the house before she passes."

Ideas flashed through Uruk's mind. He wasn't smart—not a paper man, certainly not a wizard. He could recognize a few letters.

But right now, orcish cunning screamed at him.

"Hold," he said, in English.

The clan stopped before Uruk's voice stopped echoing from the lake.

Sanford needed a couple more steps before stopping and looking back. "What?"

"Your woman—"

"Beverly!" Sanford spun to face Uruk. "Her name is Beverly! She is my wife, dammit, not just some woman I *own!*"

Sanford didn't own her? That made no sense. How could human mates stay together, raise a family, if they did not own each other? If they would not fight to keep their property?

But Sanford had fought for his woman.

Why fight for what was not yours?

No. No more struggles with human strangeness. They had no time for Sanford's madness! "Bee-voh-lee. Your wife."

Sanford gave a single nod.

Uruk's heart rattled in his chest, as fiercely as it had when Saint Clair had fought to suck him off the boat. "She does not like flowers?"

"What does it matter?" Sanford shouted.

"Answer me!" Uruk shouted, his cry echoing off the lake.

"No!" Sanford screamed. "She sneezes, they set her off. Fresh flowers, flower perfume! All of that makes her sneeze until her nose bleeds. Are you happy? What else can you possibly want to know?"

Uruk turned to look at his clan. "Kaba, can you run?"

Kaba nodded.

"Tara." Uruk slowed himself, making sure he was speaking in English. "You will carry Sanford."

"Wait a minute!" Sanford said.

Uruk whirled back on him. "The war is not over. And we will *fight*."

25

Their dragging pace chafed at Uruk. With Kaba's maimed foot, the five tired orcs needed six minutes to cover the mile back to the truck. Sanford's feeble struggles in Tara's grip slowed them more for the first few hundred yards, but the man quickly quit thrashing. Now Sanford lay belly-up across Tara's arms and met Uruk's every glance with a glare.

Fortunately, the sun's battle for freedom had not yet turned the eastern sky red. The cottages remained dark, and Sanford stopped shouting about his broken dignity. The clan could pass without opposition.

With the slow pace, though, Uruk had time to think and to give orders.

The truck still sat before the home of Sanford's brother, to the side of the long driveway. Uruk studied the wheel. He could shift the driver's seat far enough back to cram himself behind the wheel—no, Sanford had said the truck's owner required him to drive. Uruk would not fight a factory lord.

Tara gently lowered Sanford to his feet. The man lurched and wobbled for balance, immediately turning on Uruk. "You damned orcs!"

"The war is not over," Uruk said. "You drive to our home."

"Fine!" Sanford raised a fist. "And I never want to see you again, understand! You come near me, I will have the police on you!"

"When the war ends, you are free." Uruk glared down at Sanford. "Until then, you listen."

Sanford glared back. "Get in the truck. The damned lot of you!"

Uruk nodded at the other four orcs. As Sanford hoisted himself up into the truck cab, Uruk circled the front and opened the passenger door.

"What are you doing?" Sanford snarled.

Uruk answered by squeezing into the passenger seat. His knees pressed hard against the dashboard, and he had to squeeze his body down so hard that he couldn't take a deep breath. If he told Sanford to adjust the seat, the human wouldn't be able to drive.

"Oh, no," Sanford spat. "You get in the back with the rest of them."

Uruk tried to raise his chin, but the low ceiling prevented him. "Then you know where we live."

Sanford's lips tightened. "Fine." He yanked the clutch and hit the starter.

The man's anger improved him. He said nothing as the truck rolled down the miles of Jefferson. When Uruk told him to turn on Cadieux, Sanford obeyed silently. Each mile strengthened the smell of coal smoke, brought more trucks to the road, and added lit-up windows in dark houses. Each bump in the road squeezed the breath from Uruk.

By the time they reached Hamtramck, the eastern sky bled with the sun's coming victory. The gleaming Model As of Grosse Pointe and Eastpointe had surrendered to the dented fourth-hand Model Ts of the poorest human immigrants and the clattering castoffs claimed by orcs. After the openness of Lake Saint Clair and Saint Clair Shores, the air Uruk had breathed since childhood tasted... tainted.

Uruk directed Sanford through the absurdly small human homes to the most inaccessible roads, where the orcish tenements loomed.

Sanford brought the truck to a lurching stop. "Out." He didn't even look at Uruk now.

Uruk pulled the door latch. Even stretching one leg out sent a shiver of relief through him. Riding on the bare boards of the truck bed would have been a pleasure—but the clan leader didn't get the luxuries reserved for the rest of the clan.

And other luxuries. An orc had to work.

He'd claimed leadership of this war. The war was not over.

If Uruk didn't go to the dock, another orc would have his work.

If he went to the dock, he surrendered.

Uruk ground his teeth in frustration, bile burning in his gut.

One or the other.

"Out!" he called in Orcish. "Tara, Kaba—to work!" If they hurried well, they could reach their jobs. The clan would not be wholly out of work. "Oscar, Ivan—with me."

Uruk turned back to Sanford.

The man stared back with open loathing.

Loathing was fine, so long as he obeyed. "Wait."

Uruk hurried.

But when he came back out fifteen minutes later, Sanford had vanished.

Fortunately, Uruk knew exactly where the human would have gone.

26

The other houses on Sanford's street looked snug and tidy, with windows showing colorful drapes and feast-wreathes hanging on doors. The smells of expensive coal and lye laundry soap scratched within his nose. The trees had stripped their weak leaves in preparation for winter's onslaught. The humans had removed the leaves to expose bright green hibernating grass, burned free of frost by the November morning sunlight.

Even in his anger, Uruk wondered why they had bothered. In days, snow would swallow everything. Maybe their church demanded a sacrifice of leaves?

Sanford's territory had trees like the others, but layered leaves covered his grass. He spent his energy on more sensible matters. The sharp line of leaves between his territory and his neighbors' left no doubt that his neighbors did not agree, though.

As Uruk had expected, Sanford's borrowed truck sat in the man's driveway. Steam rose from the canvas bed cover as the bright cold sun burned away the night frost.

Uruk brought the clan's Model T to a halt before Sanford's home. Its cylinders came to a rattling halt, surrendering to the sound of another battered Model T pulling up behind his.

Seconds later, the other car shut off.

Uruk had taken the correct actions.

Now he only had to hope that he had guessed correctly.

No. Not hope. He had to trust his senses, his instincts. He had to trust *himself*.

The air chilled Uruk's skin, but the red-hot forge of rage warmed him within.

Rage or not, the elves had declared slow feud with the clan. He had to act for the good of the clan.

Uruk stepped out of the Model T.

From the other Model T, Azok-Snaka hobbled onto the road. The old orc's terrible arthritis crippled him today, but he still stood as straight and proud as his twisted spine allowed.

Uruk led Azok up to Sanford's door. Angry or not, he couldn't hammer down the door. Damaging Sanford's home would summon police. He raised one tired finger and delicately tapped the wooden doorframe. The door shuddered once, twice, three times.

At the edge of his vision, sunlight flashed. Uruk turned to see a human woman's face peering through the front window of the next house over.

Uruk grunted. Had she heard the knock, or the misfiring engine?

No matter. Orcs did not belong in this pretty human neighborhood. The woman would summon police officers.

Uruk heard footsteps within Sanford's house.

They paused.

Receded.

Sanford had a telephone. Was he summoning the police?

Trust your instincts.

Uruk knelt on one knee, raised one hand, and crashed his palm against the door right next to the ridiculously low-placed knob with all his strength.

The flimsy wood frame snapped in a shower of splinters.

The door flew back on its hinges and bounced off the interior wall. Uruk stopped the rebound with a straightened arm, then heaved himself to his feet and stormed inside.

The tidy, lifeless living room looked much as it had two nights before, with its pristine walls and fragile furniture. The man's soaked coat and pants steamed on wall hooks over the heat vent, and his waterlogged shoes sat upside-down on the vent itself. The same tang of blood touched the air.

Sanford himself stood at the back, fingers halted inches from the phone handset, wearing only a threadbare green towel around his middle. Rage twisted his bright red face. "Get out of my home!"

Could Uruk explain?

No—police were coming.

Uruk took two steps forward.

Sanford had just enough time for his eyes to get big, then Uruk seized his shoulders, hoisting him into the air and pinning him against the back wall. Uruk's knuckles dented the plaster.

The man's head cranked against the ceiling and his bare heels kicked against the plaster wall. His mouth hung open as his eyes bugged.

Uruk felt like an overheated boiler unable to vent furious steam, ready to rupture and take a whole building with him. Releasing that anger would be so easy: let his talons dig into Sanford's meat rather than the plaster behind him. One swipe of Uruk's tusks would mark the man's face, so the world would know his shame.

Or he could go a couple inches lower. A quick slash across the throat would rip the man's life right out of him, just like in Grandpa's tales of the Old Country.

Somehow, the man found the gall to hiss, "Get. Out. Of my home!"

"I would kill an orc now." Uruk's words vented a tiny bit of the pressure. "You said you would listen. You left."

Even with his head cricked against the ceiling, his bare feet hanging, and the towel slipping to the floor, Sanford's face blazed in defiance. "We failed. It is over, orc!"

"It is over when I say it is over!"

"Oh, is that it? Tonight lasts forever?" Pinned against the wall, helpless, Sanford sucked in his cheeks and spat.

Warm wetness struck the middle of Uruk's forehead.

Uruk instinctively jumped forward, crashing his nose into the man's chin so he could stare into the man's eyes from inches away. Sanford stank of lake water and human's vile sweat. "You want to be dead?" The police, they come. "I have cause to take your marrow!" Leave the Tai clan leaderless? A blood struggle, when the elves already hunt the clan? "Your life is mine!"

Sanford twisted his head, trying to get away—

Pain blossomed across Uruk's nose.

Sanford had *bit* him!

No—not only bit, the man was hanging on! With his teeth!

Uruk jerked his head back.

Sanford's flat teeth slipped away.

Uruk burned to slash out, to bite, to claw, to shred the man like a brick or a bear. The effort to restrain himself shook his whole body, but he managed to only rattle the man against the wall.

Sanford's feeble flat teeth gleamed, bloodless.

"You would mark me?" Uruk shrieked.

Sanford opened his mouth to speak.

Uruk shook him again, just a little, but the man's head wobbled from side to side like it might break off. "I am here for you, and you would *mark* me?"

Behind Uruk, old Azok-Snaka said, "It is as you thought."

"Ha!" Uruk said. "You hear that, man?"

"Hear what?" Sanford sneered. "That you're a stupid orc, and you're going to jail for a long time? I hear that!"

He doesn't speak Orcish, Uruk reminded himself.

Uruk's breath took in half the room's air. "Your woman."

"If you've touched her—"

"She is not sick, man!" Uruk shouted. "She is *cursed*!"

27

"What horseshit is this?" Sanford bellowed. Inches from Uruk's head, the shout was almost impressive.

"Cursed!" Uruk screamed back, unleashing his fury at Sanford. "Elvish magic! She is cursed!" His cry resounded within the tiny plaster room.

Sanford's mouth snapped twice at air.

The man is mad. Human mad.

Anger quivered in Uruk's every muscle.

If I shred him as he deserves, I go to jail.

He'd given up on explaining to Sanford earlier tonight.

But right now, the livid human was the only one who could keep the police from Uruk.

Uruk shoved his rage back into his marrow. "Azok. He is our shaman. He smells the magic on her."

"But—" Some of the tightness of Sanford's face shifted, moving from the cheeks to up around his eyes. "Why would they curse her?"

"I thought humans were smart!" No—police. Patience. The clan needed patience. He'd surrendered his work for this war. "You said Celebrimble wanted your Lord Dodge's factory?"

A bit of the tightness leaked from around Sanford's chin. On an orc, that would mean preparing to attack. When did humans do that?

"I saw you tonight." Uruk gave the man a little shake, to force his attention. "You fought the warehouse man with words. The Treasury soldiers you defeated—fourteen of them! Fourteen! With words. You are your Lord Dodge's word war wag won—" Uruk shook his head. How did humans survive with this stupid, stupid language! "You wage. War. With. *Words.*"

More tension was bleeding from Sanford's face. But his eyes had begun to bulge from their sockets. What did that mean?

"You held off the elves," Uruk said. "So the elves stopped you."

Sanford hung in Uruk's grip, silent.

Did Uruk have to repeat it?

How simple could he make it?

Sanford let out another string of English, but not normal English. Not even paper man words. Uruk had heard these words before, from some of the roughest human sailors. The most brutal dock-men had rebuked them.

Apparently a paper man could curse like a sailor.

Sanford ran out of breath.

Uruk studied the man, then lowered him to the floor.

Sanford shivered. "Close the door."

The urge for combat sang in Uruk's marrow. But better if the police saw a closed door.

The blow had warped the hinges. Uruk had to give the door a good shove to get it back in the frame, and even then the latch showed through the splintered frame.

When he turned back, Sanford had retrieved his towel and wound it around his waist to hide that silly little pinky human men called their "privates."

Then again, if Uruk had such a puny dick, he'd keep it private too.

Sanford studied Azok. "And who are you?"

"Azok-Snaka is our shaman," Uruk said. "He understands you, but he will not speak to a man."

"A curse." Sanford bit his lip hard enough that a dot of blood ran down his chin. "How would you know that?"

Slow. Simple. "Elf magic smells of spring. Flowers. Blossoms." Uruk studied Sanford's face for signs he understood, but the man seemed carved from teak. "You did not smell the compass. Not even when we broke it."

Sanford still didn't respond.

"Your woman. Your Bee-voh-lee. I smell her blood."

Sanford trembled. Fear? No—anger.

Had Uruk mentioning her blood angered him? It didn't matter—if Uruk was to explain this to a human, he had to make it *very* simple, and blood was the simplest thing of all. "Beneath the blood—flowers."

"Flowers?" Sanford glanced towards the hall, towards his woman. "But she's—"

"Flowers make her ill," Uruk said. "But she stinks of them."

Sanford jerked an insolent thumb at Azok-Snaka. "Can he break it? Can he save her?"

Outside the house, car tires squealed.

A volley of metal doors slammed.

"Police," Uruk said.

"Can that God-be-damned orc break it?" Sanford hissed.

Feet tromped up the walkway towards the door.

28

A fist hammered on the front door. "Police!"

Uruk glanced at the door, then at Sanford. "If we are taken? No."

"Sit," Sanford snarled. "Both of you, sit!"

Uruk's teeth ground at Sanford's tone, but swallowed his annoyance. The couch looked too small even for Uruk's sons, and the curved wooden legs with knobby feet wouldn't come close to holding his weight. The spindly ladderback chairs? Not a chance. Uruk squatted in place, resting on his heels.

Azok looked down at Uruk. "The man has no respect."

"He is mad," Uruk said.

"I did not come here to be insulted by a *man*."

Uruk watched Sanford tug on the door with one hand, using the other to keep his towel in place around his middle. "I lead him. He will offer sacrifice."

"Hello, officer—officers," Sanford said. "What seems to be the trouble?"

Azok studied the two stern blue-uniformed men standing outside the front door. Without a word, he crouched beside Uruk, resting on his toes, his butt on his heels.

The less the police heard from an orc, the better. Even a shaman.

"You see, Officer," Sanford said. "They've done some work for me, and apparently the bank gave them a hard time about cashing the check I paid them with."

"You gave an orc a check?" the shorter officer said.

Beside him, the taller officer kept one hand on his revolver and his gaze on Uruk.

"I give coloreds checks," Sanford said. "Why not orcs?"

"Because there is *no* orc bank," the officer said.

"That's ridiculous," Sanford said. "What about the thirteenth amendment? They have rights too."

The officer rolled his eyes. "You need to be able to read and write to run a bank. You ever try to get an orc to read?"

Uruk's rage flared anew. Not rebuking the police officer with a good slap took all his concentration. My sons are learning to *read*. They are staying in school.

Beside him, another anger flashed in Azok's eyes.

After more back-and-forth babble, the police officer said, "Your neighbors don't want orcs around here. Next time, don't hire knock-off negroes. Get the real thing, or we'll run you in."

Uruk was not a knock-off of anything.

He suddenly felt Azok's hand slide around his forearm and squeeze. The old orc's knobby, arthritis-riddled grip was still tight enough to grind muscle against bone, sparking just enough pain to seize Uruk's attention.

Azok watched him, eyes angry—but still. Patient.

Not here. Not with the police.

Not even with Sanford.

"Yes, Officer," Sanford said. "You won't see orcs here again."

The taller officer said, "And get some pants on."

"Right away, officer," Sanford said. "All this was a—surprise."

Sanford pushed the door back to the frame, but couldn't reseat it. He turned to lean against it, eyes closed. His muscles began to quiver, and his breath sped up.

Uruk stood. "I said that if you obeyed, I would see your woman to her healer. You obeyed. Unwillingly. Badly. You understood nothing. But you obeyed."

Sanford opened his eyes. The man seemed to be trying to bring himself under control. "I did."

"Then—" Softly! The police car has not started. They are here. The police are cunning, they *listen!* "Then, at the end—you disobey! You flee the war!"

"The war is over!" Sanford shouted. "We lost! Remember? You—" He caught himself, lowering his voice. "Your orcs pushed everything overboard. There was no money for the surgeon."

"There was no money," Uruk said. "But she does not need the surgeon. She needs the elvish magic broken." He raised a hand. Keep it very simple. "You say the war is over. You are disobedient. I bring our greatest shaman here, and you call on your gods to damn him. Why should I ask him to aid you?"

Sanford closed his mouth and his eyes, tightly. The muscles of his face rippled with his madness. When he spoke, his voice was a razor; small, but sharp steel. "Mister Orc. Shaman." Sanford opened his eyes to look straight at Azok's face. "I apologize. I had no right to swear at you. My concern for my wife, for losing her... it overrides my good sense. I..." His face convulsed again, and he drew a ratcheting breath. "I am sorry. Tell me how I can make this up to you."

Azok watched Sanford's face.

Sanford held himself still. He had even stopped breathing.

Azok rose from his crouch. "I will not permit his madness to offend me. This time."

Sanford looked at Uruk.

Uruk said, "Shaman Azok-Snaka has decided to not accept your insult. If you offend him again, only your blood will appease him."

Sanford breathed again. "Thank you." He licked his lips. "Can he help her?"

"No."

Sanford opened his mouth but Uruk plowed over him. "You can. He can guide you. If you marry her properly."

"We've been married for three years," Sanford said slowly. Was he trying to be patient? "Right in Saint Paul Episcopalian. With her family's approval."

"Approval?" Uruk said. "What kind of—" No. Simple. "An orc would not call that a marriage."

"You want us to renew our vows in the orc church?" Doubt filled Sanford's voice.

Frustrated, Uruk slapped his forehead. "What does the church have to do with a marriage?" Too loud. He hadn't heard the police cars start yet.

How could it be so hard to explain to someone that he was doing them a favor?

Uruk paused. What would Tara say?

"When an orc decides to marry," Uruk said, "the clan leader gathers his brothers to war. They attack the bride's home. The orc fights for the woman. If he is successful, if he can bring her to his home, she is his. The next morning, they are married."

"That's barbaric!" Sanford said. "Doesn't she have a say?"

"How does she not?"

Sanford crossed his arms. "When?"

How did humans even *breed* with minds this slow? "If she objects, she takes his heart and tusks. The clan returns her home. His name is never spoken again."

Sanford stopped. "That's—rough."

"As it should be!" Uruk said. "She knows in her marrow that he will fight for her. He learns how fiercely she can fight. My marriage fight, it lasted until dawn, with the cheers of my clan outside our door. My Vara, she could have slashed my chest to the heart the first hour. She scarred my neck, my back—everywhere she could reach, all but my face, she made me hers even as I fought to claim her."

"You want me to *attack* Beverly?" Sanford said.

"No!" Uruk said. "If you would save her, you must fight for her. You must place your marrow against the elf's magic, and break it. You must fight as if your own life does not matter, as if you don't care that your marrow has burst into flame. You have never fought for her before. Can you now?"

Sanford's eyes unfocused, and his chin started a little nod.

"Well?" Uruk said.

"Humans do things differently." Sanford stilled himself. "I gave Beverly the gift of my heart. She gifted me with hers. They beat as one. If she dies..." He shook his head. "If she dies, my life will end. And I want that life with her." He looked at Azok. "Is that good enough?"

Uruk felt stunned. He trusted Vara, as Vara trusted him—because they'd each proven their worth to the other. But if Vara died he would continue, as she would without him. He couldn't imagine tying his heart to another so tightly, without even a token battle. His trust came from certain knowledge. Sanford had to trust without that certainty.

The human gods were cruel.

Maybe that's why men ruled America.

Uruk turned to Azok. The shaman had not moved.

Breaking the curse would aid the clan, if only by frustrating the elves. When you can't claw out your enemy's heart, bite his nose.

But if Azok refused, Uruk would have to find another way.

Uruk struggled to master the leftover anger and the human-forged frustration swirling within him.

Worst, he knew that Azok had already made up his mind. He only waited to make Uruk practice his patience.

Once Uruk steadied himself, the shaman gave a single nod.

Sanford's face lit up.

"It is not done," Uruk said.

"But—"

"We go now to break the curse," Uruk said. "But the war is not over. You will obey until it is."

"And when will it be done?" Sanford said.

Uruk smiled. The man *could* learn. "Maybe tonight. Maybe tomorrow. And there will be a price. I know that you will pay it."

"Fine." Sanford's eyes were bouncing towards the hall leading to his woman, and his feet kept shifting and shuffling like a horse ready to leap into a gallop.

Uruk reached into his coat pocket and pulled out a metal flask. "Here, man. You need this."

The tiny flask looked ridiculously huge in Sanford's two-handed grip. "What is this?"

"Orcish draught," Uruk said. "You have the will. Now you need the strength."

29

Uruk watched Sanford and his woman all through the chanting and the fire and the oozing blood. The tenement basement's low ceiling made the smoke from the three brass braziers feel so thick that it threatened to trap his head like muck. The shaman's herbs and rare woods smoldered in an ever-changing blur of scents: pine replaced boar replaced sage and hickory. Uruk wanted to sit, but the witness must stand ready and alert.

Whirlwind head or not, Uruk stood. He endured.

As did Sanford.

But half an hour in, arcs of green flame flared from all three braziers to spatter against the ceiling.

Both humans screamed as one—not merely at the same time, but with the same breath, the same peaks, the same ragged undertones trailing off with their exhausted air.

Sanford had claimed that his heart was joined with his woman's, but to hear it astonished Uruk.

Blue light erupted around Sanford's woman.

The stink of roses overwhelmed the smoke.

And was consumed.

30

The dying sun had sunk into its evening grave, leaving its lifeblood spattered across the western sky. To the east, Lake Saint Clair had swallowed the light. Rush hour had come to an end, but a few late stragglers wandered up Jefferson Avenue, veering around the borrowed truck. Uruk had told Sanford to not hurry, to not attract attention. The rendezvous would not start until they arrived.

But now he wished that he'd told Sanford to break all traffic laws to get the trip over with.

"Amazing." Sanford's fingers drummed on the wooden steering wheel. "Totally amazing. She hasn't looked that good in months."

Uruk wondered how many times the man had said *amazing*. He should have counted. Humans only understood basic ideas with much repetition, though. It made sense that they would say things over and over again, if only so other men could comprehend.

"And eating!" Oncoming headlights sent a line of illumination across Sanford's wide expression. "I had to coax her to drink a cup of broth yesterday, but I thought she was going to attack that porridge your wife brought her."

If Uruk had counted *amazings*, he would also have to count the number of *broths* and *porridges*. Too many words said too many times.

Patience. With any luck, Uruk needed Sanford.

"Your shaman knows his stuff."

That was new. And was that respect in Sanford's voice? Best encourage it if so. "Yes," Uruk said.

"I mean, I saw how much blood was on the floor. You're *sure* that all came out of me?"

The man had already asked this—but only four times. Uruk should count himself lucky. "Yes."

"That draught—remarkable stuff. I should be in the hospital. Or dead."

The truck bounced across the streetcar tracks, jamming Uruk's head painfully against the ceiling. He heard Kaba and Tara shift in the back of the truck. Both were probably taking advantage of the break to catch a little sleep.

If Sanford babbled the whole way up, though, Uruk might slash the man's throat open and drain the rest of his blood just to shut him up. "Azok said that the elves will know the curse has broken."

That silenced Sanford. "Do you think that they will come for us?"

"You are sworn to your Lord Dodge," Uruk said. "If they capture his factory, they will leave you alone."

Sanford shook his head. "I'm not going to let that happen."

"You think you can stop it?"

"You called me a word warrior." Sanford's sudden smile had a comforting, predatory slant. "They attacked Beverly. Once this—this war is over, I'll find a way to crush their lawyers. They will not get away with this."

"Then Celebrimble will come for you," Uruk said. "You and your children."

The truck veered to the right, towards the lake.

Uruk stiffened. "Man!"

If the truck went into the water—as tight as Uruk was jammed into the cab—

Sanford jerked the wheel back. "Sorry. Did you say 'children?'"

"Not if you drive like that!"

"The doctors, they told us—"

"Human doctors know nothing," Uruk said. "The curse is broken. Azok told me she will bear strong children."

Sanford drove in silence, giving Uruk a moment of hope. Then:

"I can't thank you enough."

Uruk hadn't expected gratitude from a man. "There will be a price."

"What is it?"

"We will find out when we arrive."

Sanford drew a breath. "I negotiate for Dodge. They call me hard-nosed—but you've got me over a barrel."

"Nothing too onerous," Uruk said. "No matter what happens tonight, you keep your blood and your woman."

Sanford gave that annoying human snort-laugh. "From you, that's pretty good."

Uruk tried to relax, but the cramped cab wouldn't permit it. "You can start your repayment by offering me silence."

Sanford opened his mouth, then closed it.

Peace held until Uruk had to say, "Ahead. Pull to the side."

Sanford downshifted. "Isn't this where the boat is?"

"Maybe," Uruk said.

"No, it is! I recognize that cottage, with the gingerbread gazebo."

Gingerbread? Did men make buildings out of food? "It is where the boat was." As Sanford set the parking brake, Uruk opened the door. "I do not know if the boat is still here."

Uruk strode away before Sanford could ask questions, stretching his tired legs so that the man would have to jog to keep up. Light slipped between the drapes of the cottage on the right, so Uruk took a path closer to its dark neighbor until he reached the rocky beach.

Sanford came panting up a moment later. "Where's the boat?"

"I sent Oscar and Ivan out with Grandpa this morning," Uruk said. "They were to patch the hull if they could."

"Did they take it back?"

Uruk drew a flashlight from his pocket. Although built for a human, it was large enough to not feel too ridiculous in his hands. He aimed it straight out in the water and pressed the button three times.

"They're out there?" Sanford said.

"Of course. How else will they get the mirovar?"

Sanford froze. "What? Are they diving for it?"

"My boys," Uruk said. "They have small fingers. I had them tie rope around the neck of each bottle. They were to throw the bottles overboard, then the crates. Lake Saint Clair is shallow. They drag the lake to snag the line."

"Oh my God," Sanford whispered. He breathed quickly, then let out a raucous bellowing laugh that split the night and made Uruk jump.

"Quiet, man!" Uruk said. "Are you still maddened? Would you summon the Treasury?"

Sanford clapped his hands over his mouth. "I'm sorry, it's just, we worked so hard, and I thought we'd lost it all—"

"We have not found it yet," Uruk said. He turned the flashlight a degree and tapped the button three more times. "Perhaps their patch failed, and my sons have drowned. Watch for their answering flash."

That silenced Sanford, leaving the only sound the patient waves washing the shore.

Uruk swallowed his worry. We sacrificed to you, Saint Clair. We sacrificed blood and bone and booze. You are as still as you ever are. Tell me that peace was not bought with my sons' lives.

He turned the light and sent three flashes questing across the water.

The answering darkness ate his breath.

Grandpa if you must, Saint Clair.

But not my sons!

No. Orcs endure. Signal again.

"There!" Sanford said—but Uruk saw it too.

Five flashes from the night.

Uruk's spirits soared. "They have found five cases."

Sanford crammed his hand against his mouth to smother his laugh.

Uruk sent five flashes, waited a beat, and sent five more after it.

Five flashes responded.

"I have summoned them to dock," Uruk said. "Saint Clair has claimed the sixth."

"Okay," Sanford said. "*Now* I can't thank you enough."

"Half," Uruk said.

"Half."

"Go back to the truck," Uruk said. "It's time to pay for your wife's cure."

Sanford's face lost some of its color. As it should.

31

Kaba and Tara, seated on the truck's dropped tailgate, looked up as Uruk approached. They gleamed in night-sight, the plumes of their breath hazy with heat in the still air.

"They have five cases," Uruk said. "Half."

Kaba's smile split his face. Tara reached over to slap Kaba's back.

Uruk let them celebrate until Sanford came panting up behind. "This is the plan," Uruk said. "We go to the dock. We load the mirovar into the truck. Sanford, the buyer—can you find him tonight?"

Sanford gasped, "Yes, certain—certainly."

"We go together. You talk. You take money. We divide. This war ends."

Sanford nodded. "Good."

Uruk took a deep breath. Did he really want to do this? Did he have a better choice? "Let us discuss the next war."

Kaba and Tara immediately stilled. Sanford stopped. "Next war?"

"You have made an enemy of the elves. If you save your Lord Dodge, Celebrimble will come for you. If you fail your lord, the elf will claim you as his prize."

Sanford nodded.

"The elves have declared slow feud against the Tai clan," Uruk said. "We must ready ourselves to fight."

Sanford nodded again.

"Fighting them will take money," Uruk said. "More money than dockworkers make, or even a janitor." He turned to Sanford. "Or even more than a paper man."

"Perhaps," Sanford said.

"No perhaps!" Uruk said. "To be an elf is to have wealth. And you, Sanford—you will not do this again."

"Probably not," Sanford said.

"But we must," Uruk said. "It is the only way to save our clan."

"If you say so," Sanford said.

"But we cannot buy," Uruk said. "The distilleries, the warehouses—they will not talk to orcs. We need a speaker."

Sanford drew himself straight. "You propose a partnership?"

Uruk didn't want to answer. His mouth wouldn't move. Partner with a man?

He forced his chin down. Then up.

Sanford heaved a deep breath. "One question," he said.

"One fourth for you," Uruk said.

"That's not it," Sanford said. "Before we get there, even." He drew himself up straight. "Why didn't you tell me my wife was cursed?"

Uruk leaned back. "I did!"

"Before," Sanford said.

"I didn't know when I saw her."

Sanford shook his head and waved a hand. "This morning. We were walking back to the truck when you figured it out."

What was the man getting at? "And?"

Sanford's voice got hard. "If you had said Beverly was cursed—hell, if you'd said she *might* be cursed—and we were going for your shaman, I would have waited with the truck. Instead, you broke down my door and brought the cops to my door." His hard voice got a sudden edge. "*Why?*"

Uruk realized he'd pulled his lips back to expose his Greater Tusks—but the man deserved them, and more! "Because I was sick of explaining every little thing to a human!"

Sanford nodded. "As far as I knew, the war was over. My wife was doomed. There was nothing left to fight for. Why should I listen?"

The day's frustrations boiled inside Uruk, demanding he shout.

But... the man had a point.

He couldn't make himself say it, though.

"That can't happen again," Sanford said. "We talk. Before each war, and after. We talk about what went wrong, and how to avoid it next time. We talk about what went right, and how to do it again."

"We tell the saga," Tara said.

Uruk stilled his anger and relaxed his talons. This war would have a cost that was neither in treasure nor blood. "We talk."

"Neither of us could do this without the other," Sanford said. "So it's half for each."

"There are many of us," Uruk said. "One third for you."

"Two fifths," Sanford said. "But—and this is the important part—we agree on each war before it begins. We plan together. Either of us can walk away before the war begins."

Uruk nodded. "Two fifths, and agreement."

Sanford smiled. "I would draw up a contract, but that would be moot."

"Now," Uruk said, "for the shaman. The curse."

Sanford stilled. His smile dissolved into a straight line.

"Tara!" Uruk said—not too loudly, he didn't want to annoy the cottagers.

Tara straightened.

"We have a new marrow feud," Uruk said. "Old feuds, they lose their life. You brought me the name Kiva Morannod."

Tara's eyes went wide, then he made his face smooth. "Yes."

Kaba grinned like he'd taken the back side of an ax to his skull years ago and now spent his days by the fire trying to find his fingers.

"You would fight for her?"

Tara bared his teeth, all of them. "I would take her."

"This war means your life."

"Without this war, there is no life."

"Tomorrow morning," Uruk said. "Once this war is done, rest. Prepare. Your next war begins tomorrow, and it lasts the rest of your life."

"Brother."

Uruk felt certain that Tara wouldn't stop smiling for the rest of the night.

Sanford looked on, puzzled. At least he'd learned not to interrupt.

Uruk said in English, "Tomorrow, my brother takes his bride."

Sanford smiled. "Congratulations!"

"Do not congratulate him yet!" Uruk said. "Would you sour his luck?"

"No!" Sanford said. "Of course not."

"We come to the matter of your payment," Uruk said.

"And?" Sanford said.

"Tomorrow, you drive the truck."

Azok-Snaka stood by the road outside his tenement and waited for the young orc beside him to complain.

His tenement's roofline sagged, just like Azok's shoulders. The bricks had shifted in the century since their laying, making the walls bulge like the veins in Azok's legs and the sinews from his arms. Dying November offered a rare clear blue sky, illustrating the building's pock marks and scars. Just like the aged hands that poked out from the sleeves of the heavy fur-lined coat his father had worn before him. The sinus-clearing wind-driven cold punched icicles straight through coat and hide alike to settle in his old bones. He didn't have to be within the walls to know it did the same to his tenement's windows.

A car rattled down the road behind him, the engine a little rough and raspy so almost certainly an old Model T. It sounded too good to be an orcish car, though. Probably a human, cutting through the orcish slum to avoid the traffic on Caniff.

As a young orc in the Spanish-American War he'd never thought that he'd still be fighting when age had twisted his bones and packed his hips with ground glass.

He never thought he'd live to fifty-four.

But Azok always had a knack for the sagas. He'd absorbed the tales of President General Washington at Grandpa's feet. Memorizing the saga of President General Lincoln hadn't felt so much like learning, more like unearthing welcome memories thought lost. He'd bellowed the war chants perfectly after hearing them once.

And he'd come home from the war to find the gods burning in his marrow, setting him to create a saga of President General Wilson, after the War Humans Thought Would End Wars. He'd heard parts of his saga chanted back to him by younger shamans from other buildings, and felt a stir of pride that his seeds had sprouted.

The only seeds he'd leave.

No wife. No children. Not for a shaman.

Instead, a whole building full of wives and children, plus young orcs too hot-blooded to keep themselves alive long enough to grow sense.

His tenement. His because he fought for it.

Some of his chants would live on, woven into the greater Wilson saga. And his orcs would endure.

Detroit in 1927 felt as hostile as Santiago de Cuba in 1898. A quiet hostility, covered over with electric lights and boiler heat and coal smoke. Humans detested orcs, even as they hired them for labor too brutal and dirty for them to perform. Elves detested orcs almost as much as orcs did them. Dwarves—not even dwarves knew what dwarves felt.

At least he no longer needed to speak English. A shaman spoke no tongue but Orcish. He dared to hope he wouldn't need any language beyond Orcish for the rest of his days.

The orcish gods loved hope.

They loved to break it.

At least his hope of his old blankets on the floor of the basement, near the toasty boiler, looked to come true soon. Modest hopes for a modest orc.

Next to him, young Magul's feet shifted on the frozen mud. The orphan had a quick mind, yes, and a chanting voice that Azok envied. He could absorb the Sagas nearly as well as Azok himself—but he had no *patience*. Patience might not be orcish, but a shaman had to encompass more than orcishness. That was the shaman's duty, to guide the clans of the caverns through the wider world.

Even if the caverns were six stories of decrepit tenement.

If Magul didn't find that patience within himself, Azok would turn him out and pick another orphan. He had no candidates at the moment, but November would provide.

Magul's weight settled once more, with a creak of strained canvas. The child must be adjusting the weight on his back. A shaman must be strong in muscle as well as bile, but the Sagas strengthened only the liver and the blood. Each morning, Azok loaded another rock in Magul's pack as a remedy.

The child could adjust the load to find the best balance, so long as he endured.

Dark smoke rose from the tenement's chimney. The landlord had turned up the boiler after Azok's last visit. Azok would have to return in January, if not December, to demand more coal, but for now the man maintained their agreement.

Magul wasn't going to complain.

A step towards patience, at last.

Azok didn't want to turn the child out.

But whether he did was up to the child's blood and bone.

Azok set out, crunching down the frozen mud path paralleling the road to the tenement's side entrance. He was just short of the building's corner when he heard the voices. An orcish woman. "Do not need!"

Worry sparked in Azok's marrow. Why would a woman speak English?

Another voice said, "Everyone needs hope," and the spark of worry flared. At "The Lord God *is* hope," the worry burst into a full-fledged bonfire.

A human interloper?

Instincts wired into every orc screamed at Azok to charge. Open his hand. Expose his tusks and talons, even though he kept his talons trimmed.

Instead, he kept all his will on maintaining a steady pace. The shaman must not run. He must show no fury, not even righteous fury at an intrusion.

And gutting a human, even an invader, would send him to prison.

Azok rounded the corner to see a woman standing in front of the tenement's double doors, laden with a bag of meal over one shoulder. Standing before her, a human with a fine wool overcoat and a black hat. Below the coat, black pants trailed down to black shoes.

"Speak," Azok growled to Magul, then raised his voice to shout in Orcish. "Black man!"

Magul repeated his words in English. The boy's voice was too high, and he tried using volume instead of intensity, but at least he spoke clearly. The power to rend bowels with a whisper would come with practice. Or it would not.

The human turned to Azok—no, to Magul, face twisting in anger. "What did you call me?"

"You are a chaplain without an army." Magul would not be able to echo the contempt in Azok's voice, but perhaps the human would catch the tone. "What lord grants you the might to accost an orc in her home?"

The woman—Vara-Tai, from the fifth floor—couldn't stand any straighter. But she raised her chin a sliver of a degree. Good. Like every orc she disputed with her neighbors, and with the floors above and below, but every orc defended the door.

"What lord?" The man in black glanced between Magul and Azok. "You translate for him? Then tell him I bring the good news."

"A shaman understands many things," Azok said. "Including languages. But he speaks only Orcish."

The man in black scowled at Magul's translation. "A heathen shaman?" One hand waved at Vara-Tai. "Be glad I have come, for I bring salvation to orcs."

"I do not see you bringing coal or clothes, black man" Azok said. "And the little meat I see is on your bones."

The man's face twisted in anger. "I am *not* a black man. I am Father Keenan Boxer of the First Hamtramck Church of God in Christ, and I am here to save your souls."

A human shaman? Why would such a one come to orcs?

The man had to be deranged. Azok had to get this crazy human out of the tenement before something justifiable but illegal was done to him.

Azok had heard military chaplains speak of souls to their human soldiers, but Orcish had no equivalent and he wasn't going to stand in the open and declare before November that he was no orc. "This word you use. It means nothing."

"It means *everything!*" Boxer said. "Maybe the Catholics and the Lutherans say you don't have souls, but I know better. Even lowly creatures like yourselves have feelings. Hopes. You even love, I know you do, and someone has to bring you the Word of God. You can be saved!"

Bafflement whirled in Azok's skull. The *catholics* and *lutherans* were human gods. What could a human god want with orcs?

Magul's weight shifted toward his toes, and Azok could almost smell the anger fuming off the young boy. Azok gave a grunt of warning. The boy met Azok's glare, his lips tight enough to show the Greater Tusks.

Azok held the glare.

Their grandparents might have gutted humans. But their grandparents also roasted *their* grandparents over an open flame when they grew too old to work.

Not slaughtering was better than slaughtering.

Here in Detroit, at least.

Azok had practiced the shaman's brutal glare for decades. He had cowed the strongest of orcs with nothing more than an eye.

The child could not win.

After a long breath, Magul closed his lips and bowed his head in submission.

Magul had insisted on losing, rather than surrendering. Good.

Azok said, "You would stand here and declare that we can be saved? Naked to November's anger? Where the sun itself can witness your words?"

"The Son witnesses all our words," Boxer said. "Even the unspoken words in our hearts."

Foolishness. The only unspoken word the gods cared for was *hope*, and that only so they could crush it. As the gods had just crushed his dream of speaking only Orcish for the rest of his days. "Then November and the sun shall witness us both," Azok said in English.

Magul looked back up at him, mouth open in shock.

"You heard my words." Azok glanced up at Vara-Tai, who still stood straight in the doorway. "Both of you. Go."

Magul headed towards the tenement door at the quickest trot he could manage across the ice and frozen churned-up mud of the ground, following Vara-Tai inside and pulling the flimsy door shut behind them.

"I see," Boxer said. "You don't want witnesses. You lead them down the path of false gods and reap the rewards."

"The rewards?" Azok's throat and mouth burned with the unaccustomed nasal tongue-torture of English. "The rewards are those any orc needs. An orc must have work. An orc must obey the gods. Remove your coat."

Boxer stopped. "What?"

"Remove your coat." Azok buried his irritation and frustration as he reached for the top tie of his father's coat.

He'd dared to hope that he need never speak English.

He'd dared to hope for his warm, snug basement cell, up against the groaning and clanking but balmy boiler.

November must be laughing to split his ribs.

"I'm not taking my coat off," Boxer said.

"Then I will go inside." Azok kept his hand on the top tie of his furs, but stopped tugging the knot. "No other orc will speak to you. Or, you may let November and the sun witness, as you said, and those orcs who come by shall witness as well."

Boxer glared at Azok. "Crazy orc."

"But an orc willing to listen to you. If you have the courage to show November."

Boxer's lips pinched together. "Then I shall stand here and declare the Word of the Lord, and it will keep me warm."

Azok undid his coat.

The cold hit his chest like a frightened cavalry horse whose rider had been shot away, rocking him back on his heels. The blue sky seemed to suck his hoarded warmth away faster than he could pull the old worn furs off. The canvas pants and thick cotton shirt were useless against the frozen wind.

Boxer had undone the top of his coat and stopped to watch Azok strip his furs away. Azok dropped his furs to the frozen ground and said, "Your coat."

Teeth gritted, Boxer unbuttoned his overcoat and ripped it off. He immediately hooted with discomfort, even though he still had on one of those human suit jackets and a vest, both in black, plus a glowing white shirt beneath them. And one of those silly human nooses, tight around his neck, to keep the warmth from escaping around his neck.

Maybe—no, if Azok was so foolish as to tie his shirt closed around his neck, November would find a way to make him even colder than he was fated to now.

"You think to freeze me out," Boxer said. "You won't. I am here to preach the Word, and my faith shall keep me warm."

Azok nodded. "So preach."

"You can be saved," Boxer said. "Saved by faith in the Lord thy God—"

Azok couldn't help laughing.

Boxer's face clouded. "Do not mock the Lord, orc!"

"A god saving me?" Azok stuck his hands into his armpits and hugged himself, trying to hoard a few meager scraps of warmth from November's hungry breath. "Orc gods do not save. They remind us to work, to struggle, to always fight but to never hope."

"That's because you've been led astray," Boxer said. "There is only one God. One creator."

The cold was already grinding into Azok's joints, setting a cold ache that set his spine tingling and even made his throat feel swollen. Testifying to November came with a horrid price. He might never fully recover.

Still, this Boxer made demands like an orcish child. He needed to be treated as such. "Black man," Azok started.

"I am not black!" Boxer shouted. "I am a man of God!"

"You wear black. You wear black under black."

"That is the garb of a man of God! It does not make me black!"

"Man of God, then," Azok said.

Boxer gritted his teeth, but stopped shouting.

"You say there's one god," Azok said. "Would you stand here freezing and deny November?"

"Who denies November?"

"You do. You deny him every time you say he is not a god."

"November is only a month," Boxer said. "It's weather. It's nature."

"So we should not respect it?"

"I speak of the one who created November!" Boxer raised a fist with one finger pointed to the sky. "He who created all!"

"If someone created all this," Azok said, "it would make sense."

"It makes sense to God!"

"November hungers for our heat." And was reaching frozen talons for Azok's liver. "What does not make sense?"

The tenement door creaked open. Young Magul poked his head out.

"See!" Boxer said. "Your own people hunger for hope. They hope for eternal life with the Lord."

"I am fifty-four years old," Azok said. "No god is so cruel as to demand that we live forever."

"He shall heal you of your mortal failings. He shall take your cares and weaknesses and wipe them away." Boxer took a short step towards Azok. "I see your hurts. Your life of struggle. Let Jesus help you. Let hope enter your heart. All you need do is accept. And believe."

Even expecting it, the impact of a bucket of chilled water being flung over his head and chest ripped Azok's breath away with a sharp hiss through his nose. He hadn't needed to testify to November for six years, and the shock felt far worse now than last time.

Every one of his days and years felt like a fresh boulder on his back, no different than the burden he arranged for Magul.

But Boxer shrieked like a newborn who'd just received his first-breath punch. His cry ended in a gasp.

The cold threatened to paralyze Azok on his feet. His cotton shirt was already turning to ice, claiming layers of skin and muscle and delving for bone. Icy water ran down his canvas pants in lines of unspeakable cold. His gut tightened and his sagging balls slammed back up against him, desperate for warmth.

But the only sound he made was a heavy inhalation through his nose. Another.

Not even the November could say he protested.

"What is wrong with you?" Boxer shrieked.

Azok had to draw a deep breath. "You asked November to witness. It is only fair to let him answer."

"This will kill us!"

Azok shrugged. "The Sun will warm us, if he chooses."

The door thudded shut. "Where did they go?" Boxer said.

"For more water."

"You're going to stand there and have orcs dump water on us?"

"You may end your testimony any time," Azok said. "November will remember."

Boxer shuddered. His face was turning even whiter, and his teeth clattered like a tin mess kit dropped on a table. His mouth opened once, twice, and then he shouted "Ah, to Hell with all of you!" and snatched his coat.

Azok watched the human stagger away, cursing like a sailor and struggling to wrap the coat around himself as he hiked across the frozen mud. Patches of his fancy black clothes were already turning white with ice.

Just as ice was forming on Azok's cotton shirt and canvas pants.

The door thudded open. Vara-Tai and Magul appeared, each with a massive bucket of water. Vara-Tai stepped out onto the stoop to see Boxer's retreat, looking back at Azok with a hint of satisfaction.

Azok would have to warn her about that.

"Shaman?" Magul said.

Azok took three long steps to stand directly in front of the door, right before his two orcs, and gave a single nod.

The water crashed over him like a mountain of ice. Had he gone inside before the water arrived—but he hadn't. He could not taunt November by walking away. The cold stole his breath. Hammers of ice crashed into his heart, his liver, his skull, sacrificing every scrap of heat to all-powerful November. He could feel the god straining at his being, threatening to rip it from his old bones and send it plunging into some mewling babe with its first mouthful of milk.

Really, that would be a relief.

His breath slammed back into him, making him take half a step to maintain his balance. Only half a step, but enough to show that November had defeated him. His brains throbbed in their skull, and his bowels seemed to contract even further.

Azok bowed his head, signaling defeat.

Water steamed from his clothes. Fresh ice formed all over his clothing.

"Shaman?" Magul said. "What if he comes back?"

Azok's struggled to find his voice. It felt very far away. "November dies. Let him present his case to December. He shall not find her so comforting."

The human's words were madness to an orc. The human gods—

Azok's mind stopped again.

Not with cold, but with November's grace.

Rhythms and words echoed in his head, his liver, down to his balls and back up.

"Shaman?" Vara-Tai said.

Her next words would be an offer to fetch more water. November would demand Azok agree. "I have..." he said. "I have work to perform." His eyes hurt with the cold, but he forced them to focus on Mogul. "My coat." He didn't want to get it any wetter.

The chant came together in his mind.

He'd defended the orcish gods, and they'd rewarded him.

A Saga.

A small one, for a small battle, but with a message that every orc needed to remember.

Orcs could not be saved.

# DEGREASED HOPES

1

Tara-Tai had never seen any place as fantastic as the janitors' closet that served Lord Dodge's automobile factory. One wall held nothing but sturdy wooden shelves of heavy brown glass gallon bottles, each containing a unique fluid. He understood a few labels: the fir pine trees of AMMONIA, the angles and half-circles of BLEACH, the deadly cross at the end of BORAX. He'd spent the last two years mastering each, when to use them and when to not even open the bottle. What had seemed nearly elven wizardry, even an orc could master with study and hard practice.

The rack on the opposite wall held a dozen different kinds of brooms and mops, each with heavy wood handles sized for orc hands. The lathe room floor required the broom with the thick, heavy bristles that could capture metal shavings before they ruined the treads of the craftsman's boots. Walkways needed a lighter broom to herd dust and dirt and the other detritus of busy humans and dwarves as they trudged between the automobile assembly line, the factory offices, and the massive outside doors.

Not that the doors would be open wide anytime soon. November's cold had claimed the world, demanding its due sacrifices of heat and breath. An orc would open those doors wide at least once a day, releasing the hoarded warmth as tribute, but Lord Dodge was human and human gods made different demands.

Tara's pulse thudded in his throat again. He tried to will it to slow. He had reason to be excited today, but orcish excitement would harm his chances. Yesterday, Janitor Burr had done something Tara had never seen before.

He had stopped work.

Humans stopped work when they got old, but not so old that they *couldn't* work.

Tara's own father no longer labored, but he was so feeble that back in the Old Country Tara and his brothers would have been forced to eat him.

Janitor Burr was human. Unbelievably, humans hadn't eaten their elders in centuries.

And in the new world of America, orcs didn't either. Detroit's Lord Mayor considered eating the age-sick criminal. Tara would never admit that the thought of eating Grandpa made him a little queasy.

But today was not a day for thinking of orcish tradition.

Today was a day thinking of the future.

In 1927 humans ruled America as they ruled the world. Tara's brothers worked as orcs always had in peacetime, hauling burdens that would crush a human and pin a dwarf. Since he was a child, though, Tara had heard that America was the land of opportunity. Anyone could be anything. Sure, you had to be human to become Lord President, but Americans declared that theirs was the land of "self made man."

Tara's brothers were remaking themselves into bootleggers, for the good of the clan. But bootlegging went against human ways.

Tara burned to make himself more than a laborer, more than a criminal. If humans ruled the world, he would work his way up in their world. After wearying months of hauling bales all day and knocking on factory doors all evening, he found his apprenticeship.

And yesterday, Janitor Burr had "re-ti-red."

When a master was eaten, the lord selected an apprentice to take his place.

Tara didn't let himself glance at his fellow apprentice, Gashmor-Morannod, who stood next to the wheeled table Janitor Burr had used for loads too heavy for his human back. Tara and Morannod had both apprenticed the same day. They both worked hard, but being a janitor wasn't about working hard. Being a janitor meant using your brain. It meant knowing which broom to use, which mop, which cleaners stripped away grease and oil from the giant presses and which cleaners scoured the filth from the humans' absurd indoor shit-stools.

Being the janitor meant knowing not to mix the ammonia and bleach.

Today, Tara's thinking would be judged.

What would Tara's new bride say when he came home and declared that he was now the factory floor's Master Janitor? It would mean more money for the clan, and some for him as well, but the real prize would be the pride in Kiva's eyes. She'd seize him hard enough to crack his ribs.

Tara shoved the thought out of his brain. Proper orcs didn't dream. They didn't expect. They held no hope because orcish gods only demanded, never gave. And they so loved to demand what an orc had the temerity to hope for.

But if Tara was not made master?

Morannod was not unworthy. Obeying an orc from another clan would feel wrong, but that's America. You obeyed the clan, then you obeyed the Lord you chose to labor for. If that Lord declared that another orc spoke for him, you endured.

And Lord Dodge would find no flaw in the janitorial closet. Last night, Tara and Morannod had scrubbed the floor and the walls. The overhead pipes, each a different temperature and width, had been scrubbed as well—even the top of the pipes, where an orc couldn't see without a boost from another orc. The steel buckets had all been polished back to their original shine. They had scrubbed every shelf and rack with diluted bleach, strong enough to kill every spot of mildew but feeble enough to not overwhelm delicate human senses. Both had worked late into the night combing lint and string and stubborn steel shavings from the bristles of every broom and the head of every mop.

On their own time, of course.

The heavy steel door rattled.

Tara made himself breathe.

The door swung silently, on hinges oiled only hours before.

At first glance, all humans looked alike. Tara needed to study the man's face carefully before determining that no, he did not know this one.

Strangely, the man wore a janitor's uniform, sewn of lighter material than the heavy canvas Tara wore. The man had a sharp nose and a broad, high forehead.

Lord Dodge's emissary would appear in a human suit, not a janitor's uniform.

Maybe the man was a new apprentice janitor. Most businesses employed human janitors, but surely they had to learn their trade from someone.

Disgust twisted the man's features. "So you're the orcs."

This man could disrupt this important morning. And a leader slashed through problems. "May I help you, man?" Tara felt a touch of satisfaction that he'd spoken before Morannod.

Don't start thinking you're the master. Don't taunt the gods.

"Yeah," the man said. "You can help a lot by quitting."

Who was this man? "We are apprentices."

Morannod said, "We stay until we are declared masters."

The man grunted. "Then you best get to work."

"I do not know you, man," Tara said. "Who are you to command us?"

"I'm Miller," the man sneered. "And I'm the new janitor here."

2

Usually, Tara took deep satisfaction in scrubbing the fascinatingly complex machinery. Each massive steel press and drill and blade had its own intricacies, intimate crannies where grease and shavings and shreds of rubber and leather gathered. Tara could comfortably polish a lathe while it was still hot enough to cook a man's skin. The foul stink as the heavy degreaser hit the metal irritated his nose badly enough that Tara found himself breathing through his mouth to keep his revolted stomach from dishonoring him.

Tara's brothers said that apprentice janitor was not work to make Tara strong, but he felt certain that even his oldest brother would get a lungful of Miracle Shine Degreaser on a hot press and discover that his own guts were as feeble as a human's.

Using the tiny brush to dig into the crevice where the lathe's flywheel met the chassis always gave Tara a flicker of annoyance. If he stopped trimming his talons, he could dig in and scrape the sludge away in a tenth the time.

But if he kept his talons, the human police would declare him a rogue and bring out their shotguns. Orcish talons could rip a man's meat from his bones with a thoughtless swipe.

Even Janitor Miller. His meat would come right off.

No, that way is death.

I joined Lord Dodge's fiefdom. He made his decision.

Supervisor Sharpton confirmed Miller's word.

Tara had dared to hope. The gods had no choice but to refuse him the prize.

The lathes on either side up and down the line were in use, men and dwarves completely focused on their craft, turning out parts for the assembly line in the main hall. Most of the men had stripped to their shirt sleeves and still sweated. Tara found the shop almost warm enough. But if he stayed here too long, the shriek of dozens of different metal stocks being shaved filled his skull with a throbbing ache. An oil boy dashed down the aisle with his can with the ridiculously long nose, dabbing lubricant onto the drive belt of each active lathe as he passed.

If Tara asked the craftsmen what they were making, some of the men would answer.

But right now, Tara felt as if his shame radiated from his very skin. He tried to huddle before the idle lathe, as if an orc half again the height of a man and twice as tall as a dwarf might vanish from humiliation.

If he'd been skilled enough, if he'd quashed his hope, he would be Janitor.

Nothing had changed.

Tara would find his way in the human world.

He massaged degreasing lube into the heavy leather belt that looped up to the drive shaft mounted near the ceiling. Once a span was soft enough that he could easily flex it, but not so slick that it slid between two tight fingers, he tugged the next length down.

Tara spent every free moment looking at how the factory distributed *torque*—the fancy human word for circular leverage—all through the machines. The lathe room had a massive steam engine right up against the outside brick wall. A shaft next to the ceiling distributed *torque* to the small wheels along its length that drove the belts that ran down to each of the lathes in this shop.

Tara had earned the duty of making sure that those belts remained supple and would not break under the strain of shaving spinning metal.

Their first month, Janitor Burr had spent an hour demonstrating to Tara and Morannod proper care of the drive belts. Burr had watched as both orcs had practiced on old, useless belts, correcting their technique. It had been one of the most difficult and painstaking tasks of Tara's first month in Lord Dodge's fiefdom.

Grooming the drive belts was when Tara first recognized that being a janitor was wholly different from being a laborer. No other orc had worked this way. Squeeze too hard and you would weaken or snap a belt costing more than an orc's daily wage. Too much lube and the belt would slip, robbing the lathe of torque. Too little and the stiff belt would snap.

And constantly inspect the belt for wear.

Tara had never seen a belt snap. A belt was as long as five or six orcs standing on each others' shoulders, and spun thousands of times a minute. Men consciously stood out of the line of the spinning belts. Janitor Burr had said that a snapping belt could kill a man or cripple a dwarf.

Caring for the belts was a position of trust.

"Hey! Orc!"

Tara stilled his hands on the slippery leather.

Miller stood behind him, fists on his hips. "What are you doing?"

Tara pulled his mouth tightly closed, fighting his instinct to expose his tusks. Humans took the slightest hint of tusks as a threat. Even Janitor Burr hadn't understood that showing only the Lesser Tusks was merely a warning, not a threat to disembowel. "I am main—tain—ing the drive belt."

At the next lathe over, the dwarf mounting his next piece of stock slowed. Tara glimpsed the dwarf's gaze flickering at him.

"You're using way too much lube on that belt." A human snarl was far more dangerous than it sounded. "You're wasting money. You need maybe half of that."

Tara's jaw tightened. He had practiced to Janitor Burr's satisfaction. Did machinery change when the janitor changed?

No, Tara was getting ahead of himself. Tara forced himself to swallow a hot lump of frustration. If his skills had been sufficient, Lord Dodge would have declared Tara janitor. He had more to learn.

Janitor Burr, at first, had inspected every belt that Tara touched. He'd offered minor corrections. Once he had stopped offering corrections, he came by twice a an hour. Then once an hour. For the last six months, Burr had satisfied himself with a brief inspection at the end of each workday, only reaching out to caress a handspan of one or two belts.

Janitor Burr had trusted Tara.

Not only did Janitor Miller not trust Tara, he wanted the work done differently.

Tara didn't even allow himself to take a deep breath. Orcs lungs were so large that merely inhaling intimidated humans.

Instead, he bent his head. "Yes, man."

Janitor Miller crossed his arms. "Let's see you get on with it."

Tara slid his hands up the heavy leather belt, letting the loop squeeze between his fingers. He done this before, many times, Long hours of practice under Janitor Burr's tight, attentive supervision and constant correction had trained Tara's hands in the true way to lube up belt. His hands could apply the grease and pluck stray shavings on their own. An orc's intelligence was in his hands.

Somehow, Janitor Miller's glare changed everything.

Tara's head pounded as he fought his hands, deliberately spreading lube thinly across the leather. His hands knew what a belt should feel like. It should be smooth, supple, and slip between his fingers like money. It shouldn't drag at his hands.

The leather felt wrong.

But under Janitor Millers burning glare, Tara stretched the lube as best he could. Finally, shoulders tight, Tara stepped back and awaited Janitor Miller's decree.

Janitor Miller used the crank on the lathe's flywheel to roll the belt through a complete loop, inspecting each finger length with his eyes narrow and lips twisted. Janitor Miller's lips always seemed twisted. Many humans occasionally twisted their lips around orcs, but Janitor Miller always had his bent. Was he deformed by birth or blood?

Janitor Miller's hands danced across the belt, then he gave one of those tiny human grunts. "Better."

"Hold, man."

Tara turned, but didn't see the speaker.

Janitor Miller whirled and glared towards the floor. "What?"

The dwarf had abandoned his lathe and stood perhaps two arms' length away. He wore thin blue machinist's coveralls, with the heavy boots that the dwarves loved, and blue and yellow beads knotted in his stubby beard to represent his clan and chosen Lord. "That belt."

"What about it?" Janitor Miller said.

Miller spoke to the dwarf the same way he spoke to orcs. Most humans liked dwarfs.

"That belt is far too stiff." The dwarf's voice lacked all passion. Tara found it unnerving how Lord Dodge's dwarves spoke so flatly. He couldn't understand how anyone could become a master of such a complex tool as the lathe without a deep longing for the craft.

"The belt is fine." Janitor Miller stood a little straighter, as if he didn't already loom over the dwarf. "I do know what I'm doing."

Of course Janitor Miller knew what he was doing. Lord Dodge had declared him Master Janitor. The Lord would not have done that unless he understood the craft at a level beyond any others.

The dwarf might have been cast in concrete. "I have spent my life with lathes. A snapped belt can crack a dwarf's skull."

"We're taking care of them!" Janitor Miller said.

As if Janitor Miller had not spoken the dwarf said, "If that were to happen, I would be honor-bound to inform Mr. Dod of what I have witnessed here today."

Tara's frustration mingled with puzzled excitement.

Was this the dwarf declaring that Tara knew better than his master?

Janitor Miller stretched his shoulders to make himself broader. "Are you telling me how to do my job? Are you threatening me?"

"Dwarves do not threaten. But if one dwarf, or a man, or even an orc, suffers injury by a snapping belt, then I will do this thing."

Miller's face turned bright red

Tara tensed. A human fist couldn't hurt an orc, but metal stock was everywhere in the machine shop. A light blow from Tara, even merely to defend himself from an enraged man with a bar of steel, would both cripple a man and send Tara to prison for the rest of his life.

Tara shifted his stance as quietly as he could, preparing to do the most un-Orcish thing he could imagine: running away.

Janitor Miller's face contorted further.

His fists twitched as if to clench.

Tara bent his knees, readying himself to launch into flight.

"Fine!" Janitor Miller whirled and jabbed a finger like a knife at Tara. "Lube that belt so that our friend here is happy." He turned to stomp away. "And be quick about it! I want this room finished within the hour!"

Tara split his gaze between the dwarf and Janitor Miller's retreating back. When Janitor Miller stormed out the door, the dwarf looked up at Tara. "You have groomed the belts many times. Do as you always have."

As leather passed through his hands, Tara's brain worked harder than ever before.

3

Tara's heavy wool coat could keep out November's ice-laden wind, and his thick knit cap the chill from his bare scalp, but nothing could protect his nose from the mechanical stink of hundreds of autos funneling through the factory gate at the end of the day. The dying sun had dropped below the factory, but still cast its red and gold through the clouds scudding across the sky.

A river of automobiles, mostly shiny new Dodge models with their walls of protective glass but a few rusty old Model Ts just short of the scrapyard, flowed from the plant so thickly that even a human wouldn't fit between bumpers. When the metal river stopped, jammed up somewhere far ahead, Tara squeezed between two shiny Dodges without scratching their paint to start the trudge towards home.

Orcs were meant to carry burdens.

But the weight of his failure felt like a boulder chained to the back of his tongue, an internal weight too heavy for any orc.

He'd felt ready to be declared Janitor.

Instead, he'd learned—what? That his skills were inadequate? That would hurt, but something worse had happened. Should he believe the dwarfish craftsman's words, just because they matched Janitor Burr's? Or Janitor Miller's?

Tara wasn't surprised to see Gashmor-Morannod waiting just outside the fence. Tara didn't want to talk, but he wanted to fight even less. "No blood today." After all the slippery English today, speaking Orcish felt a relief.

Morannod dipped his chin an inch, a habit he'd stolen from humans. "No blood today." He matched his stride to Tara's as naturally as if they were called to war, moving more quickly than the paralyzed herd of grumbling cars on the road beside them. The cold, exhaust-tainted air tasted cleaner than the factory's metal polish and belt lube.

They walked half a block in silence before Morannod said, "I clean the *bathrooms* –" in English, for there was no orcish word—"today. He declares that my water is not hot enough, and that I use too little bleach."

Morannod's words stirred Tara's embers of anger. "Today, I deep clean lathes and lube the belts."

"As you should on Wednesday." Morannod's tone was un-orcishly flat.

"He tells me I use twice as much lube as needed." Just remembering stirred Tara's frustration. "The belts should be drier, he declares."

Morannod spat a thick lump of phlegm to the edge of the road, more eloquent than even Orcish could manage.

Tara hesitated. The world gave small punishments for what an orc held in his head and heart, but once he spoke? Once he gave his thoughts flight? November was not the cruelest month, but the frozen wind told Tara January listened. And right now—not only could the sky see them, but both the sun and the night?

Tara had to speak with care and thought.

"A dwarf machinist spoke to me," Tara said. That unusual event merited words.

Morannod grunted in acknowledgement.

"The dwarf told Janitor Miller that he was wrong." Again the truth, told in such a way that not even the Moon could take that Tara had raised himself.

"Dwarves and humans argue."

"The dwarf threatened Janitor Miller," Tara said.

Morannod laughed. "What, to chop his legs off at his knees?"

The weak joke reminded Tara of his grandfather's tales of the Old Country, where life was simpler and shorter. Remembering sitting at the aged orc's feet in the sweltering tenement where he'd grown up cast a shadow of warmth in his heart. "Not at all." This is the part that might get him in trouble, if he seemed to take sides. "The dwarf declared that the belt was to be greased in the manner of Janitor Burr."

A few more steps, and Morannod said, "I re-cleaned the *bathrooms* in obedience to Janitor Miller's commands."

"As proper."

"Once I declared them ready for his inspection, he asked why I had not cleaned the factory wall behind the line."

Tara barely kept his step from faltering. Men on the assembly line made the trek to the bathroom only to empty their bowels. For mere water, they used the useless brick wall behind the line. The factory's warmth made it evaporate harmlessly, and the stink meant nothing next to the mechanical reek of the line's grunting, tusk-rattling machinery. Tara and Morannod cleaned the wall once a year, during the August shutdown.

After another stride Tara said, "More work is always welcome." A true statement for any orc.

Morannod did not seem to notice Tara's weaker step—or, if he had, he held his silence on the matter. If the world noticed Tara, they might notice Morannod as well. "The men of the line became angry."

Janitor Burr had told Tara that Lord Dodge had built the factory specifically for assembling autos. It was exactly the size it needed to be, no larger and no smaller. The long room that held the assembly line was full of machines and men, all working together in a dance more intricate than the Winter Melt Festival that thanked January for permitting the clan's survival.

An orc working at the wall next to the line, wielding a massive mop and a bucket of hot water, dissolving half a year of urine into salty slipperiness, would be as welcome as a spear thrust between the Melt Chief's legs during the final leaps.

Tara could not think of what to say, so he grunted.

"I told the foreman I obeyed my master. He sent for Janitor Miller."

Tara had figured out that the human word "foreman" was short for "formidable man." He felt sure that the foreman intimidated other humans. "I am sure you obeyed."

Morannod spat on the path behind them, all the acknowledgement Tara's words rated. "Janitor Miller declared me disobedient."

Only quick thought kept Tara from tripping on his own boots.

Morannod had declared to the frozen November wind, to the sky and the approaching night, that his master had deceived him.

Morannod had not declared marrow feud with Janitor Miller. Not quite.

It was a declaration that Janitor Miller was unworthy of Morannod.

If Lord Dodge heard those words, Tara felt sure Morannod would find himself cast from the fiefdom.

But Tara's heart whispered that Morannod spoke the truth.

Beneath the sky and the last rays of the sun's light, though, with November's cold breath carrying his words to the distant but approaching night, Tara said, "It is every orc's duty to obey his worthy master." A catechism taught to every orc, in case they attempted to become a shaman or a warrior.

He didn't dare emphasize the word *worthy*.

But Morannod dipped his chin in silent agreement.

At the end of the block, where Tara turned left and Morannod turned right, Morannod said "My respect to your family."

Tara had taken Morannod's sister as his bride. Asking after her, in the human manner, would be un-orcish. "My clan will grow," Tara said—the closest thing he could offer to *she is well*. "No blood today." Tara crossed the street and headed towards their rented room.

With November seeping in through his skull, Tara didn't dare let his thoughts come together into a plan.

4

Tara had always known himself as more full of thought than other orcs— not smarter, never that, but his skull seemed to echo with so many ideas. His new bride's fierce attentions pushed them away for a time, but once she surrendered to sleep they returned and pinned him awake.

He had to be better.

He had to develop a deeper understanding not only of being a janitor, but of how humans worked. How they thought.

Perhaps Morannod would stand beneath the sky and declare Janitor Miller unworthy. Tara would not, could not.

Humans ruled the world. He would master their world.

He would make a place in it above any an orc had claimed before.

Tara opened the door to the janitor closet early the next morning, only to discover that Janitor Miller had beaten him there. Yesterday's rags and mop heads sat in a petrified lump in the laundry bucket, adding a hint of mildew and weak human piss to the air. The sturdy pegs where the orcs hung their coats stood empty; Morannod had not yet arrived.

Shockingly, Janitor Miller had moved a chair into the closet.

Janitor Burr had never sat, except during the midday meal all humans took. And he certainly had never rested in the closet, behind a closed door, shamefully concealing his weakness rather than overcoming it. Even as his body became too frail for labor, Janitor Burr had always stood respectfully.

But Janitor Miller sat in the closet with a leg folded over the opposite knee, a broadsheet newspaper folded open in one hand and a steaming cup of coffee in the other.

Was coffee part of Janitor Miller's morning ritual? Tara had tasted coffee once, but Janitor Burr had preferred tea. He'd often offered them a mug before beginning the day's labors.

Tara felt certain that Janitor Miller would not invite him or Morannod to drink anything in his presence.

Before Tara could open his mouth to offer the ritual greeting, Janitor Miller said "Don't get comfortable, orc. Some moron spilled light oil right by the lathe room engine. Get it cleaned up, then get on the with restrooms."

The restrooms? Did Janitor Miller intend to rip Morannod's labor away? Was he so displeased? "Yes, Janitor Miller." Tara slipped out of his coat.

"Hurry up now!"

Moving as quickly as he dared, Tara loaded the rolling table with solvents, buckets, and clean rags. He carefully placed a fifty-pound bag of sand at the end opposite the handle.

"Quickly!"

Did Janitor Miller want Tara to rupture the sandbag by tossing it? Or a bottle? Maybe spill ammonia and bleach together and fill the closet with poisonous *chlorine*? Best to get out as fast as he could.

Tara grabbed the oil mop and pushed his load out the door.

The lathe room was just starting its day. Men and dwarves were settling in at the machines lining the main walkway. At the far end, two men worked at the monstrous engine that drove all the lathes.

Tara's rolling table clattered as it bounced over and across the irregular floor. Once the great engine started its growl would silence all lesser sounds, but now the rattle echoed off the tall windows in the high walls. The table's tiny wheels wanted to wedge between the bricks, so he had to tow it like he would a truck with a dead engine. The burden wasn't heavy, but he needed more than strength to carry all these different things.

The thought gave him grim satisfaction. Most orcs just heaved and hauled.

"There he is," one of the human craftsmen called as Tara lumbered past. "The Terror what's going to keep us from breaking our necks."

Humans couldn't pronounce his Orcish name, so they called him Terror. The unexpected respect after Janitor Miller's coffee and ambush sparked a flame in Tara's heart. Despite Janitor Miller, with his coffee and broadsheet, Tara had found a place in the humans.

Tara said, "No blood today."

"That's the hope," another man said.

Tara wasn't on his way up. Not yet.

But Janitor Miller would not defeat him.

Neither would the oil stain.

One of the great drums of cooling oil had leaked in the night. The whole fifty-five gallons of thin lubricant had gushed out, leaving a broad amber pool soaking into the bricks and mortar at the foot of the great engine. Remedying would take hours, and multiple trips to the closet as well as the waste heap.

Janitor Miller would not be pleased.

Tara would have to work as hard as he could, on his knees before the great engine.

The engine stood almost three times as tall as an orc. He'd heard one of the craftsmen say that it came from a locomotive, and if that wasn't truth Tara felt it should be. The engine loomed like a human god of steel and coal and grease, great interlocking wheels and gears spinning together to drive this wing.

And Lord Dodge's factory had six of these beasts!

His brothers might succeed at bootlegging, but they'd never understand the wonder Tara felt at the engines. It was as if the humans had built an orcish god, served by two shamans disguised as mechanics.

Tara settled the cart next to the pooling oil and easily bounced the fifty-pound sack of sand in one hand. With a carefully trimmed edge of a talon, he cut a small slash in the canvas and began soaking up the spill.

The great engine started up, its floor-thudding thunder loud enough to make April jealous. The craftsmen claimed their lathes.

Tara got as far as cleaning up the oil-drenched sand and spreading degreaser before the disaster.

5

Greasy sand covered Tara's hands and heavy orcish sweat had soaked through his janitor's uniform. The labor itself wasn't hard, but the concentration and attention to every detail, every line of mortar and every crack in every brick, was its own work, and the great engine cast a wall of greasy heat more intense than any he'd ever felt. The stinks of oil, coal dust, and hot shavings filled his nose.

Tara had gotten the oily sand hauled to the waste heap—what orcs called the bone pile. Degreaser worked on one section of brick while he scrubbed another. The usual degreaser left oily slime. He'd have to try one of the others on his cart.

It only drove home how much more he had to learn.

Tara had grown numb to the great engine's noise, to the throbbing growl that rattled his bones in their joints and his tusks in his skull. The thirty lathes further down the room formed a second note, higher pitched, all the screeches of metal carving metal joining together into a drill that threatened to punch a hole in the top of Tara's skull. Occasionally he heard a man or dwarf shout above the chained storm.

That sharp snap didn't belong in any of that noise.

Tara jerked his head up.

The dwarf at the lathe closest to the great engine had stumbled off his raised work platform, trundling backwards on those stubby legs, arms wobbling for balance as if someone no taller than Tara's knees could fall over. It would look ridiculous, if the lathe's flywheel wasn't slowing down from a missing belt.

Horror clamped Tara's lungs.

Belt snap.

He'd checked that belt yesterday! He'd passed every inch of the leather through his fingers, letting them feel for weak points.

Metal screamed overhead.

The great engine's shamans added their own shouts.

Kneeling on the knobby brick, Tara felt exposed to an angry god.

The belt had flown up into the ceiling. One end tangled around the drive shaft, the other spun round it like an orcish babe being whirled by his father.

The great engine's pitch dropped. The men were working the gears, stopping the flow of torque.

Tara's hand reached out and grabbed the handle of his mop.

His brothers would piss themselves laughing at his un-Orcish habits.

The flopping end of the severed belt caught between two gears.

Faster than Tara could blink, the spinning shaft and wheels drew the belt tight. He heard and felt another snap, this time mixed with a clang and crash deeper than any he'd heard before.

Tara's guts clenched so hard they tried to suck his balls back up into his body.

Metal rained down—no, it was flung down, thrown with force far beyond anything even an orc could manage. A gear tooth bounced off a brick, the broken edge gleaming in baleful red heat.

The Great Engine *was* a god.

The snapping belt had angered it.

And Tara knelt at its throne.

The ceiling erupted in noise, not quite enough to drown the shouts of men and dwarves.

Tara heaved himself forward, boots slipping on the oily brick, scrabbling upright.

Next to him, one of his glass bottles shattered. A spray of bleach spattered his face.

Something small and sharp and metallic ricocheted past his vision.

Over the lathes and between the belts, Tara saw men fleeing.

Tara's lips were peeled back, instinctively exposing the Greater and Lesser tusks, but there wasn't an enemy to fight here, nothing but rupturing metal and flying death.

The coal door. He could turn around and hurl himself straight out the back of the room, out into the shelter of open air. Let the Great Engine scream its wrath.

Something crashed into the brick right next to Tara. He instinctively jerked to look.

A metal shaft, as big around as his arm, had hit the ground and already bounced back up but in the wrong direction, the Great Engine's nearly magical gift of torque sending it spinning an unnatural angle, back towards the aisle of lathes where men and dwarves were already a panicked mass crushing themselves out the far door—

No.

Not all of them.

A pair of short legs, feet clad in heavy dwarfish boots, stuck out from behind the closest lathe.

The dwarf who had stumbled back from the snapped belt?

Tara's body was already staggering towards the coal door. His bone and blood screamed for him to go on, to flee the angry engine.

But he'd checked that belt yesterday.

That dwarf?

Tara's fault.

And if the Great Engine demanded blood, Tara should be the one to pay it.

Tara lunched back, the oil-slick soles of his boots barely providing any traction. Something infernally hot and sharp slashed at his face and bounced off a Lesser Tusk, sending blinding pain up into his skull and making his eyes spasm, ricocheting away into the rising heat.

The dwarf lay slumped, thick red blood on his shirt. Tara bent to scoop him up, his feet still moving.

Tara's hands met the dwarf—and stopped.

Like they'd hit a cliff.

The rest of Tara's body kept moving.

The Great Engine granted Tara the gift of torque.

For an eternal second, the brick floor rose in Tara's vision.

Then Tara was down, rolling, arms flopping uselessly under him before he crashed up against a stock bin, the crash of steel shafts against each other not loud enough to penetrate the Great Engine's furious roar but forceful enough to echo down Tara's spine, pummeling the air from his lungs.

The lathe room rocked and wobbled.

The Great Engine smoked.

The degreaser Tara had spread to clean the oil?

Aflame.

Thick green smoke rising.

The fire spreading to Tara's rolling table, with all the cleaners on it.

Ammonia and bleach.

What else couldn't be mixed?

Tara struggled for breath.

The blow had confused his lungs.

If Tara waited to breathe, he'd die of flame or poison or flying metal.

He'd breathe again. Or he wouldn't.

Tara rolled himself over. One hand landed on the dwarf's leg. Head pounding, Tara clenched his jaw, seized the leg, and pulled himself upright.

One hand under the dwarf's shoulders.

The other under the legs.

Something struck Tara's lower back, a punch of pain that turned his guts to liquid.

One foot beneath him, one knee.

The compact dwarf felt as heavy as a cow.

Rising.

His ribs shrieked in complaint, demanding he inhale, but his lungs refused so he turned and lurched towards the far door, heading past the machines towards freedom with that stupidly heavy dwarf—must be full of lead. Eyes tearing with burning rubber and hot metal and that awful green cloud of flaming degreaser. Lower back a lump of pain growing hotter and hotter, sinking down his legs like warm thick porridge.

Tara's lungs spasmed. He hauled a breath in, but it burned his nose and mouth, making him cough as he staggered out of the lathe room and down the hall, out through the double doors into November's gift of fresh clean frozen air.

6

The Great Engine's shamans had somehow soothed their god to sleep. The factory's fire brigade still tromped in and out the lathe room's coal door, protected by their heavy leather armor and steel helmets. Black smoke poured out the open windows, but had thinned in the last few minutes.

Most of the lathe men remained in the muddy lot, huddled together for warmth. November's wind had slowed, replaced by a chill that promised a memorably stern December. Even the brilliant noontime sun couldn't get its heat through the ice blue sky.

Tara stood between the factory and the crowd of men. His back would bear a fine bruise from the falling debris. His shoulders hurt where he'd tried to casually scoop up the impossibly heavy dwarf. He'd discovered a nasty chip in one of his Lesser Tusks, explaining the ache deep in his jaw. He hadn't been this dirty since his fourth spring, when he'd discovered the mud pit behind the tenement—and the filth of fire was a whole different filth, one he doubted even his Kiva could clean.

But those aches were nothing next to his spirits as he watched the firemen roll up their hoses.

If everything else wasn't bad enough, he'd even denied the Great Engine its dwarfish sacrifice.

Tara had disappointed his new bride. Himself, his clan, yes, but his new bride. How had he thought himself worthy to claim a wife?

"Terror!" a man shouted.

Tara was so deep in thought, he didn't react until the man shouted, "Orc Terror!"

His human name. Tara wouldn't need a human name much longer.

Tara looked over his shoulder, sending a line of pain from the back of his skull down his spine. When had he hurt his neck?

Supervisor Sharpton marched towards Tara, Janitor Miller trailing behind him. Two dwarves followed, studying a mangled length of leather belt between them. And with them—

Lord Dodge himself! Tall for a man, in a human suit that fit him like a second skin, but with his weird blue noose only loosely knotted.

Tara made himself face his sworn Lord. He had one last duty.

Before Lord Dodge could get close enough for a man to speak Tara declared "The belts were my responsibility." He raised his chin to expose the tender veins of his neck. "I have failed. I submit myself to Lord Dodge's justice."

He had unmarried brothers. One would claim Kiva. She would be well.

"See!" Janitor Miller shouted, storming closer. "He admits it!"

Tara hoped Janitor Miller wouldn't be the one to administer the final cut.

"Hold yourself, Miller," Lord Dodge said. His voice was higher-pitched than most men, almost elvish but without their music. "I wanted to see this myself."

"Worthless orc," Janitor Miller spat. "Get rid of him. I know people who do better work and what deserve the job."

Tara watched Lord Dodge, refusing to turn his eyes from his fate.

Lord Dodge looked *furious*, even by orc standards. "This is the orc?"

"Yes, sir," Supervisor Sharpton said.

One of the dwarves said, "He hauled Bomlin out before we knew he was hurt." Tara only knew dwarves as flat and emotionless. The anger burning in this one's voice would have shocked Tara any other time, but he didn't need names.

"I did not inspect the belt properly," Tara said.

"You are finished," Janitor Miller said.

Lord Dodge turned his gaze to Janitor Miller. "Mister Gimrin. Please repeat what you told me."

One of the dwarves stepped forward. "Sir. This belt was weakened with a shallow cut across its width."

Janitor Miller's eyes got round, and he whirled back towards Tara. "Sabotage? You—"

Tara's fists clenched. He could accept his failure—he had no choice—but to be accused of betraying his oath?

"I said hold yourself, Miller!" Lord Dodge thundered. "Terror! You as well."

Tara focused on keeping his aching feet to the floor.

Lord Dodge glanced between Tara and Janitor Miller. "Gimrin. Proceed."

"The cut was made with a knife," Gimrin said. "Not an orcish talon."

A layer of Tara's tension bled out. His name was clear. He would die a failure, but not a traitor. The clan would mourn his loss.

"You can't tell the difference between a talon and a blade," Janitor Miller said.

Gimrin said, "Mister Miller. I fought orcs in war for almost four hundred years. I know orcish talons."

Grandpa had told tales of those wars. Maybe Gimrin would cut Tara's throat. He knew how it was done.

"Then, then he should have caught it," Janitor Miller said.

"Sharpton," Lord Dodge said. "Repeat what you learned."

"The first man in this morning," Supervisor Sharpton said. "He saw Miller in the lathe room. The oil drum was still leaking."

"I found it on inspection," Janitor Miller said.

"It had just started leaking," Supervisor Sharpton said.

Dangerous hope flared in Tara's chest.

He wanted to lower his head to look properly at Janitor Miller, but Lord Dodge had not declared judgment.

"Orc Terror has cared for our belts for the last year," the other dwarf said. "No belts broke in that time."

"Old man Burr covered for them," Janitor Miller shouted.

Even Tara could hear his desperation.

"Supervisor!" Lord Dodge said.

Supervisor Sharpton drew himself straight. "Sir!"

Lord Dodge studied Tara. "Take four of the men. Take Mister Miller to the police station. I want him arrested for sabotage."

Janitor Miller—no, *Man* Miller now—shouted in outraged protest.

Tara's heart thrilled.

Supervisor Sharpton paused. "I... don't know if there's a law against sabotage."

Lord Dodge whirled. "Then arson! Willful destruction of property." He jerked a finger back into the crowd. "That dwarf—Bomlin, was it? He tried to kill Bomlin." He raised his voice to overcome Miller's shouting. "Lock that man up, Sharpton!"

"Sir!"

Miller turned to run, only to face a wall of men.

Tara watched Miller's struggles with silent satisfaction.

Once Miller's shouts were distant enough for a man to speak over, Lord Dodge said "Terror."

The pain in Tara's back had made him slouch. He hauled himself upright. "My Lord."

"Mister is fine," Lord Dodge said.

How was he supposed to put these words together? "My Lord Mister."

Lord Dodge raised his eyes to gaze at the sky. Tara thought he heard the Lord murmur, "Orcs." More loudly, he said, "You saved the life of a dwarf today. You demonstrated loyalty nobody expected." He nodded. "And you took responsibility." He glanced over his shoulder at the crowd of men dragging Miller away. "Something many humans could learn." His gaze turned back to Tara. "How can I reward you?"

If Tara hadn't been so tired and beaten. If he hadn't almost starved for air. If the Great Engine's anger hadn't almost destroyed him. He wouldn't have said it. Not anywhere, but especially not here, beneath the open sky, with the Sun itself as witness.

"My Lord Mister Dodge," Tara said, "I would serve you as the plant floor head janitor."

Silence reigned for a breathless moment.

Then the sun and sky and November all witnessed Lord Dodge erupting in laughter.

Supervisor Sharpton joined in.

All the men laughed, each nudging the one next to him so that the mockery spread beyond the sound of Tara's voice.

Tara's soul shriveled.

To be told no? Life was hard. Failure was normal.

But this—this—derision?

The two dwarves studied him solemnly. One shook his head.

The tallest person in the crowd, Tara felt the smallest.

But Lord Dodge had not declared judgement. And Tara had sworn an oath.

He stood with his chin raised, allowing the laughter to wash over him.

In a moment, Lord Dodge wiped his eyes. "Mister Terror," he said. "I applaud your ambition."

Fresh hope flickered in Tara's heart.

"Orcs can withstand heat that would main a man," Lord Dodge spoke as if to a child. "You can clean machinery too hot for a man to touch. That's why we hire you. That's why we value you. But an orc responsible for the whole floor?" He shook his head. "Orcs do not have what we need."

Tara withered within.

All his plans of the last two years? Gone.

To be told no for now? Endurable.

But to be told no forever?

Tara's shoulders started to slump—

No. He would stand.

Tara lived full of thoughts, and those thoughts had led him badly.

They'd led him into hope.

And the gods so loved to take hope.

Ignorant or uncaring of Tara's secret revelation, Lord Dodge said "But you are the greatest assistant janitor I have ever had. With your bravery and loyalty, I will always have a place for you."

Tara would have a place... shackled at the end of the social chain.

Living on the scraps left by those ahead of him.

He could taste his bitterness.

The urge to rip off the greasy, smoke-stained canvas of the janitor's uniform filled Tara. To fling it to the ground at Lord Dodge's feet. To march away, naked to November. To find work hauling barrels, or crates, or oxen.

Lord Dodge smiled, carefully not showing his teeth. "You look like you've had a ton of bricks dropped on you. Take the afternoon off—paid, of course. Come back in the morning."

But where would Tara go? Home? Tell Kiva his shame?

"Lord Mister Dodge?"

"Yes, Terror?"

The words tasted like vomit. "I would work today."

Lord Dodge studied him for a long breath. "Mister Sharpton."

"Sir," Supervisor Sharpton said.

Lord Dodge nodded at Tara. "Double this orc's pay."

Five minutes ago, that would have delighted Tara. Instead, the words only twirled amidst the sickness in his gut.

Supervisor Sharpton's eyes got larger. "Sir."

"That'll put him up with a line worker, correct?"

"Yes, sir."

Lord Dodge nodded once more to Tara. "Would that I had a hundred men like you."

Tara watched his lord walk back into the crowd.

Supervisor Sharpton looked to Tara. "You're one lucky orc. You know that?"

Tara didn't trust himself to speak. A lucky orc? Maybe.

But humans ruled the world.

And they would keep it for humans.

Tara lowered his head. "I have work."

He needed to find another way.

Every moment, Uruk-Tai regretted letting the paper man talk him into this.

He knew in his bones that orcs did not belong in human places. Not even in the liberated year of 1927.

A downtown Detroit tailor's shop was more human than any place he'd ever been before. Especially after closing hours.

The smell wasn't too bad. A human might only smell cotton and wool. Uruk's sharper nose picked out the underlying taints of the acids and solvents used to torture those acres of raw materials into the fancy textures and colors humans preferred. And a human would need a very sensitive nose to pick out the traces of urine—mostly horse, but some human—from the leather belts and shoes.

At least the shopkeeper hadn't tried to cover up the smells with sickly-sweet perfume. The three bowls of dried flowers placed discreetly around the shop were something Uruk's wife Vara might use, if the clan had money for luxuries and she wanted to add a sweet scent.

Besides, Uruk could drown that smell with one good fart.

And the clothes? Uruk dressed properly for an orc: sturdy canvas dungarees. Heavy boots. A double layer of shirts, both burlap, plus his heavy third-hand wool coat to hoard heat against November's breath.

Here, rolls of fabric hung on wall hooks like bottles of whiskey in a crate. Wool should be white, or stained a color that wouldn't show the muck, but these were pale brown and dark blue and even a rich ruby red. What kind of man would wear red clothes? Humans didn't like to fight hard enough that they needed clothes that could hide blood.

Maybe upper-class humans snuck off somewhere orcs couldn't watch and held knife fight tournaments. He might like them more if they did.

No, their blood dried dark brown. They had some other use for red.

The shop felt too narrow for Uruk. The ceiling was high enough for him to stand comfortably, but the gap between the sacrificial dummy wearing a dress covered in tiny white beads and the impossibly feeble couch was so narrow that Uruk had to turn sideways *and* watch his feet to squeeze between them.

Everywhere Uruk looked he saw something fragile.

If he sneezed, he'd ruin a month's wages.

Let his dick got hard and he'd shatter something expensive. He'd been wise to demand his wife stay home.

"See?" Sanford said. "You are doing fine."

Sanford didn't look like a bootlegger. Even a small snarl would frighten him. But, much as Uruk loathed to admit it, he needed the paper man.

Sanford was a human word warrior, a *law-yer*. His spindly arms had all the strength they needed to lift a few pages of paper, and the shade of his skin reminded Uruk of the meat of that salmon he and his father had caught in the Detroit River so many years ago.

And Sanford talked far too much.

But the paper man could talk to men. He knew human respect chants. Those skills didn't help him get whiskey across the Detroit River.

Uruk and his brothers could move the whiskey but couldn't sell it to men.

Their alliance brought the clan money.

If Uruk needed a man as an ally, he wanted one whose marrow burned hot. He knew from hard experience that when roused, the scrawny paper man would fight to the limit of his strength, so he contented himself with grumbling "This is stupid."

Sanford smiled. "Not at all, my friend."

Friend? Uruk bit back his outrage. To an orc, a friend was one who fought at your side. Humans threw such intimate words around without meaning.

Oblivious, Sanford said, "Once the new buyer sees you dressed like a businessman, we'll get twice as much."

Humans got upset so easily. Uruk needed to be gentle. "Then humans are stupid."

Sanford only laughed. "I can't argue with you."

The door in the back of the shop opened. Uruk wasn't sure if the thing that emerged was a man or, perhaps, a possum that had learned to walk upright. No, Uruk had seen stronger-looking possums. The man's whole face seemed pulled back from his nose. Blotchy red and white skin shone through the pale hair swept back over his scalp. He wore wire frames over his eyes, filled with thick round windows—*glasses*, men called them, as if you'd make a window out of anything but glass. "Come in, good sirs!"

The man sounded like a possum, too: high and nasally and just a little bit coarse.

Sanford held out his right hand. "Hello, Reginald."

Reginald? Too long for a name. How would Reginald's victims accuse him with their dying breath? No, it made sense. A man-possum would never attack someone unless cornered, and even then he wouldn't finish the fight.

Besides, this was America, not the old country. Despite Grandpa's tales, such things didn't happen here.

Still: the man's parents had cursed him at birth.

"My dear Mister Sanford! What a pleasure this is!" Reginald came forward, holding both his hands out to grip Sanford's one.

"Reginald." Sanford raised his free hand, palm up.

Uruk tensed. Had Reginald already offended Sanford? Would the paper man strike down the opossum at their first greeting?

If Reginald fought fiercely, he might harm the paper man. And Uruk needed Sanford. Uruk shifted his weight onto the balls of his feet.

Something brushed against his back at the motion. The sensation quickened Uruk's pulse. Random smashing bored him, but he didn't want to accidentally topple one of these expensive displays.

Rather than striking Reginald down, Sanford held his free hand towards Uruk. "Permit me to introduce my associate." He cleared his throat and attempted to growl, "Urka-Tai."

Uruk blinked. Sanford had once again failed to pronounce Uruk's simple Orcish name, but he'd never gotten so close before. Still, he could not let the mispronunciation stand. "Uruk-Tai."

"Mister Tai," Reginald said.

Uruk tensed. Only those from a feuding clan called an orc by his clan name.

Whatever was brushing against Uruk's back wobbled.

Uruk froze. If he destroyed this shop, the police would come. By dawn, Uruk would be on his way to a Jackson chain gang.

But rather than declaring feud, Reginald crossed one arm over his chest and cradled his chin in the other. "You are *quite* the challenge." His nose even twitched. Just like a possum. "I don't know that any tailor has ever attempted to craft a proper suit for an orc."

Uruk didn't know of an orc that needed a man-suit. Even if Sanford had this stupid idea, why would this tailor even try?

Uruk let out his breath and tried to shift his weight forward without toppling whatever fragile things were precariously heaped behind him.

"Sir requires my undivided attention. I fear my fitting rooms are far too small, but I've cleared a space in the back." Reginald waved to the stockroom. "If sir would be so kind as to come with me."

Sir? Wasn't this about getting Uruk different clothes? If Sanford didn't need Uruk for this, why had the man brought him along?

Sanford glanced at Uruk, then at Reginald's retreating back. "I think it best if I come along."

Reginald glanced over his shoulder. "If sir has no objection."

Wait—Reginald was calling *Uruk* sir?

Sanford leaned close, coming almost up to Uruk's chin. "You said you've never seen a tailor. I can help with some of the more confusing parts."

Uruk swallowed. Why was his mouth dry? "You are the paper man."

Sanford glanced at Reginald. "That's a yes."

"Come along," Reginald said. "I don't mind staying open for sir, but I'm certain sir would prefer to be at home as expeditiously as possible."

What was the possum saying? Uruk answered with a grunt. Humans thought a grunt meant whatever they wanted it to mean, when it always meant *I'm not going to kill you now.*

Not that orcs in America killed humans.

Any more.

Following Reginald, Uruk crouched to get through the door to the back room and down an uncomfortably narrow hallway with textured, patterned walls. That wasn't paint—was it paper? Had they put colored paper on the walls? Uruk's talons, even as neatly trimmed as he kept them, would gouge plaster, but one of his *hangnails* would shred paper.

Entering the next room felt like an iron band loosening from around his chest.

The ceiling ran up a good twenty-five feet above the concrete floor. Heavy wooden shelves lined the walls, burdened with bundles of cloth in more colors than Uruk had ever imagined. Yes, he'd seen men dressed like songbirds every day of his life, but all this cloth gathered together in tight little rolls and bundles seemed a rainbow of a hundred different shades, especially with November's gray choke on the outside world. Bright lights hung from the ceiling, directly over mysterious tabletop machines.

Reginald waved Uruk to a cleared section of floor in the center of the room, large enough to park a Model A in. "If sir would be so kind as to stand here so that I could take proper measurements."

Was Reginald *really* calling Uruk sir? Uruk caught himself glancing at Sanford, and immediately jerked his gaze away. You've faced down men with machine guns and angry cows. Why does this opossum unnerve you?

Humans called orcs *pigs* or *grunts*. They didn't call orcs *sir*. Uruk would rather be back out on Lake Saint Clair gripping a gunwale and peering out over the black water for an approaching powerboat full of thugs with machine guns than let Reginald call him sir again. At least then he'd know what was happening.

Sanford said, "He's just going to measure you." His voice got quiet. "It won't hurt."

Not only had Sanford noticed—the man thought he was afraid? Uruk bit back a roar, but didn't trust himself to form an answer. Instead, he stomped to the cleared concrete floor and glared at Reginald.

Reginald didn't seem to notice Uruk's glare, instead plucking a pad of paper and a pencil off of a desk. "Exactly so, sir. If sir would be kind enough to stand there as I work?"

Standing was a kindness? Perhaps it was. He could crush an opossum with a step.

Sanford claimed a nearby seat and folded one ankle over the opposite knee. His body seemed relaxed, but his eyes never left Uruk. He had almost orcish attention.

Reginald stuck out his lips and hummed, staring at Uruk.

Uruk's heart picked up and a tight knot formed in the back of his chest. Humans saw orcs all the time, but they never really *looked* at orcs. The sensation of Reginald so intently studying him left Uruk uneasy.

"If sir would please relax," Reginald murmured.

Did the opossum want Uruk to lie on the floor? No, Uruk's shoulders were tight. His right hand had tensed, as if he hadn't trimmed his talons.

Treat it like waiting for an attack. Empty your thoughts. Look at nothing. Endure.

Reginald hummed again and stepped to the side.

Uruk shifted to face him.

"Please stay still, sir," Reginald said. "I must see all of sir if I am to ensure sir's suit fits sir properly."

From his chair, Sanford said, "Why don't you look at me?"

"If sir likes."

Uruk stilled his hands. An orc who ripped off a human's head went to prison, and stayed there forever. "Stupidity."

"Humans place great faith in appearance," Sanford said. "If they see you in those canvas pants, they'll think you're dumb muscle. If they see you in a suit, though—you'll be someone of power."

"Orcs have power," Uruk said.

Reginald had circled behind him, but Uruk could feel the man's opossum-vision against his back, studying him like a cow carcass hanging in the slaughterhouse.

"You have strength," Sanford said. "And nobody can question your bravery. The…" He paused. "What did Tara call it—the respect chant? That's the orcish term?"

Uruk grunted. Sanford had paid attention during that conversation, he shouldn't be killed now. "Yes."

"Wearing a suit is part of the human respect chant. It means that you expect respect."

"Indeed it does, sir." Reginald had almost completely encircled Uruk. "The clothes, as they say, make the man."

Uruk let his Lesser Tusks show as he glared at Reginald. "I will *never* be a man."

Reginald's eyes fixed on Uruk's face. He turned even whiter.

The orcish word for human meant *pale meat*, from the days in the Old Country. To call an orc pale meat meant that they were fit only as food. And in America, nobody ate anyone.

"Not human," Sanford said quickly. "But male. A husband, a father. That kind of man."

Uruk glared at Reginald for a beat, just to make sure the man understood Uruk was choosing not to take offense. "Your language is as stupid as your clothes."

A thin line of tension bled out of Sanford. "Utterly true. I spend entire days arguing about the meaning of words."

Reginald circled back to the front. His face was still pale, and sweat dotted his scalp beneath his thin hair. He kept his attention below Uruk's face.

Good.

Reginald pulled a thin cloth tape from his pocket. "If sir would extend his arm for me? So I can measure?"

Uruk eyed the man—but this was what he'd come here for. He slowly raised his arm straight out from his shoulder.

Reginald gulped. "If sir will excuse me, I must fetch my stool."

Uruk said, "Man Sanford. You think other men will offer me respect because of my clothes. Men do not respect orcs."

Sanford gave a small nod. "I respect your abilities." He tightened his jaw. "The men we deal with, they respect competence. They respect money."

Uruk let himself glance down at Reginald. "A man does not know *how* to respect an orc."

"True." Sanford said. "They will make mistakes. But you, Urka? You're a smart orc. You know the difference between being insulted because of ignorance, and someone wanting to insult you."

A smart orc. Like other orcs were stupid. And what did the intent matter? An insult was an insult. "A child knows the difference." But not a man.

Reginald set a short wooden stool down beside Uruk. "Here we are, sir."

"The suit is a start," Sanford said. "It says that you expect respect."

Uruk left his arm straight out as Reginald struggled to circle his bicep. "Do men not expect respect?"

"It depends on the clothes," Sanford said.

Human foolishness.

Reginald made a *tsk* noise, wrote something on his notepad, and scuttled off his stool. "If sir could raise his other arm, I must take a chest measurement."

Was Uruk a shaman's doll, to be arranged before stabbing the enemy through the heart? Not even his wife took such liberties.

But Vara clenched Uruk in her arms every night. She knew exactly how big he was.

"Zhan-ford." Uruk raised his other arm, allowing Reginald to loop the tape around his back. "This war needs you. I allow this out of respect."

"I know," Sanford said. "And it helps that I'm paying for this first one."

Uruk's chest swelled with tension. "First one?"

A tiny popping noise. "Oh, dear, sir." Reginald hopped off the stool, holding both ends of a snapped measuring tape. "A moment, sir."

"Once you see how wearing that suit changes things," Sanford said, "you'll want another. Also, if things should..." He eyed Reginald, scurrying through the clutter on a nearby table. "Go wrong during a discussion. If your suit was to need repair, or pick up stains too... difficult to clean. You'd need another."

The clan needs Sanford. Speak politely. "You are wrong."

Sanford shrugged. "If I am, then it costs me a measure of your respect and the price of a very custom suit. I'm more concerned about the former."

Sanford understood priorities. Uruk grunted.

Reginald stepped back, swallowed, and looked up at Uruk. "I fear, sir, that your clothing keeps me from obtaining an accurate measurement. It is most loose. Wherever does one obtain such... garments?"

Uruk raised his chin. "My wife sews them."

"And very fine work she does, sir. Truly skilled needlework. Very strong. To craft you a suit, however, sir, I must have your measurements. Not the measure of your garb." Reginald took a deep, shaky breath. "Might I ask sir to remove his outer layer of clothing?"

Uruk cocked his head at the opossum. *Outer* layer? How many layers did men wear? With quick, deft motions Uruk stripped his shirts off over his head, untied the rope that held his pants up, and let them fall.

"Oh my, sir."

Sanford averted his gaze. "Good lord, Urka, have orcs ever heard of underwear?"

"No. What is *under-wear*?"

Reginald said, "Traditionally, one wears smaller clothes beneath one's outer garments, to protect one's clothing from the body's natural processes."

Uruk said, "You mean, a fart makes your clothes dirty?"

"Indeed, sir."

Why would even humans wear such fragile clothes? Humans farted. Uruk couldn't spend a day in public without one of them letting off a good rip.

"Reginald," Sanford said slowly, "let's add two sets of underwear to the order."

"Very good, sir. If sir would be so good as to remove his boots as well? We must arrange footwear for sir."

"Can you take those measurements?" Sanford said.

"Certainly," Reginald said.

"Can you acquire the shoes?" Sanford said.

"Boots," Uruk said. No orc wore *shoes*. The tiny ropes men used to tie them together wouldn't last an hour on an orc's feet.

"But of course," Reginald said to Sanford. "A suit such as sir's will require the most special shoes."

"I said *boots*," Uruk snarled.

Reginald blanched.

"It is all right, Urka." Sanford's voice shivered.

Good. "It is not all right. Boots."

Sanford made an obvious effort to calm himself. "If you require boots, then you will have boots."

Uruk glared. "You will not ignore me."

"Sir..." Reginald fluttered his hand in front of his face, as if trying to generate a breeze against the sweat that had cropped up there. "No, sir. I would never ignore sir."

"You did ignore me." Uruk's hands itched. "Never again."

"As sir says." Reginald looked like he might faint.

"Do orcs not wear shoes?" Sanford said.

"They are too weak for orcish feet." Uruk could haul cargo all day, wrestle with his boys, ravish his wife—twice!—and *still* feel less tired than explaining the simplest facts to a human. "Even you must hold them together with string."

"Indeed, sir." Reginald's eyes didn't leave Uruk's face—good. "I shall rise to the occasion. Sir shall have boots with his suit. The finest hand-crafted boots. They will fit sir's feet perfectly."

"Steel-toed," Uruk said.

Reginald glanced down at Uruk's feet. Uruk could tell exactly when Reginald realized the strength of Uruk's trimmed talons. "Yes, I do believe sir is most wise. Steel toes."

Uruk grunted.

Reginald squeezed his elbows to his side as if he was trying to hold his ribs in place. His replacement tape measure was wound so tight around his hand that the fingers were turning even whiter. His notepad shook in the other. "If sir would allow me to proceed?"

Uruk raised his arms.

Reginald scurried in.

"He will finish soon," Sanford said. "Reginald's father made my father's suits."

The flimsy tape tickled Uruk's chest. He didn't bat it away. "Do you try to make me like you?"

Sanford laughed. "Urka my friend, even divine intervention couldn't make you like me."

If Sanford so wanted to be a friend, then Uruk could arrange a fight. Let Sanford prove himself at Uruk's side. Perhaps this new buyer would give them trouble.

Sanford said, "I brought you to my family tailor because I want you to have a suit as good as mine. We are partners. Neither of us can succeed without the other."

Uruk grunted.

"If sir would fully inhale? Sir's suit must have enough space for—just so, sir."

"Our customers must see us as equals," Sanford said.

Uruk frowned. "Why is this important to you, man?"

"I'm not a strong person." Sanford stared into empty space. "Alone, some of these people would force me to work for them. But if I have a partner..." He focused back on Uruk. "A strong, fast, cunning partner. If we're halfway through a run—a war, as you say, and something happens to me... if a buyer betrays us, you would make them pay. It would be literal, bloody war."

"Something you cannot do for me."

"You've seen what I do with the law," Sanford said. "If you went down, I'd attack their business. A human without money, without friends, without family? Your brothers would handle what remained."

Uruk grunted. "Then this suit protects you. It does nothing for me."

"Oh, no," Sanford said. "You can't dress like a dockworker and demand big money. Dressing the part shows you can deliver."

Yes. Sanford knew better than to carry a cow on his own. Uruk needed to learn to not war with words against a *law-yer*.

Or to get better words.

Reginald knelt, running the tape measure down the outside of his leg.

The gesture made Uruk strangely uncomfortable, like a surrender he hadn't earned. He fought down the urge to scream at the man to stand, to endure.

Rising, Reginald said, "If sir would care to dress again, sir can select his fabric."

Uruk reached for his pants. "Fabric? Would you dress me in red?"

"Not at all, sir!" Reginald fanned his face. "Sir must have a serious suit, for serious business. That leaves many fabrics for consideration. Also." He licked his lips. "How does sir feel about suspenders?"

Uruk frowned. "Suspenders?"

"For sir's pants."

Uruk's frown deepened.

"I fear sir is flat-seated."

Uruk's frustration at the possum's tedious speech was starting to sizzle up his spine. "Say what you mean, man."

Sanford said, "He means you have no butt."

"And you have no dick," Uruk said.

"The way a suit is cut," Sanford said. "You can either tie it up with a belt, or with suspenders. They clip to your belt and go over your shoulders. Like on overalls? I've seen orcs with overalls."

"As sir says."

"What's wrong with them?" Uruk said.

"I make the finest suspenders," Reginald said.

Don't claw the human. Don't claw the human. "Why do you *ask*, then?"

"Some people do not care for them," Reginald said. "They feel suspenders are... lower class."

"So important humans have bigger asses?"

Sanford bellowed a laugh.

"Sir! Not at all, sir."

Why had the man even *asked*, then? "I am an orc. Orcs wear overalls."

"Sir?"

"That's a yes," Sanford said. "Two pairs of suspenders."

Reginald drew his first full breath since he'd started measuring. "As sir wishes." Once Uruk had his boots on, Reginald said, "I took the liberty of laying out some fabric samples that I felt might be suitable. If sir would look this way?"

A nearby table held a dozen scraps of cloth, from a few inches on a side to almost a yard. While the room held fabrics of hundreds of colors, these were all dark blues and browns and blacks.

Uruk eyed a swatch the same blue as the Detroit River on a dark day. Thin parallel black lines ran through it.

"If sir would care to examine the samples, sir could express his preferences. If none of these will do, I have many others."

Uruk picked up the blue swatch. The softness sent a revolted shudder up his arm. He instinctively flicked it away.

Reginald scuttled back a yard.

"Uruk?" Sanford said.

His tusks were showing—not merely the Lesser, but the Greater as well. Uruk felt the iron-hard tension in his shoulders and down his spine. His weight had shifted onto the balls of his feet, and his toe talons scratched against the steel lining of his boots.

Uruk had never felt anything as repulsive as that cloth. "You wear that?"

Sanford took a step back, arms raised. "It's okay, Uruk."

"It is not okay!" No. He was shouting in Orcish now. His heart pounded against his ribs and his breath felt a fire in his lungs. The need to upend the table, to slash that horrid softness to shreds, burned his marrow.

No—no. Uruk clamped his mouth shut and pulled his hands into fists to conceal his talons. Was he going to let a piece of cloth send him to prison? Hurt the clan?

It took all his will to stand in place and push the revolted fury away.

The opossum slowly inched to put a table between himself and Uruk.

Sanford, to his credit, did not retreat further.

"If sir—"

"Hush!" Sanford said. "He will speak when he is ready to."

Uruk needed another moment before he could say, "That cloth is... no. It is..." He had to forcibly loosen his jaw to say, "It is the most awful thing I have ever touched."

Nobody spoke for a moment. Then:

"If sir would care to say how?"

Uruk's hands were fists. Orcs fought with talons, not fists. His talons were trimmed—but to a human, he'd look like he was ready to fight. He deliberately unrolled his hands, not far enough to use the talons, but enough that he didn't look ready to punch a man's head to Canada.

Uruk raised his pinky and dragged one neatly trimmed talon across another sample. It parted like porridge. "This—*cloth*. It is soft like rotting fungus. It is not orcish."

Reginald eyed Uruk's clothing, nodding. The fear had left his face, replaced by a thoughtful expression. "If sir would wait a moment, I shall fetch some samples sir might find more suitable."

Uruk concentrated on banking the fire in his heart.

"Orcs are so tough," Sanford said. "It never occurred to me that fine cloth would... distress you."

"That's not cloth," Uruk said. "That is torture."

Sanford spoke slowly. "I told Reginald that I wanted you to have a good suit. Made with good cloth. A human would find that material most pleasant. His intent was to please you."

Intent, intent, intent! What was with humans, thinking that intentions meant *anything*? "You declare that this... *suit* is a necessity. I will not allow myself to be offended." Uruk drew a breath. "This time."

"Thank you."

Reginald scurried back, holding a decrepit box with bits of cloth poking out. "I've gathered some samples that sir might find more pleasant. The colors are not correct, but if sir would care to find a fabric that pleases him, I will arrange dying."

If anyone would arrange any dying, it would be Uruk.

The box thudded onto the table.

Uruk couldn't help pausing as he looked at the box—no.

He was an orc. Orcs endured.

He thrust a hand into the box.

Nothing appalled him.

In another minute he had chosen a chunk of coarse wool. The fibers dragged at his skin, and the cloth felt heavy enough to withstand a sneeze. "This."

Reginald took it, eyebrows raised, and rolled the material between his pasty white fingers. "When Mister Sanford asked me to sew a suit for an orc," he said slowly, "I thought, if I can accomplish this, I would be the greatest tailor in Detroit. I did not expect... how great a challenge." The man's eyes burned with hunger for a worthy battle, the first expression Uruk recognized. "If sir would care to return in a week for sir's first fitting?"

"What is a first fitting? I thought I was getting a suit?"

"I'll have the first cut of sir's suit ready, but it will require adjustment. It must fit sir perfectly, as sir deserves."

"Eight days." Uruk nodded. "We work one week from tonight."

Reginald said, "Eight days would be suitable, sir. And for the underwear? Most men would prefer soft cotton."

Uruk tensed.

"But for sir, might I suggest—canvas?"

Uruk grunted, letting the tension bleed away.

"As sir wishes."

"Anything else?" Sanford said.

"I suspect sir would not care for a tie."

Sanford said, "You suspect correctly."

"You do not speak for me," Uruk said. "What is this *tie*?"

Sanford reached up and flapped the ridiculous red noose that dangled around his neck.

Sanford had guessed well—but Uruk would never say that. "No tie."

"As sir wishes. Eight days, then?"

"Until then," Sanford said. "Urka shall we? Go, that is?"

Uruk looked at the possum and made his mouth form the words, "No blood tonight."

Reginald glanced at Sanford.

"It's an orcish fare-thee-well," Sanford said. "Sort of. Good night, Reginald."

Uruk retrieved his heavy wool coat and trudged after Sanford into the front of the store.

Sanford stopped next to a display of those absurd ties to button his coat. "Thank you, Urka. I know that was very..." He looped a scarf around his neck, clearly buying himself a moment to think. "Un-orcish."

Uruk grunted. "You want me to have a suit to protect you."

"And to bring us money," Sanford said.

"But to protect you."

Sanford frowned and faced Uruk, looking straight up into his face. "Listen to me, orc." He folded his arms across his chest. "We're bootleggers. And if we're going to bootleg, we're going to be the best bootleggers in Detroit. That means we deliver the best booze. We demand top dollar for it, and a suit is part of that. And, most important?" He raised a finger. "I go home to Beverly. And you return home to your clan, to Var—Vaha—" He raised a hand to cover his cough. "To your wife, your sons."

The man understood. "Yes."

"Sorry." Sanford cleared his throat. "I'll practice your name, but there's no way I'm mispronouncing your wife's name."

Uruk couldn't help his nod.

The man could learn. Uruk could work with that.

"If this suit brings more money," Uruk said, "I shall buy another."

 # A DEBT OF MEAT

Men had built an orcish god, and Lord Dodge had chained it to serve his automobile factory.

Tara-Tai knew men didn't think of the Great Engine that way. Humans cared nothing for orcish gods. They probably didn't know orcs had gods. They would never think of the Great Engine as anything but the old locomotive engine that powered Lathe Room Four. Men lacked the spirit to gaze at the massive steel boiler and the whirling flywheels distributing miraculous *torque* to the thirty lathes around the machine shop and realize that the Engine had a power that could never be compromised, never placated, never tamed. You accepted the Great Engine on its terms or it slaughtered you.

The men sacrificing endless rivers of coal to the Engine were no different than priests.

The human and dwarven craftsmen laboring at their lathes beneath the bright electric lights, its acolytes. The steady vibration through the brick floor, its voice.

Orcish gods could not be argued with. Disrespect December and she froze your blood to your meat, even in this modern year of 1927. Challenge the Detroit River and it swallowed you. Taunt the Great Engine's drive shaft with a finger, and it would claim your hand. Lean against the boiler and it would instantly cook your flesh to the steel, adding the stink of cooked man to the god's incense of coal smoke and heavy grease and metal dust.

Two weeks before, a man had disrespected the Great Engine. Its wrath had struck down men and dwarves. The priests had completed their cleansing rituals only yesterday, and today the acolytes again worshipped at their lathes.

Tara owed the Engine a debt of meat.

The thought weighed him more than it should. Orcs always owed their gods.

Tara-Tai tried to focus on his heavy-bristled broom. If he brushed too hard, the endless metal shavings would scatter. If he brushed too softly, the shavings would remain wedged down in the mortar between the bricks, only to work their way free under the Great Engine's constant vibration and get caught in the craftsmen's boots. Metal shavings ate boot soles. Lord Dodge paid the craftsmen well, but even their unnatural salaries could not afford new boots every week.

If Tara had kept his mouth shut, he might have had different labor.

Tara had dared hoped for a higher future. He studied the janitorial craft. He mastered the different broom and all three mops. He understood the secrets of *Ammonia* and *Bleach* and *Alcohol*, the Four Degreasers and the Three Solvents. He could lubricate the lathe drive belts as well as any.

But standing before Lord Dodge and the heads of his factory, beneath the Sun itself, and declaring that he hoped to become head janitor? Tara-Tai had left the Sun no choice but to destroy him. He might as well have declared he would become President of the United States. His foolishness weighed his bones.

Movement at a lathe caught Tara's eye.

One of the dwarves stepped down from his station. Tara knew this dwarf's name—Bomlin. Tara knew nothing more than his name, but that one fact was enough to make Bomlin more familiar than any other dwarf.

Two weeks before, the Great Engine's wrath had struck Bomlin unconscious. Tara had carried him to safety before the Engine's smoke could smother him. Lord Dodge had doubled Tara's pay in gratitude, even as he'd declared Tara's hopes impossible.

But Tara had denied the Great Engine its sacrifice. The Engine would claim that debt.

Bomlin caught Tara's eye and pointed at his lathe, telling Tara he had time to clean it. Surely Tara didn't glimpse discomfort in Bomlin's square face? Dwarves were as feeling as granite.

Tara nodded, accepting Bomlin's command. A dwarf could not demand an orc's service, but the head janitor had told Tara to clean the lathes when the craftsman permitted. Tara put the heavy-bristled broom back on his cart and wheeled it over to Bomlin's lathe.

Lathes were fascinatingly intricate. Tara's gaze could trace the workings of *torque* from the drive belt into the gears and down to the rotors and blades, imposing the Great Engine's will upon the metal. The craftsmen might steer that will across metal, but it was the Engine that shaped steel and aluminum stock into automobile parts. Oil and grease and metal shavings would fly from the blades, wedging in countless crannies and mingling with the leather shredded from the massive drive belts. Restoring the machines to a pristine state, ready to evoke the Engine's will, had always satisfied Tara.

But not today.

As his brothers would die hauling bales at the Port of Detroit, Tara would die cleaning lathes.

Tara took a rag from the bag and reached for the lathe—

—and stopped.

The dwarf had abandoned the lathe's teeth on the workbench.

Dwarves always put their tools away when they left their lathe, even when they only went to the wall to make water. Bomlin had left the lathe teeth out amidst the metal shavings, two dozen different bits of cunningly curved hard steel scattered almost randomly amidst the metal and grease.

The tooth case sat to the side of the bench, open.

Teeth were expensive. Was Bomlin so well paid that he could be careless with Lord Dodge's tools?

Tara was not so well paid. He could not clean the lathe around the teeth. He would have to put them away.

The tooth case sat at the end of the bench, closed against the shavings. Tara had just enough of a talon on his thumb to flip the latch open, exposing two dozen identical six-sided holes.

How did the craftsmen store their tools? Tara carefully put his thumb and forefinger around a minuscule tooth. His fingers were far larger than a man's, or a dwarf's. The tooth felt like small as a newborn's tusks, slick with light machine oil. He wrapped his rag around the tooth, gingerly wiping away the dust and leather and metal.

His fingers told him that one end of the tooth had six sides, just like the holes in the tooth case. With all his attention, he slid that end of the tooth into the first hole in the case.

It fit as well as his own tusks in his jaw.

Picking up the next tooth was no easier. Unlike the first, though, this one had a curved edge; a meat tooth, not a grinder. He put it in the first empty space of the second row.

The third tooth had a straight edge like the first, but it was a tiny amount longer. Wiping it down, he placed in next to the first.

The third tooth was also straight, but shorter. Surely the teeth went in order, just as in a mouth? Should he move the first two over? No, he would spend all his time shifting lathe teeth from one socket to the next, and be unable to clean the lathe before the dwarf returned. Shamed by speaking his dreams or not, he had to clean the lathe.

Fast as he dared, he laid the loose teeth out on the workbench. Twelve were straight. Another ten, curved. The last two were long and square, totally unsuited for eating metal.

No, he couldn't let his thoughts take him astray. Tara-Tai wasn't any smarter than any other orc, but so many thoughts filled his skull that they kept him from working properly. The purpose of those lathe teeth did not matter. All that mattered is that the contoured lid of the tooth-case had a space where these would fit, at the end of the first row. The ten curved teeth must go in the first row, not in the second as he had placed them.

Mouth dry, Tara ordered the teeth by size. If he moved any more quickly, his massive fingers might pinch too hard and shoot a tooth out into the lathe room. He would never find it, and the cost of the tooth would be taken from his pay. The oily teeth seemed almost alive in his grip, but he wiped each down before putting it in its place.

The oil had soaked through this rag. Tara turned to put it in the soiled bucket and grab another.

Bomlin was standing right there. Canvas coveralls or no, if Tara had turned any faster his swinging balls would have cracked the dwarf's skull.

Tara stilled himself. A surprised leap would give the Great Engine a chance to claim the debt Tara owed it. Instead, he shifted his weight back to give himself a breath of space. Had putting the teeth away taken him so long? Truly, he'd been a fool to hope to become a full janitor. If the teeth not been left for him—

No.

Orcs did not get excuses.

Tara made himself say, "I am slow, dwarf." The words tasted like the filthiest ballast from the most disreputable freighter he'd unloaded at his first job. "The lathe is not yet clean."

Bomlin took two steps back, then waved a hand for Tara to lower himself.

Why would a dwarf want Tara to kneel? A dwarf's voice could penetrate the Great Engine's roar. A dwarf had no rights over an orc, not like a man. Did he intend to strike Tara for touching his tools? They weren't the dwarf's personal tools, they were Lord Dodge's. Even an orc knew to not touch a dwarf's tools.

The only way he would learn what the dwarf wanted would be to kneel.

Tara compromised by bowing, putting his hands on his knees so that he could bring his head even with the dwarf's. If the dwarf attacked him, Tara would have to stand again to defend himself.

Bomlin's voice was pitched just loud enough for Tara to understand, and as flat as any dwarf's. "The fault is mine."

Why would a dwarf take an orc's fault? What could Tara say to such a thing?

"Return to your work," Bomlin said.

Tara shifted his weight to stand.

No louder, Bomlin said "Accept that this place will never let you escape your role."

2

December's ice-laden wind gnawed at Tara-Tai all through the two mile trudge home, but not even the Sun-Eater could devour the shame and frustrated fury burning in his blood. The cramped concrete stairs down to his basement apartment seemed even more treacherous than usual, the narrow treads meant for humans made slippery with blown snow.

He ached to throw the door open and declare his presence the way his father had. If he broke the door, though, the landlady would demand he pay for it. Instead, he seized the knob as delicately as he had the lathe teeth and eased it open.

Any orc would call his basement room luxurious. Worn-out burlap feed sacks covered the floor, offering soft footing and insulating against the dirt below. They had their own iron stove, with a chimney out one of the narrow windows up by the exposed rafters of the ceiling, and the landlady granted them an entire bucket of coal every day. Her bedroom was above. Tara's fire warmed her aged feet. While men had lived here, once, it had been long enough past that the pervasive stink of cabbage and beans and man-sweat had surrendered to the wholesome smells of an orc family: sweat, porridge, the occasional hint of lard or even bacon. And the subtle scent of his joy. His new wife.

The room was not big enough for Kiva to charge properly, but enthusiasm made up for speed.

Tara barely stepped inside before she crashed into him, ignoring the snow on his patched wool coat to savagely kiss him.

More days than not Tara responded by kicking the door shut and unleashing his own gentle savagery, ending an hour later with Kiva trying to discover where he had flung her dress, but today he only wrapped arms around her and kissed her back.

Kiva ended the kiss and stared into his face. "My warrior." Her Orcish words always kindled a pleasant fire throughout his body. Today, it could not ignite. "What is wrong?"

Tara carefully closed the door and stripped off the old wool coat. His breath came hot in his sinuses. "I am not a warrior today."

"You do not fight with talon." Kiva came back into his arms. The Lesser Tusks rising from her jaw were cool against his neck, her breath warm between them. "You have chosen a war for the world we live in."

Tara glanced around the room. Old feed bags covered the windows, shielding their room from December's sight. The stove burned low. Despite his instructions, Kiva always hoarded most of the coal against Tara's return. More burlap shielded his feet from the Earth. The gods would hear what he said. They always did. But words spoken in the full privacy of the hearth were not weighed so heavily.

And along with the obvious pleasures of marriage, a woman had responsibilities to clan and family. Fulfilling them required she know her husband's secrets. Even if they reminded her of his failures.

Tara made his heavy tongue form the words. "Today, the dwarf whose life I saved reminded me of my shame."

Kiva stiffened in his arms, her breath turning hot against his skin. Her fingers straightened against his back, ready to slash the enemy. "Why would he do such a thing?"

She had not scorned him for his failure. Tara let his own breath out. "Does saving a dwarf's life grant him power over me? Does he resent his breath? Would he have had me leave him to breathe fire? Lord Dodge—" No, he would not speak of Lord Dodge's approval. Even here, in the privacy of the hearth, the gods would hear. They would have no choice but to take it from him.

Kiva's Lesser Tusks nuzzled at the pulse of his neck, quickening his pulse even further. Usually that would send his hands roaming down her back. Not today.

Another breath, and Kiva said, "What were the dwarf's exact words?"

The windows were still blocked, the fire still low. He still barely dared breathe, "Accept that this place will never let you escape your role."

"Dwarves do not understand shame." One of Kiva's trimmed talons trailed across his janitor's coveralls, right over his heart. "He would not try to remind you. He intends something else."

"Intentions mean nothing," Tara growled. An orc catechism, among the first things taught. Only results mattered.

"Has this dwarf ever spoken to you before?"

"No."

"Then why today?"

Tara made himself tell the short saga. Starting was hard, but by the time he said "I cleaned his lathe the next time he left," his blood had somehow eased.

Kiva squeezed him fiercely. "The dwarf made an error," she murmured. "He made an error in front of an orc."

"He did." Murmuring into the knitted wool cap over her scalp would not hide his words from the gods, but it felt good.

"Dwarves do not treat with orcs," Kiva said.

Tara nodded.

She took half a step back, just enough to look into Tara's eyes. "I say that he tried to cover his own shame at his failure by reminding you of yours. I say that this war is one of will, not muscle. Will you let him unbalance you? Or will you ignore his trifles and continue to serve Lord Dodge as honorably as you always have?"

Kiva's words kindled the familiar orcish urge for battle. Maybe Tara didn't fight with talon and tusk, but America presented its own strange battles. "My woman," he said. "I think you are right."

"My warrior," One hand reached up to cup his cheek, her thumb stroking his tusk. "Sometimes, you let your thoughts overwhelm you. Do not make me hold your head in the river until you stop thinking so much. Those thoughts drew me to you. I would miss them."

Tara's laugh shattered his heavy heart. "You would do that?"

"I do what I must," Kiva said. "For the family, for the clan."

"Then I shall stop thinking, the best way I know how." Tara made his face stern. "Give me that dress."

Kiva bared her tusks. "Come and take it."

3

Walking to the plant the next morning, not even dark December hurling raging snow against his face could steal the warmth from Tara's heart. Perhaps he was only an assistant janitor, but he had a home any orc would envy and Lord Dodge paid him more than any orc could hope for. Not even a fool like Tara would dare voice his hope that there would be children, but if orc meat and blood could manage them, his Kiva could. Lord Dodge demanded his presence when the lathes began work, but like any orc Tara showed up early. An orc's labor defined him, but he took an un-orcish delight in the factory's quiet.

The Great Engine was just waking from its overnight rest, the priests sacrificing coal and water in their prayers for its efforts. It had been kept warm but idle through the night, but now the steel boiler pinged and creaked as the pressure within it surged. Five rows of lathes sat silent, their drive belts disengaged and rotors safety-locked. Tara had cleaned every lathe before he left the night before, and they still gleamed. The stink of coal and steam were only starting to overwhelm the cold smell of metal polish.

Perhaps he'd cleaned them a little too forcefully. The steel of the lathes could withstand any amount of scrubbing, but the leather belts that connected the lathes to the Engine were fragile. Men and dwarves checked their own belts each day, but grooming and lubricating them was his duty.

If a belt broke because Tara handled it roughly, Lord Dodge would rightfully discard him. Tara could not fail Kiva that way.

The factory awoke around him, the clatter of men and machines and waking engines filling the air. Tara was checking the fourth belt, slipping the long greased leather between his probing fingers, when a flat voice behind him said "Orc."

Bomlin. Again.

Tara stiffened. Dwarves did not arrive at the factory early. They marched to the gate as a group, arriving exactly when the start whistle blew. When the stop whistle blew, they departed as one. Why would a dwarf come here alone? How? "Yes, dwarf?"

Bomlin had a small wheeled cart behind him. Not one of the factory's carts, but one like Tara had seen man-children playing with. It was half-full of grungy, rusty metal bolts and screws and nuts, junk you might collect from the bone pile behind the factory. Lord Dodge would never allow such parts in one of his automobiles.

"I will inspect the belts." Bomlin pointed a finger at the cart. "You will attend this."

"You demand my labor?" Tara cursed the surprise in his voice.

Bomlin's voice had no inflection. "I can request help when you are not otherwise working."

Any of Lord Dodge's men could make that request. Tara supposed a dwarf could as well, but no dwarf ever did. Most dwarves knew better. Did saving Bomlin's life make the dwarf feel entitled to him?

But the rules were clear. The orcs would aid all who served Lord Dodge. "Yes, dwarf." He could haul the scrap to the bone pile—the waste heap, men called it.

He saved a dwarf's life, and the dwarf sent him into the cold?

Tara should have left Bomlin to burn.

Bomlin said, "Some of the bolts have matching nuts. Mate each nut to its bolt. Use the oil to loosen the rust. Screw them together. Do not force any. Place those parts without mates in a separate pile."

Tara froze. This was not orcish labor. This was... he had no idea what this was. His thoughts, always crowded into his head, huddled against the sides of his skull in confusion.

"Do you understand."

Was that a question? Spoken so flat, it didn't sound like one.

Bomlin's mouth twisted. "Do you understand?"

"Yes, dwarf."

Bomlin pointed over to a corner near the Great Engine. Tomorrow's shipment of metal stock would fill the space, but today it was half-empty. "You will work there. You have until the men take coffee."

If he spent that long doing the dwarf's work, the floor would be filthy! He wouldn't have time to finish the floor before he needed to start on the bathrooms. Tara opened his mouth to protest—

No.

Protest was for a full janitor.

When Janitor Kowalski came to check on Tara at the start of shift, Tara would explain.

The absurdly short cart's handle barely came up to Tara's knees. He had to bend nearly double to get one finger through the round handhold at the end and gently tug the tiny thing. It skipped and danced across the bricks, threatening to overturn each time one of the tiny wheels caught against a gap or a crack. After only a few steps, Tara straightened.

Bomlin still watched.

Tara bent his knees, seized the cart, and hoisted it into his arms. It weighed almost nothing, not even as much as a cow. Ignoring Bomlin, Tara marched to the corner and lowered the wagon without spilling any.

Running his fingers through the hundreds of bits of metal, they came away filthy with decaying grease and rust and plain old oily dirt. Had the dwarf taken it from the waste heap? What could he possibly want with it? And how was he going to sort this trash before Man Coffee?

He'd start by discarding everything that was not a bolt or a nut. That would go into a pile of its own. Then he would separate nuts from bolts. He would line them up by size, exactly as he had the lathe teeth. Then he could test each nut against the bolts, finding those with the same threading. He would soak them with the oil, and thread them together.

Thread them as best these scraps could fit.

Then he'd clean the floor, before the oil soaked into the brick.

Tara bent to work.

The Great Engine's grumble became a roar, washing him with almost enough heat to be comfortable. Men strolled to their machines, laughing and chattering with each other. Tara ignored their curious gazes. Moments after the start siren, the squad of dwarves marched in the main door and split off to their lathes.

None of the dwarves looked at him. Tara couldn't decide if that was better than the men, or worse.

The bolts demanded most of his attention.

He sorted away the scrap easily enough, but fitting the nuts to the bolts was difficult. Many of the nuts were tiny enough to frustrate his fingers. So close to the Engine, its heat was enough to illuminate the threads in orcish night vision. The smallest bolts, he had to pinch the head between two fingers and meticulously turn it into a bolt laid flat against the floor, then raise the pair and roll the nut along the length of his arm to turn it. Grease and oil stained his sleeves. Kiva would struggle with these stains.

The task was near impossible for an orc.

Was that why Bomlin had demanded this labor? Was he trying to remind Tara that being a craftsman required more than putting lathe teeth in a box? Tara was not so foolish as to need that lesson.

Tara worked as fast as he could. The metal of the bolts was so soft! Any but the softest twist would force a nut onto the wrong bolt, stripping both. Bomlin had almost certainly believed Tara would use brute force.

Tara would not give the dwarf the satisfaction.

How long until Man Coffee? Men knew.

An endless time later, Tara glimpsed Janitor Kowalski walking down the main aisle, scowling at metal shavings like a blizzard across the floor. Tara held the man in the edge of his vision as he tested another tiny bolt against two different nuts. How did such tiny sticks hold Lord Dodge's autos together?

Kowalski saw Tara.

Tara would get a chance to explain. Kowalski always asked for explanations.

Before Kowalski could take more than two steps, though, Bomlin turned from his lathe and shouted for him.

Even an orc could recognize the irritation on Kowalski's face, but he turned to Bomlin. Man and dwarf conversed. Tara took care to keep his eyes on the bolt he was trying to clean, but still saw Kowalski shake his head at Bomlin, wave a hand in frustration.

Finally, Kowalski turned and marched towards the door.

Tara dropped a nut. By the time he found it between two bricks, Kowalski was gone.

The head janitor had fled the conflict? Had he gone for reinforcements?

Moments later, another orc assistant janitor trudged into the lathe room, with his own cart, and began sweeping.

Surprise almost unbalanced Tara. Kowalski had given Tara's proper labor to another? Would he declare that Tara was no longer needed? Was Lord Dodge's pleasure with Tara so fleeting?

No—the floor needed sweeping, and Bomlin had somehow convinced Kowalski that the dwarf's claim on Tara's labor had more weight than the head janitor's. Tara's legs were beginning to ache from kneeling on the brick, and frustration with the tiny parts made him want to snarl, but the swirl in his thoughts pained him even more.

At the end, he had three bolts so tiny that his fingertips swallowed them, and three nuts too minuscule to hold. No orc could fit such tiny parts together.

But no orc would surrender to them.

When the lathes' battle shriek softened and the men stepped away for Coffee, he had a set of bolts with their matching nuts lined up, arranged by length, width, and threading. The three impossible bolts lay at the end, with their matching nuts at their heads. Legs tingling with a million tiny stabs, he rose to his feet. Tara kept his face blank, betraying none of his annoyance, as Bomlin safetied his lathe and tromped over to him.

The dwarf studied Tara's display.

Tara waited. He could not do the final three bolts. That would satisfy the dwarf's need to prove his superiority. Tara could return to his duties, and try to forget this humiliation.

The dwarf took a step back and met Tara's. "You do not belong here."

Tara belonged with the brooms and mops, not with this pathetic heap of scrap metal. Did Bomlin say this before the Engine in hopes that it would claim Tara's debt now?

Tara held silent through the rage bubbling in his heart. Let the dwarf have his boast, then return to work.

"I will deal with these," Bomlin finally said. "Return to your work."

Tara nodded and took a step.

"Do you know where Test Bay Four is?" Bomlin said.

Tara stopped. He'd heard of the test bays, but he'd never had to clean one. "No, dwarf." At least such ignorance was no shame for an orc.

"Along the Main Line," Bomlin said. "The fourth alcove from the beginning. Where the engines are bolted into place."

Tara nodded. He could find it—but why was the dwarf asking? Was he not satisfied?

"After your lunch meal, you will join me there."

No. Bomlin was not satisfied.

And Janitor Kowalski had surrendered Tara's labor to the dwarf.

Tara said the only thing he could. "Yes, dwarf."

Rather than return to his station, the dwarf abandoned his brothers and walked out of the hall.

4

Lunch was a tripe and turnip pasty the size of his hand, baked by Kiva the night before. She had even added a few shreds of bacon, both to give him strength and to warn him that she would demand that strength from him tonight. Tara's mind whirled so much that he could not give the delicious treat the attention his wife deserved.

What did Bomlin want?

What would satisfy him, so that he would leave Tara to his work?

What did saving a dwarf's life mean?

If the dwarf continued these senseless demands, Lord Dodge would soon decide Tara did not work hard enough. At best, his extra pay would be lost. At worst, Lord Dodge would discard Tara. He had to solve this. Today.

Two days from now was Sunday. The plant was shut. If Tara had not freed himself from the dwarf's demands, he would have to hike nine miles to the clan's tenement. The shaman would understand what Tara had entangled himself in, and how to free himself.

Tara devoured the pasty before he truly tasted it, licking crumbs off his fingers and washing it all down with a modest bucket of water. His Kiva deserved better.

He must stop this before she suffered.

The Main Line was the heart of Lord Dodge's plant. Conveyor belts ran down the factory's longest room. A pair of orcs heaved the rectangular bottom chassis of automobiles onto the beginning of the conveyor. Every minute, the belt dragged the frame one stop forward. Men and dwarves attacked the frame, adding bolts and frames and engines and transmissions and wheels and all the other mysterious parts that made up an automobile, until they drove off the far end under their own power. Every man, every dwarf, had one task, and they did it all day, grunting and shouting and twisting as they bolted and welded metal against metal.

The Great Engine was a god, but a god that served the Main Line.

Would that make the Main Line a god as well?

It was unstoppable. The whole factory was built to keep the Main Line rolling forward. Even the death of a man wouldn't halt the line. Lord Dodge had people on *standby*, which meant that they got paid simply to be present in case they were needed. The men and dwarves rotated that duty every day. If they were here, how could they not work? Even one of the orcs heaving chassis onto the line would pick up a broom if he had no other labor.

The Line could not be argued with. It claimed trophies from those who thoughtlessly put themselves in its path. And every Great Engine in the plant served it.

Perhaps it was an orcish god, then. But a god made of men and dwarves?

Tara shook the useless thought out of his head and found Test Bay Four. Bomlin waited outside for him.

"I am here, dwarf."

Bomlin said, "Follow."

The test bay was perhaps thirty feet square. A wall short enough for Tara to comfortably sit on fenced it away from the Line, but the Line's rattle and clang filled the air almost as much as the Great Engine and its lathes. One wall was made entirely of chalkboards, mostly covered in the arcane symbols used by Lord Dodge's engineer-shamen. Near the Line, someone had clumsily chalked a figure with an absurdly large dick, as if half-man half-orc. A man must have drawn it; it was far too high for a dwarf.

At least men were jealous of orcs in one thing.

Greasy mounting chains dangled from tracks mounted on the exposed girders beneath the ceiling. A black machine hung on those chains, a stubby cone as long as Tara's arm and as thick as his chest at the base. A long table, big enough for a whole clan of orcs but far too short, filled the center of the room. Greasy gears and cables and metal shells covered half the table.

What could the dwarf want of Tara here? This was not a place for an orc. Lord Dodge did not allow orcs to even sweep the floors of these spaces.

Bomlin turned a crank on the wall, lowering the cone-shaped machine to where he could reach it. He heaved, and half the case came away in his hands. The effort made him grimace, but he lowered the casing without complaint.

Tara burned to ask what the dwarf demanded now. He would not give Bomlin any cause for a feud, though. Lord Dodge would hear nothing bad of Tara.

An incredibly complex mesh of gears filled the casing.

"Look at this," Bomlin said.

What else would Tara be looking at? "I see it."

"On that table are all the parts in this transmission." Tara had always thought a dwarf's dispassionate voice amusing, as if the tree stumps had no feelings. Bomlin's flat tones had grown to infuriate him, however. "You will take these parts. You will put them together, to match this transmission. You have until shift end."

And Tara had thought the task with the bolts was impossible! Gears and bolts and curved bits of metal lay everywhere, right next to each other. He'd come too close to succeeding with the bolts. The dwarf would not be content until Tara had failed in a more grand manner. Well, this was a feast of failure here. All he had to do was fumble a few parts—

No.

An orc always tried. When he failed, it would be because he'd reached his limits.

Tara quickly saw that parts fit together, or not. He would see a gear attached to a shaft in the *transmission*, and find two similar gears on the table. One slid easily onto the shaft. One did not. But the parts were too numerous, the transmission too complex. He would attach a gear to a shaft, another gear to another lever, and find that he had to take them both apart to fit all four together.

The whole time he worked, Bomlin watched.

Tara refused to let him know how much the dwarf's gaze irritated him. The table was so short, he had to work on his knees.

Eventually, Tara had thirty different assemblages of gears lay across the table. Each belonged within the *transmission*—but none were connected to each other. He had a frame filled with gears in one hand and an assembly of gears and shafts in the other when the shift siren finally blew.

Tara lowered them both to the table and turned to the dwarf. "I have failed." *Are you satisfied?*

Bomlin shook his head. "No."

"I did not assemble the *transmission*."

"You could not." Bomlin had his head tilted far back to meet Tara's gaze. "The transmission must be assembled in a very specific order. I wanted to know how you would fail."

Tara flared with the need to snatch the gearbox he'd assembled and smash the dwarf's face with it. "Are you that angry with me for saving your life?"

Bomlin said nothing for a long moment. "Perhaps I am."

As if a dwarf would know anger! Tara's brothers insisted he lacked proper orcish passion, but next to Bomlin he was a volcano. "Let us end this, dwarf. What is your demand?"

Bomlin studied Tara's face. "If I owed a dwarf my life, I would craft him a gift in thanks. I would hone my craft to create that gift. It might take a century."

That was foolish. Who would remember a debt after a century?

"An orc would not live so long," Bomlin said. "And yet, I must pay my debt."

"By giving me work I cannot succeed at?" Tara struggled to keep his voice from a roar.

"Your hands are smart," Bomlin said. "Your eyes see how metal mates metal. Do you know of the Renault Straight Twelve?"

If this was how dwarves conversed, no wonder orcs avoided them! "I know of no such thing."

"It is an engine," Bomlin said. "Twelve cylinders, arranged in a straight line. The unique thing about the Straight Twelve is that there is so much space around the cylinders that I believe even an orc could work on it."

Tara's frustration crumbled into angry confusion. "Nobody would ever let an orc work on an engine!"

"I owe you my life," Bomlin said. "If you will accept, I propose to teach you."

"Still!" Tara said. "Even Lord Dodge would not let me forget myself."

"A factory is about people working in their place. You showed that you want another place."

Tara could not help bellowing, "NONE WOULD HIRE ME!"

He suddenly became aware of workmen talking outside the test lab, as their voices swelled and quieted.

Tara had to calm himself. Men were quick to call the police on orcs. He forced his breath out through his nose, trying to smother the fire in his heart.

"You misunderstand," Bomlin said. "You cannot work on the tiny parts used by human cars. I propose to teach you to build an orc car."

Tara's thoughts came together.

An engine big enough to be worked on by an orc.

Big tires.

Big seats. A big steering wheel.

"Bolts for my hands," he murmured.

"For your *tools*." Bomlin emphasized the word, somehow giving it intensity without raising his voice. "Tools are a gift from the teacher. I do not know that a dwarf has ever gifted an orc a set of tools. Finding them will be a challenge."

Tara looked over the maze of gears and shafts. "I will make mistakes."

"If you cannot learn," Bomlin said, "I will finish an orc car for you. But I believe you can build two."

"What would I do with two?" Every time Tara thought he had corralled his thoughts, Bomlin added another to the stampede!

"You will sell the second."

The money would please Kiva, almost as much as the family having its own car.

Bomlin said, "And you will use the money from it to buy the parts for two more cars."

Tara's jaw fell open.

He looked out at the sleeping Main Line.

Bomlin nodded. "If you wish."

Tara's pounding heart threatened to rupture from his chest. "When would we do this?"

"Evenings. Sundays."

Tara grimaced. Spend that time away from Kiva?

He made his breath slow, ordering all those thoughts. Thoughts of their future, their children.

And he owed the machines a debt of his meat.

That made the choice easy.

He held out a hand, as men did when they made contracts.

Bomlin studied the hand, then clasped it with his own.

If orcs needed gods, it was only right that they built their own.

Want more orcs?
Look for *Frozen Talons*,
the first Prohibition Orcs novel!

ABOUT THE AUTHOR

https://mwl.io

Never miss another new release!
Sign up for MWL's mailing list at
https://mwl.io.

NOVELS AND COLLECTIONS (AS MICHAEL WARREN LUCAS):
Immortal Clay
Kipuka Blues
Butterfly Stomp Waltz
Terrapin Sky Tango
Forever Falls
Hydrogen Sleets
Drinking Heavy Water
$ git commit murder
$ git sync murder
Prohibition Orcs
Frozen Talons
Vicious Redemption
Devotion and Corrosion (coming 2023)

NONFICTION (AS MICHAEL W LUCAS):
Cash Flow for Creators – Relayd and Httpd Mastery – PAM Mastery
FreeBSD Mastery: Advanced ZFS – FreeBSD Mastery: Specialty Filesystems
FreeBSD Mastery: ZFS – Tarsnap Mastery – Sudo Mastery – PGP & GPG
Networking for Systems Administrators – DNSSEC Mastery
FreeBSD Mastery: Storage Essentials – Absolute OpenBSD – Ed Mastery
SSH Mastery – Network Flow Analysis – Absolute FreeBSD
Cisco Routers for the Desperate –FreeBSD Mastery: Jails
SNMP Mastery – Letters to ed(1) – Domesticate Your Badgers

The Networknomicon
Only Footnotes

See your favorite bookstore for more!

MY FANTASTIC KICKSTARTER BACKERS

Ada Kerman
Adam Thompson
AFresh1
Alexander Shendi
Alexandra Brandt
Alexandra Fluskey
Algot Runeman
Alyssa Rose Farver
Ami Parikh
Amy Claflin
Andrew Wainwright
Ann R. Kist
Annie Reed
Anthea Sharp
Appalachian Orcish Outpost
Author Amy Campbell
Ben Korvemaker
Berat 'The Tornado' Arik
Bill Albertson
Bill Kohn
Bonnie Elizabeth
Brad Ackerman
Brigid Collins
Brooks Davis
Caleb
Carolyn Rowland
Ceredwin
Charles B
Charles Childers
Chris Pullen and Mia Tokatlian
CJ Jones
Claas P.
Craig Maloney
Craig Small
CrispyMayhem
Cyberfossil
D. Moonfire
Dan S.
Dave Cottlehuber
David "Handsome Dave" Bishop

David Bowden
David H Hendrickson
DeAnna Knippling
Dustin Laughlin
earless wondercat
Eric Barry
Ericka Kahler
Erik DeBill
Erin
Eva Holmquist
Fatima Fayez
Felicia Fredlund
First Wildebeest
Florian Obser
Fshhhbone Spineshiver
g
Gaël Vander Schelden
Gaston Phillips
Gergely "algernon" Nagy
ghostDancer
Gil André
Gordon Carrie
Grawg Skullaxe
Jay Hannah
Jeanette Brewer-Loebig
Jeff Marraccini
Jessica Marquardt
Jim Cheetham
Jim Kosmicki
Johanna Rothman
John Gilligan
Jonathan Mendonca
Josh Grosse
Josh Washburne
Karen Fonville
Kate MacLeod
Kate Sheeran Swed
Kelly Hays
Kelly Smith
Ken Strong

krinsky
Kristine Kathryn Rusch
Laura Bickle
Laura Ware
Leigh Saunders
Linda Jordan
Lisa Owen
Lisa Silverthorne
Loren L Coleman
Louisa Swann
Lukasz Bromirski
Luke Kolata
Mark Damon Hughes
Mark Moellering
Mary Jo Rabe
Mary Sue
Mason Egger
Matthias Schmidt
Merrie Destefano
Meyari McFarland
Michael "You *Wish* You Were Half-Orc" McComas
Michael A. Stackpole
Michael Cieslak
Michael Hannemann
Michael Mock
Michelle A Freeman
MJ Silversmith
Ms. Anonymous
Murray Bollinger
Natasha Swift
Niall Navin
Nic Neidenbach
Niels Kobschätzki
Olivette Devaux
Pam A. Herbster
Patrick Muldoon
Phillip Vuchetich
Prince Eric Vickers
R.S. Kellogg
Ranthoron
Ray Percival
Rebecca M. Senese

Rhel ná DecVandé
Rhonda Lane
Ricardo M.P. Martins
Richard "President of the MWL Depreciation Society" Jones
Rob Szarka
Rob Vagle
Ron Collins
Ruthenia
Ryan M. Williams
S. J. Schuchart Jr.
Sarah Clark
Scott Murphy
Scott Peters
Sean Watson
Seth Hanford
Shaun Davidson
Shawn K. O'Shea
Shayne Power
Sherry D. Ramsey
Stefon Mears
Stephannie Tallent
Steven Martindale
Steven Saus
Stinkthorpe Bogwoncher
Stuart Griffiths
sungo
Tao Wong
Tifaine Highly
Tobias "rixx" Kunze
Tom Rini
TommiP
Trip Space-Parasite
Veo Corva
Walter Parker
Wes Frazier
Willard Goosey
Wolf Duttlinger
yam655.com

and the Anonymous Thirty-Seven

www.ingramcontent.com/pod-product-compliance
Lightning Source LLC
Chambersburg PA
CBHW020637110726
47899CB00002B/804